"You're not getting to Des Moines tonight..."

Rowan bit into a cookie. It was flaky and buttery and everything a Christmas cookie should be.

Ellory idly wiped the counter. "They're saying it's going to snow like this for a couple of days at least. If you're not already home for Christmas, you're probably not going to be."

"Why does everyone wax so sentimental about being home for Christmas?"

"Oh. Is that not why you're going? I just assumed."

"I don't do Christmas."

"What does that mean?"

He gestured around the room. "The lights and decorations and..." He held up a cookie. "All the hullabaloo and the notion that everyone is merry and bright. It's just not for me."

"It's true that I'm merry and bright," she said, but he could have sworn that there was a forced feeling behind her words.

As if she wanted to be merry and bright...but she just couldn't quite get there.

Dear Reader,

Here in Liberty, Missouri, we have enjoyed a very snowy winter. I say "enjoyed" because there is no weather event that I love more than a good snowstorm. How fortunate I felt to literally be snowed in eleven times while drafting this novel. I was able to feel the chill of the wind and the warmth of the fire, and see the diamond-like sparkle of the post-storm sun on the snowy ground.

One thing I love even more than a good snowstorm? Christmas! I was also fortunate to be writing this novel during the holiday season. The cookies, carols, gifts and joyful memories were all at my disposal.

For these reasons, I felt like I was "in the story" with Ellory and Rowan, experiencing their excitement, nostalgia and romance right along with them. I truly connected with them, and when it comes to writing, there is no better feeling.

Grab a comfy blanket, stoke the fire, nibble a sugar cookie and dive right into the Haw Springs blizzard! I hope you enjoy the storm.

Merry Christmas!

Jennifer

SNOWED IN FOR CHRISTMAS

JENNIFER BROWN

Harlequin

HEARTWARMING

If you purchased this book without a cover you should be aware that this book is stolen property. It was reported as "unsold and destroyed" to the publisher, and neither the author nor the publisher has received any payment for this "stripped book."

Harlequin® HEARTWARMING™

ISBN-13: 978-1-335-46022-6

Snowed In for Christmas

Copyright © 2025 by Jennifer Brown

All rights reserved. No part of this book may be used or reproduced in any manner whatsoever without written permission.

Without limiting the author's and publisher's exclusive rights, any unauthorized use of this publication to train generative artificial intelligence (AI) technologies is expressly prohibited.

This is a work of fiction. Names, characters, places and incidents are either the product of the author's imagination or are used fictitiously. Any resemblance to actual persons, living or dead, businesses, companies, events or locales is entirely coincidental.

For questions and comments about the quality of this book, please contact us at CustomerService@Harlequin.com.

TM and ® are trademarks of Harlequin Enterprises ULC.

Harlequin Enterprises ULC
22 Adelaide St. West, 41st Floor
Toronto, Ontario M5H 4E3, Canada
www.Harlequin.com

HarperCollins Publishers
Macken House, 39/40 Mayor Street Upper,
Dublin 1, D01 C9W8, Ireland
www.HarperCollins.com

Recycling programs for this product may not exist in your area.

Printed in U.S.A.

Jennifer Brown cut her storytelling teeth by letting her imagination run wild in the fields, forests and farms of her youth. Her love of weaving romance and nostalgia into stories that feature simple, small-town living runs deep. Nearly all of her novels—young adult, middle grade, women's fiction, inspirational romance or heartwarming romance—feature connection between people, a sense of belonging and a love of community. Jennifer lives and writes in Liberty, Missouri. Visit her at jenniferbrownauthor.com.

Books by Jennifer Brown

Harlequin Heartwarming

A Haw Springs Romance

The Cowboy's Dream Family
The Veterinarian's Perfect Match

Love Inspired Inspirational Mountain Rescue

Rescue on the Ridge
Peril at the Peak
Hunted at the Hideaway

Love Inspired Inspirational The Protectors

Kidnapped in Kansas

Visit the Author Profile page
at Harlequin.com for more titles.

For Scott, always.
There is no one I'd rather be snowbound with.

Acknowledgments

Thank you to all who have gifted me with your time,
energy, enthusiasm and expertise
when it came to writing this novel.

Thank you to my agent, Cori Deyoe,
who lavished me with armloads of gifts: a listening
ear, unwavering belief, great ideas, endless
encouragement and so much more. You spoil me,
and I'm so lucky to have you at my holiday table.

To my editor, Johanna Raisanen, thank you
for the gifts of patience, understanding and
unrelenting kindness. To the entire team at Harlequin,
thank you for the gift of helping to ensure that
Snowed In for Christmas is the best, most well-written,
most beautiful book it can possibly be.

Thank you to my family for the gift of being there
for all the snowy days and all the Christmases
and all the love.

And thank you, Reader.
Your support is the biggest gift of all.

December 22

THE ANIMALS POKED their heads out of their dens, sniffing at the sky.

There was weather coming.

Big weather.

The kind of weather that would trap the humans in their own dens and nests, cowering against the driving wind and the pelting snow and little bits of ice that hurt their human skin and made them shiver and emit their breathy, surprised human noises.

The animals would retreat into their dens and nests as well, grateful for their reserves of fat and food and fur. They would curl around their partners and their young, snooze into a comfortable warmth, and hope that they wouldn't have to wait too long for the weather to pass and their lives to continue the way they always did. They would venture out only on a need-to basis. And would do so warily.

If they ran into trouble, they could only hope for friend, not foe, to greet them on their precarious paths and to help usher them to safety.

A reminder that perhaps they weren't so different from their human counterparts after all.

CHAPTER ONE

ELLORY PLACED BOTH hands on the counter and leaned over a bowl of half-stirred batter, eyeing a nearby wooden spoon but not wanting to pick it up. Maybe she physically couldn't pick it up at this point. She wouldn't be surprised. Her mixing arm felt like a warm, wet noodle, and she'd become aware of an ache in her shoulder that threatened to wind its way all the way up the back of her neck and into her head. Well, the stress of the weather forecast was going to give her a headache, so she might as well go wholehog and bring on the arm ache, too.

She glanced at the spread of cookies she'd already made. There were hundreds of them, everything from traditional Christmas cookies to pecan sandies to peanut butter blossoms and windowpane sandwich cookies. Her kitchen looked like a blizzard had already hit, with all the flour on the countertop, her clothing, the floor.

She'd been at it for hours upon hours, and she was tired.

Not that she could blame this on anyone but herself. She was very well aware that volunteering not only to head up the Annual Haw Springs Main Street Christmas Carol Crawl Planning Committee but also to bake all of the cookies for said Crawl had been her decision, and that hand mixing the cookies—with a wooden spoon no less—had also been her decision. Furthermore, she was well aware that she did those things precisely to wear herself out. To take out her frustrations. To distract herself from the ache in her chest and the gnawing in her gut that made her not want to eat a single one of the cookies in front of her. And that ache had nothing at all to do with the weather.

Her Christmas spirit had never been dampened before, and she was determined to keep her fa-la-la at full volume, one grinning gingerbread man at a time. So far, however, she'd only managed to create an ache in her shoulder, a wet noodle arm, and a callus on her palm where the wooden spoon rubbed as she stirred. Fa-la-la-la-ouch.

Didn't matter, she told herself. If she had it to do over again, she would have done it the exact same way. She wanted the Dreamy Bean to be the place where the carolers would get cookies and cocoa and warm their hearts and bodies. She had her regulars, but she was still newish to town and still trying to entice every customer she could get a coffee bean into. If the Carol Crawl was like every other celebration put on in Haw Springs, the entire town would be there. Haw Springs liked its celebrations. And Haw Springians liked their neighbors. In Haw Springs, if you were a friend, you were basically family.

Ugh. Family.

Haw Springians don't shut a family member out of Christmas just because of a breakup, she thought bitterly, and at this thought, picked up the wooden spoon and went back to stirring. *A year-old breakup, at that. Ancient history!*

As if on cue, her phone buzzed. Her little sister, Daphne.

Are you still mad, Ell? Don't be mad.

Ellory wiped her hands off on the tea towel that was stuffed into the waistband of her apron.

Why would I be mad? Just because my own family doesn't want me to come home for Christmas? What is there to be mad about?

She knew she was being flip. And she knew it wasn't precisely Daphne's fault that she'd been cut out of Christmas this year. She didn't care. She was hurt. Beyond hurt. And Daphne was the one family member that was talking to her.

For the last time. We want you home. We just don't think it's the best idea with the Wittfelds here.

"Of course, it didn't occur to any of you to maybe tell the Wittfelds not to come over because *I* would be home for Christmas," Ellory said aloud. She stirred like her life depended on it. "Molasses cookies," she muttered. "Focus on molasses cookies."

But her phone continued to buzz.

You know how Mommy feels about Danny.

"Oh, I know very well," Ellory said to her empty kitchen. *Stir, stir, stir.* "And, unfortunately, I now know how Mommy feels about me."

You know that Danny is still grieving, Ell.

"Oh, is he? I guess I didn't realize that breaking off our wedding was so hard on *him*, given how easy it was on *me*. I only moved to an entirely different town, all by myself, because my own family chose to support *him* in *his* time of need. And chose to ridicule me for the things I wanted in life, by the way." *Molasses, molasses, molasses...*

If you'd tried to work things out, you might be here right now.

"Oh-ho! So that's how it works, huh, Daphne? Just go ahead and marry the guy who mocks me and my dreams so I don't inconvenience everyone in the family at Christmastime. Because heaven forbid they not get to play their annual game of Christmas charades with their besties. That would be terrible. Selfish, selfish Ellory. You should have stuck it out and created a lifetime of misery with a bully, you selfish girl."

I can't talk to you when you're being like this, Daphne texted, and for a wild second, Ellory thought maybe Daphne had heard everything she'd said. She put down the bowl and the spoon and picked up her phone, swiping around to make sure she hadn't accidentally called her sister. Another message popped up.

It's childish not to answer my texts.

Ah, no, Daphne was just unhappy with being ignored.

"Well, see how it feels? Not good. Not good at all," Ellory said. "At least you're not being told you can't come home for a *family* holiday, Daphne."

She swiped a fingerful of batter and ate it, then sighed. It wasn't Daphne's fault that their parents were lifelong best friends with Ellory's ex-fiancé's parents. She was just the messenger, trying to smooth things over. Trying to make Ellory feel better.

Christmas back home in New Hampshire had all the trappings to warm the heart. It was like living inside a Christmas card. Ellory's parents would be so busy with all of their fancy dinners and good china and crystal wineglasses, Ellory wasn't sure they would even notice her absence. But Daphne would feel it just as Ellory was feeling it. She and Daphne had too many Christmas traditions of their own for their distance from each other not to hurt just a little.

Ellory pasted on a smile and took a selfie in front of the giant platters of cookies.

I'm keeping busy and am filled with Christmas cheer! It's all good!

Keeping busy? Truth. All good? Maybe not as true.

Filled with Christmas cheer? She was trying. Ellory loved Christmas, which was part of why she volunteered to head up the organizing committee for the Carol Crawl in the first place. No matter what time of year, if something had tinsel, glitter, lights, and a sentimental message, she was all in, all day long. Just...right now? Mustering Christmas cheer was, well...a muster.

Whew. I thought you stopped talking to me. That's a lot of cookies, though. Remember, a moment on the lips.

"Ugh. I swear, Daph, you have turned into our mother."

A lifetime on the hips. I know. Don't worry, they're for a gathering.

A gathering? Are you having a party?

The bells that Ellory had hung over the front door jingled.

Oops, gotta go. A customer just walked in. Talk later!

She dropped her phone back on the counter and hurried out into her coffee shop.

"Welcome to the Dreamy Bean," she said brightly.

Marlee West, her best friend who happened to own the flower shop next door, stood just inside the doorway, stomping snow off her shoes. Her cheeks were pink from the wind and cold, her boots covered with snow just from her few minutes outside.

"It's really coming down out there," Marlee said. "I'm going home before the roads get too bad to get anywhere. Thought I'd stop by and say Merry Christmas before I go."

"That bad, huh?" Ellory chewed a nail and craned her neck to look out the big front window. "I was hoping the forecasts would be exaggerated."

"Not this time," Marlee said. "Do you want to come home with me? I've got a little air mattress that I bought when Morgan and Archer used to stay over."

"No, I'm sure it'll be fine. The snow will die down eventually, right? Those forecasts are famous for making things seem worse than they are. Besides, I have Mr. Crowley to attend to."

Mr. Crowley was a sweet, elderly regular customer who didn't own a car and walked everywhere he went—including to the Dreamy Bean, where he would read an actual newspaper over a good cup of black coffee every single morning. Mr. Crowley's wife had just been moved to a nursing home a few weeks ago, and he'd been so despondent it practically broke Ellory's heart. The nursing home was on the outskirts of town—way too far for him to walk—and he missed Mrs. Crowley terribly. What was worse, their sixtieth wedding anniversary was coming up on Christmas Eve, and he was beside himself with the thought of not spending the occasion together. Ellory had promised Mr. Crowley that she would help him surprise Mrs. Crowley at the nursing home on Christmas Eve with a nice, candlelit dinner.

But that was before the storm moved in. Now

it looked like nobody was going anywhere. She wasn't sure what she was going to do, other than hope and pray that the worst of it moved out before December 24.

Marlee stomped around on the welcome mat. "I'm sure everything will be fine. Are your machines fired up? I'd love a large flavor of the day, please. The hotter the better!"

"Gotcha. White Peppermint Mocha, coming right up. I'm calling it White Christmas."

"Fitting. We will for sure have one of those."

Ellory grabbed a cup and began making Marlee's coffee. "One minute it's two to five inches, the next minute it's three to six. Last I heard, they were predicting over a foot. They're making it sound like we could be snowed in for days."

"Don't look now, but I think we might be," Marlee said. "And I have a backlog of poinsettias that people haven't picked up. My store looks like Christmas exploded in there." Marlee glanced around at the decorations that Ellory had been dutifully hanging for weeks. "Kind of looks like that in here, too, to be honest."

"You can never be too festive." Ellory handed Marlee her drink over the counter. Marlee wasted no time taking a sip. "And try to look on the bright side—poinsettias are iconic."

"Poinsettias are expensive. If people don't pick

up their orders, they don't pay for their orders. This is delicious, by the way. One of your best."

"Thank you. Hey, you know what? I'll buy some of those poinsettias if it comes down to that. I could use some color to liven up my sidewalk for the Carol Crawl."

Marlee took another sip of her coffee. "Oh. Um…"

"Oh, um, what?"

She swallowed. "It's just that I did see Katherine Messing this afternoon. She came in to get her poinsettia."

"Oh, no," Ellory said.

"Oh, yes."

"And?"

Marlee winced. "I don't want to say it."

"Don't want to say what?"

"She was being very Katherine Messing about all the snow." Marlee gave another pained look and took another sip of her drink. "I'm sorry."

Katherine Messing was the dour, no-nonsense head of the Haw Springs Chamber of Commerce and the person who Ellory reported to on all things Carol Crawl. Ellory may be head of the committee, but it was Katherine who truly called the shots.

"What exactly did she say?" Ellory went back to wiping down the counter, trying to look busy so Marlee wouldn't see her stress and disappointment ramping up. First her dis-invitation home, then her promise to Mr. Crowley being threatened, and now, after she'd baked north of five hundred cookies, the Annual Haw Springs Main Street Christmas Carol Crawl being in jeopardy? Fa-la-la-la-come on now!

"She was saying that the Carol Crawl might have to be canceled. It would be the first time in over one hundred years. She didn't reach out to you?"

Ellory recalled missing a phone call while she'd been elbow deep in cookie dough. By the time she'd washed her hands, she was getting texts from Daphne and had forgotten all about it. She didn't even look to see who had called, and they hadn't tried again.

"No, I haven't talked to her. But she can't cancel it. I've been planning for months. And the trees were just delivered yesterday."

She glanced through the big front window again at the four-foot, potted spruce tree that stood on the sidewalk in front of the Dreamy Bean. She, personally, had made sure that one was delivered in front of every shop on Main Street. In her mind, a line of sparkling, baubled Christmas trees standing sentry down the length of Main Street would add an extra bit of cheer to the event. But there had been a delay in transit, and they'd only just arrived. All of them, including hers, were still bare. She'd already resigned herself to the idea that they might stay bare. But snowy spruces were Christmassy all on their own, right? They were not a sign that everything was falling apart at the most inopportune time, right? Right?

"Ugh. I can't talk about it. I can't even think about it. Do you want a cookie? It's on the house."

"Sure," Marlee said. "What kind?"

Ellory hurried into the back and returned with a platter of assorted cookies. "Every kind," she said.

She and Marlee locked eyes, and then they both burst into laughter.

"You should maybe take two," she said, and they laughed harder.

"Only if you take two poinsettias."

"Deal."

Marlee plucked two cookies off the platter and took a bite. "So good," she said. "That reminds me. I came up with a new name for your café."

Ellory waved her away. "That was just talk. I'll never actually do it."

"What? Why not? You are a whiz in the kitchen, Ellory. Haw Springs needs you to start selling food for real. Not just sometimes and not just for Mr. Crowley."

"Nah, it's just a silly idea."

"This—" Marlee held up her cookie with the

missing bite "—is not silly. And I thought you could change the name to the Dreamy Baker. What do you think?"

Ellory made a face. "You're being nice, and I appreciate it."

"Okay, okay, the Dreamy Cream Puff. Better? Worse? I don't know."

"Marlee…"

"Café Dream. Cloud Café? I could come up with them all day." Ellory could feel her face fall with every word. It must have shown, because Marlee stopped talking and frowned.

"Thank you for always being so supportive," Ellory said. "Really. But it's okay for this to just be a coffee shop that sometimes has baked treats."

"Okay, okay, I'll let it go." Marlee chewed and swallowed. "But just know I'm letting it go under duress."

"Thank you."

Marlee waved her cookie around. "All these cookies…all these decorations…you've been busy."

"I've been trying to distract myself."

"Is it working?"

Ellory placed the tray on the counter and rolled her shoulder. She couldn't hold it up any longer, her arm was so tired. "No. Not especially."

"What were you distracting yourself from?"

For a moment, Ellory considered taking a seat, telling Marlee the whole story from start to finish. How she began her life lying in a crib next to the baby who would become the cruel fiancé that her family chose over her. Marlee was her best friend, after all. But it was Christmas. And she didn't have the energy to tell the story. And her oven was beeping.

"Cookies are done," she said. "Be right back."

"There are more?" Marlee asked. "How much distraction do you need?"

"If only you knew…"

IF HE HADN'T been dragging his feet about going home for Christmas in the first place, Rowan might have paid attention to the weather forecast. But, no, he was too busy finding little tasks at the firehouse. Sweeping, mopping, scrubbing the bathroom from one end to the other. Cleaning out a drawer here, a cabinet there, going over the equipment one more time. And then one more.

If he'd looked at the forecast, he would never have gotten into the car at all. Pointless to try to get from Tulsa to Des Moines with a massive storm settling in over the entirety of Missouri. But he didn't think to look until he was hours into his journey and the first bits of sleet ticked against his windshield. Within minutes, the sleet turned to snow, and another two hours in, he was smack in the middle of a blizzard.

Not that there was much to see in the fields of

nowhere, Missouri, but now it was vast whiteness for miles on end. Bleak. He hadn't even seen another car in an hour, at least. And he was pretty sure he'd taken a wrong turn. He shouldn't have been in the middle of nowhere at all. He should have been on the highway. And this white wasteland surrounding him was no highway. It was no…anything.

It was a little scary, honestly. Like the end of the world.

Worst of all? His car was starting to make a funny noise. A knocking and whirring noise. Rowan was nobody's auto mechanic. The best he could do was change a taillight, and he was pretty sure that a busted taillight didn't make the noise he was hearing. Or create the strange revving and slowing that he was feeling as it made the noise.

Why on earth did he have to choose today to take a wrong turn?

His phone rang in the center console. He pawed at it, afraid to tear his eyes away from the road.

"Rowan?" It was his twin sister, Megan, aka the only reason he was out in this mess to begin with. She was very pregnant with her first baby, and her husband, Johnny, was in New Jersey on business until Christmas Eve day. Rowan loved his twin and didn't see her nearly enough, and even though he despised all things Christmas, he agreed to come help her finish decorating and cooking. His plan was to scoot out of there as soon as Johnny returned, in hopes of being back in Tulsa and alone for Christmas Day, the way he always was. He was pretty sure he could get away with it, as long as he promised to return as soon as the baby was born. Megan wouldn't like it, but she would just have to live with it.

"Hey, Megs."

"Are you on your way?"

"I'm trying."

"Where are you?"

He studied the landscape around him, hoping to see anything that could help give him a clue what the answer to that question might be. There was nothing but snow on top of snow. And sometimes snow on top of things that were no longer recognizable as things, only as larger, lumpier lumps of snow. In between him and those things? Snow. And a sky that was saturated with snow.

The only thing Rowan disliked more than the holidays themselves was snow during the holidays. While the rest of the world was getting all misty-eyed about their White Christmas, he was internally bah-humbugging that Christmas was intolerable, and snow only made it even more so.

"No idea. Somewhere in Missouri."

"Like...northern Missouri? I hope?"

"I haven't even gotten to Kansas City yet. So, no."

She let out a frustrated groan. "Why didn't you leave earlier?"

"Trust me, I'm asking myself that question every time my car slides dangerously close to what I think is probably a ditch somewhere under all that snow."

"Wait a minute. What do you mean, you have no idea where you are? Are you being serious?"

Rowan didn't want to answer. For a twin, Megan sure had Big Sister Energy and was definitely not afraid to mother him at any and every chance she got.

"Rowan? What did you mean by that?" A brief pause, and then, "Are you lost?"

"I wouldn't say lost, so much as…exploring."

"Exploring. In a blizzard."

"Admittedly, not the best timing, but every exploration has its little inconveniences."

She took a breath and let out a sigh. "I have a bad feeling about this. I'm worried about you. I mean, I was already worried about you. But now I'm like, really, really worried about you, Rowan."

"I've been driving for a few years, Megs. This isn't my first time traversing in bad weather. I've got this. I'll re-find the highway and be there in no time." He didn't want to mention to Megan, or even admit to himself, that the funny noise that his car had been making could possibly have something to say about that plan.

"Even if you re-found the highway right this second, I'm thinking you won't even get here in time for Christmas."

"It's December 22. I'm driving slowly, and I'm a little bit lost, but surely I can make a six-hour drive in three days."

"Unless you're forced to stop and wait it out. And I hate the idea of you spending Christmas alone in a hotel room. I think you really need Christmas this year."

"Why? I never do Christmas. What makes this year any different than any other year?"

"Well, for one, the baby. Maybe he'll come while you're still here."

"He's not due for weeks yet."

"I know, but wouldn't that be amazing? A Christmas Day baby! And his uncle-slash-godfather giving a rare Christmas appearance."

"Would that mean you'd have to buy double the gifts every year?" Rowan asked.

"Ooh," she said. "I don't know. But we could have birthday cake with our Christmas dinner. And…you would be forced to come for Christmas every year, no matter how you feel about it. Forced to see your sister. Will you survive it?"

"It's not about me not wanting to see you, you know," Rowan said. One of his windshield wipers began to freeze up and was just dragging slush across the windshield that quickly turned to ice, making it impossible to see. He fiddled with the defrost dial, even though he knew it was maxed out. And that revving and slowing sound was getting louder and more frequent. "It's about—"

"I know what it's about. It's about Christmas itself and the unrealistic standards of happiness and *blah blah blah*. You've told me a million times."

"Not just that."

"It's also about Mom and Dad and all the fighting. But Dad is dead, and Mom's gone on one of her cruises again. Remember, she hates Christmas just as much as you do. She's never here in December to ruin it for the rest of us. So, you know, you could get rid of your Christmas hate if you really wanted to. Just release it like a balloon. A red and green balloon. Or silver and gold, if that's what you prefer." She started singing a song from a popular animated Christmas movie from their childhood.

"I don't have hate to release. I just don't see the point of all the fuss and the food and the parties and the decorations and the singing and the gifts."

"Yeah, sounds terrible when you put it that way. Who would want all that? Gross."

"I'm coming, aren't I?" He let out a frustrated

grunt. "Great. Now my other wiper is starting to freeze."

"I don't think you're gonna make it here, Row. The weather doesn't look good. And now I'm feeling all sorry for myself because I'm stuck here alone on December 22, my tree is half decorated because I can't reach the top, and I can't even bake myself a Christmas cookie because my huge belly gets in the way of the oven door and my feet hurt and I don't have anyone to drink cocoa and watch Christmas romance movies with."

"Ah, so now the truth comes out. You want me there to bake cookies for you."

"No," she said defensively. "Not just bake them. You have to decorate them, too."

He slowed even more, peering through the rapidly closing hole of clear windshield. He wasn't even sure where the road was anymore. He glanced in his rearview mirror to make sure he wasn't weaving his way off pavement but found that the back windshield defroster was having just as much of a hard time as the front.

"Megs, are you watching the weather forecast right now?"

"It's all I've watched all day."

"How far until I'm out of it?" he asked.

She paused, clucked her tongue. "December 26."

"Huh?"

"It's just a wall of green on the radar. You aren't going to drive through to the other side. Your nephew will be so disappointed."

"My nephew is still living the good life swimming around a heated pool on the inside. I doubt he'll be too broken up about it. I'll come up after the New Year, and he and I will party all night long. It'll be okay." Rowan felt equal parts guilt and relief that he had been gifted a Get Out of Christmas Free card from the meteorological powers that be. He just had to find a place to turn around, then figure out how to get back to the highway, all while hoping that the engine troubles weren't actually engine troubles. No problem.

"Still. I'm disappointed. I'll just have to be cookie-less, with a half-decorated tree, waiting for Johnny, until Christmas Eve."

"I'm disappointed, too." *So why are you smiling? Stop smiling.* "Guess I'll find somewhere to turn around and head back to Tulsa."

"I don't know, Rowan. I think you should pull off as soon as you possibly can and find a place to hunker down until this passes."

"Right." Wrong. But what Megan didn't know wouldn't hurt her. He would call her as soon as he got home, safe and sound. She could lecture him about safety after the fact. "I'm sorry, Megs. I really am."

"It's okay. You can't help the weather. Do you see any town at all? Or a street sign?"

He did see a sign ahead. He slowed to a crawl and rolled down his passenger side window to read it. "Haw Springs," he said. "Population 652."

"Haw Springs, Missouri. Sounds quaint. Call me when you get settled. And Rowan?"

He slowed to a stop and rested his forehead on the steering wheel. He didn't like disappointing people. But especially not Megan. She'd been there through all the bad Christmases, and she managed to keep a positive outlook. She also managed to fall in love and get married and have a baby on the way—three other things he couldn't imagine allowing himself to do. "Yeah, Megs?"

"Merry Christmas."

"Yeah. You, too."

"Come see me after the baby is born?"

"Of course. I wouldn't miss it. He and I have party plans."

Megan chuckled. "Love you, Rowan."

"Love you, too, sis. Don't worry. Everything will be fine. It's just a little snow."

But his car didn't agree that it was *just a little* anything. Now that he was stopped, the revving was followed by sputtering. He worried that he would never get the thing rolling again.

He hung up. He just had to get to Haw Springs, and then he would turn around and be back home before bedtime. He rolled up the window and pressed the gas.

His tires whirred uselessly in the powder beneath them.

"Come on, come on," he said, trying to resist the urge to floor the gas pedal, knowing that flooring it would only entrench the tires deeper into the snow. It took patience and a soft touch to get out of deep snow in a car like his. "But I don't have time for patience," he said, looking into the sky through the windshield. He'd never seen snow this heavy before, not even growing up in Iowa.

He kept working the pedal, and finally, the car slowly, slowly inched its way forward. He smacked the steering wheel with his palm triumphantly. "Atta boy! Come on, now. I know you're cold and tired, but just get me to Haw Springs, little buddy. That's all I ask."

In the end, the car hadn't quite made it all the way into Haw Springs. But it made it close enough that he could see Main Street and one little shop that had lights on inside. He got out of his car, shouldering his duffel bag, and was immediately ripped through by the cold.

"You couldn't have made it another few hundred feet?" he asked his car, then shut and locked the door. He patted the top of the car, which was already getting iced over. "Don't worry, I'll find a way to get us out of here tomorrow. There's got to be a mechanic somewhere in Haw Springs, Missouri. Good luck, little buddy. Hope you don't get too cold tonight." He gazed down the deserted street. "I hope the same for myself."

Rowan quickly found himself wishing he'd worn more layers, though he was grateful that he'd worn his parka and boots, at least. He hunkered against the wind, reminding himself that he'd endured way more difficult surroundings than this. He tried to conjure up memories of being surrounded by flames and sweating under 50 pounds of turnout gear, in hopes that it would help him feel less cold.

It didn't.

Instead, he just walked faster, slipping and sliding, despite his boots, feeling the wind drive little pellets of ice and snow into his face. During a particularly strong gust, he heard the groan of tree limbs. There would be breaks soon if this snow didn't let up. Power lines down. This could get bad.

At last, he found himself standing in the middle of Haw Springs's Main Street. He paused, his hands pushed deep into his jacket pockets, and gazed up one side of the street and down the other. Darn if Megan wasn't right: this town was charming.

But it looked a little like Haw Springs residents

needed to take the Christmas cheer down a notch. Every light pole was wound with red and green garland, and every shop had a potted spruce in front of it. There was a plastic Santa in one shop window, and another decorated like the inside of a gingerbread house. A gust of wind wrenched a chunk of garland from the light pole nearest him and threw it against his neck, showering snow down the collar of his jacket.

"Bah!" he cried out, clawing it away and throwing it onto the ground. He looked up just in time to see the last light in the one open shop extinguish. He watched as a figure flipped the OPEN sign to CLOSED and walked away, disappearing into the shadows of the store. "No!" he said. "No, no, no, no…"

He raced across the street, losing his footing and going down to one knee. He pushed himself back up, getting snow inside his gloves. He ignored it. He had to get to the store before whoever was inside couldn't hear him.

He was unable to get any real traction beneath him, and he was trying not to fall again, which made his trek to the door seem like it was happening in slow motion. When he finally reached it, all he could see inside was the dimmest of lights in the very back of the store.

He pounded on the door with his gloved hand,

quickly yanked off his glove, and pounded with his freezing, bare fist. "Hello?"

His stomach sank as nobody stirred inside. He pounded harder.

"Hey! Hey! Is there anyone in there? I need help!"

Finally, he saw a silhouette against the dim light. He continued pounding until the silhouette got closer and closer, pulling itself out of the shadows.

A young woman appeared on the other side of the door. She was decked out from head to toe in red and green and was holding an armload of garland that caught little glimpses of light and projected them onto her creamy skin. She blinked at him with impossibly blue, impossibly big eyes, her mouth dainty and pink, her bottom lip tucked into her teeth contemplatively, her long, white-blonde hair cascading over the shoulders of her Christmas sweater. She made no move to open the door.

His hand froze in midair, and suddenly he didn't feel the cold at all.

CHAPTER TWO

THE WOMAN AT the door finally smiled, wary and fleeting, and the blizzard swam away for the briefest second. She pointed to the CLOSED sign with a curious expression.

"I know. I'm sorry. I'm stranded. Can I come in? It's cold out here." His breath fogged the glass, and he realized he'd been standing too close. He took a step back and held his arms out wide, as if that somehow would make him look more disarming.

She bit her lip again and glanced around, clearly unsure whether or not to let him in.

"I'm safe, I swear," he shouted, and then realized that this was exactly what someone who wasn't safe would say. "I'm a firefighter. You can trust me." Ugh. It was like he was only allowing himself to say all the things that would lead him to not being allowed inside. What would come out of his mouth next, he wondered. *I swear I won't murder you? I promise I'm not on the run from the police?*

She gazed at him a second longer. Just long enough for the wind to gust again, only this time lifting a sheet of ice and snow from the awning above him. It slid over him like a blanket, its fingers stretching down the length of his back, inside his shirt. He let out a frustrated cry and found himself doing a little jig. He opened his eyes again just in time to see her stifle a laugh with her hand.

"Oh, come on," he said, drawing close to the door again. "Is there someone you can call? Somewhere I can go? I'm freezing out here. I'll go anywhere warm. There can't be any place worse than out here."

Tentatively, she reached down and unlocked the door. She pushed it open, shoving a wedge of snow over his boot. He let out a sigh of relief.

"Thank you. Thank you."

She took a step back, letting him inside. The scent of coffee warmed him instantly.

"Brrr," she said, shutting the door behind him. "It's as cold as it looks out there." As tiny and delicate as she appeared, her voice was surprisingly rich and warm, crackling through his chilled skin and bones.

"Yeah. Colder." He stomped to rid his shoes of excess snow. "Thank you for letting me in."

"What are you doing walking around out there in a blizzard?"

"My car is down the road. I got stranded." He

blew into his hands and rubbed them together. "It's a long story that really just starts and ends at the same place: I should have looked at the forecast."

"Can I get you some hot coffee?"

"Yes, please." Finally, fortune was favoring him.

She flipped on the overhead light, and Christmas burst around him in an annoying barrage of sights and sounds. "Whoa."

She froze with her hand still on the light switch. She glanced up at the ceiling. "What?"

"You've got a lot of Christmas going on around here."

She shrugged. "It's the most wonderful time of the year."

I was wrong, he thought. *There is someplace worse than out there, and I managed to find it.* But he didn't want to be rude, so he forced a smile. "That's what they say."

She had gone to the other side of the counter and was winding an apron around her waist. "I have a feeling you're not actually a fan," she said.

"Well, there's fan, and then there's..." He trailed off as he spun in a circle, trying to take it all in. "You've got a lot of decor."

"Oh," she said. "I love decor."

"I can see that." Photos, paintings, wall hangings, ceiling hangings, tchotchkes and dolls and statues and pots and license plates and sea glass and yarn and random items seemed to be clinging to every square inch of spare space. It gave Rowan the dizzying feeling of having fallen into someone's junk drawer. "Lots of clouds and rainbows. It's like..."

"Like a dream?" she asked, putting the finishing touches on his coffee. "Like a Christmas dream?"

More like a fever dream. No, he couldn't say that. He needed this place right now. He would have to save his visceral reaction to clouds and rainbows for later, when he was warm and had a hotel room secured. "Yeah, sure. Like a dream. That's exactly what I was thinking."

"Welcome to the Dreamy Bean. My dream." She pushed a cup across the counter with a tentative smile. "Are you hungry? I have cookies."

He just knew they were going to be Christmas cookies, little Santas and snowmen, probably floating on clouds and sliding down rainbows, and he would have to *ooh* and *ahh* over them as if Christmas cookies were the best cookies ever invented. Normally, he would wave them away. But his stomach rumbled loudly, taking the decision away from him.

The woman gave another tentative smile. "Sounds like you're hungry. I'll get you a plate. I was also just getting ready to put some soup on for dinner. I'll make it for two. Just...um...get comfortable? You can take off your wet shoes, if you want."

She scurried away through a door behind the counter, her hair bouncing off her shoulders as she moved. She came back quickly and handed him a plate piled high with cookies. Rowan couldn't help noticing how delicate her hands were, how her fingernails were pink and smooth and shiny, matching her lips. It almost distracted him from the pile of red-and-green confections on the plate in his hands. Almost.

"Anything else I can get you?" she asked. "Do you need to use a phone?"

"No, I have a phone. I just need a minute to figure out who to call," he said. "Thank you for these." He bit into a cookie. It was flaky and buttery and everything a Christmas cookie should be. The last time he purposely ate a Christmas cookie, he was a kid. He forgot how delicious frosting could be.

"So why were you out there?" she asked again. "You're not from around here, and Haw Springs isn't really on the way to anywhere. Are you visiting someone?"

"Something like that," he said. "Only that someone is in Des Moines, not Haw Springs. I took a wrong turn."

"Oh, you're not getting to Des Moines tonight.

The blizzard is stretching all the way up to the Iowa border, and it sounds like it's staying put."

"That's what I hear."

She produced a towel out of nowhere and idly wiped the spot where the cup had just been. "They're saying it's going to keep doing this for a couple of days at least. If you're not already home for Christmas, you're probably not going to be."

Thank you, I know what staying put *means*, he wanted to say, but instead simply made a balking noise. "I don't care about being home for Christmas. Why does everyone wax so sentimental about being home for Christmas? If anything, Christmas is an inconvenience when you want to go just about anywhere."

"Oh. Is that not why you're going to Des Moines? I just assumed."

"In my sister's mind, probably, but not in mine. I don't do Christmas."

"What does that mean, you *don't do Christmas*?"

He gestured around the room. "The lights and decorations and…" He held up a cookie. "All the hullabaloo and the notion that everyone is merry and bright. It's not true. And it's just not for me."

"It's true that I'm merry and bright," she said, but he could have sworn that there was a forced feeling behind her words. Like she meant to be merry and bright, and wanted to be merry and bright, and knew she should be merry and bright, but she just couldn't quite get to actual merry and actual bright.

He finished his cookie. "Well, then, the sooner I get out of your hair, the better. As soon as a plow comes through, I'll get my car towed to the nearest mechanic, get it fixed, and zip right on out before the snow can build up again, and you can get back to your revelry."

"There's not going to be a plow," she said. "Or a mechanic. Junior Feeny owns the only garage in Haw Springs and also owns the only plow, and he's gone home to his mee-maw's for the holidays. Out in Riverside. He's a good hour away, and that's in clear weather. Nobody's going anywhere. I'm sorry."

Rowan made another, weaker, balking noise. *Way to go*, he thought to himself. *Dragging your feet put you in a world of mess, and here you are. Stuck in a Christmas- and cloud-covered coffee shop with Miss Merry and Bright.*

Now, instead of happily ignoring Christmas like you wanted to do, you're literally stranded in it.

WELL, SHE'D WANTED a distraction from her Christmas woes, but Ellory hadn't exactly been expecting the distraction to have so many…muscles.

She'd been getting ready to heat up some soup when she heard the pounding on the front door.

It had startled her, and when she peeked around the corner to see a large figure standing on the other side, her heart gave a little panic pang; she considered turning out the remaining lights and pretending that nobody was home.

But he had seen her lurking in the shadows. She knew it.

Plus, once her eyes adjusted to the hazy gray outside, his shadow didn't seem as large and looming as it had at first. He was just a tall man bundled up in a parka. And, from the sound of things, he was freezing anyway.

She opened the door against her better judgment, reminding herself that this was Haw Springs, and it just wasn't like everywhere else in the world. Everyone here was friendly. Everyone was friends. And she was still new-ish to town. This may be someone she just hadn't met yet. Besides, she let strangers into her business all day every day. That was just part of having a business.

You never met a stranger in your life. Of course you want to open a coffee shop. What better way to immerse yourself in whole crowds of strangers, her mother had said when Ellory had first divulged her vision for the Dreamy Bean. But Angeline DeCloud hadn't said it as a compliment. Quite the opposite, with an exasperated sneer. Ellory could only imagine what her mother would have to say about her letting this man in.

When he stepped inside, and she turned on the lights, she had the singular thought, *This man is what the term* devastatingly handsome *was meant for*. He was damp and rosy cheeked and snow covered, but she had a feeling that the slightly disheveled look about him was somewhat purposeful, as if he was one of those guys who artfully looked as if they just tumbled out of bed and slipped into the first formfitting sweater and jeans they came across. His jaw was strong; his neck and shoulders were muscular. He carried himself a little stiff and taut, as if he was ready for an emergency to break out at any second. But he also had the sharp gaze of someone who would spot an emergency coming before it fully arrived.

But also? He was a little grumpy. He looked around the Dreamy Bean as if he was judging every last inch of it and it wasn't quite up to his standards. He made a comment about the decor that he thought she didn't hear—she did—and turned his nose up about Christmas as if she didn't care—she...did. He was grumbly and muttery and seemed completely out of sorts. Even after a white peppermint mocha, extra whip. *Who stays grumpy after extra whip?*

She locked the kitchen door behind her when she excused herself to heat up the soup, leaving him tentatively perched on the very edge of a cloud chair as if happiness was going to jump up and bite him. He way-too-casually flipped through a cooking magazine, still wearing his parka, his gloves tossed to the side. She watched him through the pass as she worked. He bit into a cookie, his eyebrows raised as he gave the cookie a second look, and then he practically devoured the rest of it. Even the way he rhythmically and determinedly chewed his cookie engaged her. She couldn't look away.

Get a grip, Ellory. You don't even know his name.

She hurried to finish the soup and took it out to him, pausing only to hit the remote so Christmas music bubbled through the speakers, as it had been all day.

His curiosity turned to a frown.

"I'm sorry," she said. "You don't like music?"

"I don't like *Christmas* music," he said.

"What? How can you not like Bing Crosby?" She really didn't understand how this could even be possible. She looked forward to Christmas music every year and waited with bated breath for the day after Thanksgiving, when she felt like she could "officially" start listening to it.

"It's not him specifically, it's just...you know what? Never mind. Christmas music is fine. Beggars can't be choosers and all that."

"Too merry and bright."

"Definitely."

"Right." But she didn't move to turn the music off.

She set the soup on the table in front of him and then curled up with her own bowl in a nearby bean bag chair, tucking her feet up into the warmth of her flared pants. "I'm Ellory, by the way. Ellory DeCloud. Hence…" She gestured toward the ceiling, his eyes following.

"Oh! The clouds!" he said. "Got it. Very clever. Dreams. Clouds. DeCloud."

"And the shop itself was a dream I had to fight extra hard for, so it all just sort of came together perfectly. And you're…?"

"Huh?" He paused with his spoon dangling over the soup bowl.

She raised her eyebrows. "Your name?"

"Oh. Rowan Kelly."

"Happy to rescue you, Rowan Kelly."

"Hmm. I'm not accustomed to needing rescuing. Usually, I'm the rescuer."

"Yes, you mentioned you're a firefighter."

"That's right, I suppose I did. I'm sorry. I'm a little bit scattered. You've caught me on a very special day." He took a bite of soup. "This is good," he said, then dived in for another bite.

Ellory blew across the top of her spoon. "Thanks. I've been trying out some new recipes. So, what's so special about today?"

"Huh?"

"You said I caught you on a very special day. What's so special about it?"

"Oh." He took another bite. "I was being sarcastic. What's special is that I was so irritated about having to go to Des Moines for Christmas, I left home without thinking about what might lie between the two places. Like, I don't know, four feet of snow and ice. Normally, I'm a forward thinker. Aware. I'm a firefighter, for goodness' sake. Being prepared is literally what I do. So it's a special day, but not in a good way."

"Oh. I'm sorry. Where is home?"

"Tulsa."

Now it was Ellory's turn to pause. "So you're already quite a few hours away from home. And definitely a few hours away from Des Moines."

"A few hours away from sanity," he muttered across the top of his spoon, before taking another bite. "I thought my sister was going to kill me for not leaving earlier. I'm supposed to be helping her with final touches on the nursery and—what in the holly jolly is that?"

Ellory followed Rowan's gaze. Her cat had come downstairs and was lazily making his way toward them, the bells on his collar jingling with every step. "That's Latte," she said simply. She tapped her leg and Latte expertly jumped into her lap. He plopped down and eyed Rowan curiously, tail swishing.

"He's wearing clothes."

"He's wearing Christmas pajamas," she corrected. "He likes to be cozy. And he likes Christmas." She scratched Latte's ear and then went back to her soup. "This is an old building. It gets drafty in here."

Rowan regarded Latte for a long time before going back to his soup. "Uh-huh," was all he said. They ate in silence, and when Rowan was done, he dropped the spoon back in the bowl. "Thank you. That warmed me up."

"Of course," Ellory said, letting her spoon drop, too.

Rowan stood and reached for his wallet. "So I'll get out of your hair now. How much do I owe you?"

Alarmed, Ellory stood, tipping Latte back to the floor. He landed with a curt *meow* and went on about his business. "You're going back out there?"

"I just thought I would check into the nearest hotel. Since I'm at the mercy of Junior Feeny, it sounds like. It's getting dark outside, and I'll have to renew my efforts in the morning."

"I'm afraid you can't," Ellory said, following him to the door.

He wound his way back into his parka. "Why

not? Surely a hotel in Haw Springs isn't full." He picked up his bag and shouldered it. "And now that I'm all warmed up, thanks to your soup, I can just walk to it. Leave my car where it is."

"It's just that we don't have a hotel in Haw Springs," Ellory said.

"Not even a bed-and-breakfast?"

She shook her head.

"An Airbnb? Vrbo?"

"Nope and nope."

"How is that possible?"

She shrugged. "We're a small town."

"I'm sure there's a neighboring town with a hotel in it."

Ellory thought. "There is, but it's too far. These small towns are miles and miles apart. You're not going to walk it."

He sighed and visibly slumped. "So I'm sleeping in my car tonight. Great. Very special day indeed."

"But you'll freeze out there."

"Thanks for the reminder. How much?" He had pulled cash out of his wallet. "For the soup? And the coffee?"

"Nothing," Ellory said. "It's on the house. I was making the soup anyway."

He raised his eyebrows, as if he was surprised, then tucked the money back in his wallet and returned it to his pocket. "Thank you. That's very kind."

"Sure," she said. "Consider it a Christmas gift. On your very special day."

"I don't really do Christmas gifts, but how about I'll just consider it a kind gesture."

Ellory frowned. She prided herself on her ability to read people, but she couldn't quite get to what was going on with Rowan Kelly and Christmas. "Would you like some coffee to go? Hot cocoa? Something warm? It's so cold out there."

"You've done enough. I'm sure I'll be fine." But the crease in his forehead didn't seem quite as sure that he would be fine. The crease in his forehead seemed to think there was a strong possibility that he would be the exact opposite of fine. Maybe even less good than that, if that was possible. He opened the door, letting in a whoosh of icy air. "Thank you again for the coffee and soup. And the, ah…" He peeked at Latte again. "The company. It's been interesting, Mrs. Clouds."

"Miss," she said, pulling forward on her toes without meaning to. She found that she didn't want him to go and not just out of worry for his health but also because she was so curious about him. "And it's DeCloud. Ellory, actually."

"Yes. DeCloud. That's right. Thanks for the hospitality, Ellory of the Clouds."

"You're welcome," she said, but she trailed off at the end as he plunged back into the snow, the sky having gone to dusk while they ate their soup. The wind ripped through Ellory's sweater. She hugged herself, unsure of what to do. It wasn't like her to open her shop to strangers overnight, but she felt compelled. *Ellory of the Clouds. Was he making fun of her? Maybe. But also, she didn't hate it as much as she would have thought she would hate it.*

Latte rubbed against her legs, and she bent to pick him up as she let the door swing shut.

"Can you believe he judged you for your pajamas, Latte? Me, either. I think you look very handsome in them, and he is a big, old Christmas crankypants."

The cat purred, his fluffy tail swishing against her arm, tickling her.

"And who needs a crankypants hanging around, especially at Christmastime?" She held Latte's nose up to her own. "Not us." She set the cat down on the ground and peered out. Rowan had already all but disappeared in the snow, his footsteps frosting over almost immediately. All Ellory could see was a gray blob pushing through the blizzard, head bowed against the wind. "Nope. Not us," she repeated, her breath fogging the window and blotting him completely out of sight.

CHAPTER THREE

THERE WAS NO more lipstick left to put on this Christmas pig. Rowan was freezing, his car was going nowhere, and he was probably going to die on the side of the road in Missouri.

All because he made the mistake of trying to go home for the holidays, like all those sappy songs say is so great.

Check that, not home. Home was in Oklahoma. Home was the firehouse where his buddies were. Home was his tiny, quiet apartment, where he could be alone when he needed to be. Home was his space, a space completely free of…joy.

"No, not joy," he argued with himself aloud. "I have plenty of joy."

But did he? He wasn't sure. At the moment, he was too cold in this icy, tomb-on-wheels to try to decipher exactly what joy looked like. He only knew that it definitely didn't look like this.

He thought about Ellory. She seemed like someone who positively thrived on a constant internal stream of joy, with her rainbows and glitter and things that went ho-ho-ho. Yet there had been something guarded about her. Something heavy. Something keeping her from her joy at the moment.

"Joy to the World"? Bah, the best we could hope for is joy to ourselves for one fleeting second.

His phone buzzed. Megan.

"Hey, Megs, can you remember the last time you felt joy?" he asked upon answering.

There was a long pause. "Are you okay?"

"Yeah," he said, tucking his hands into his armpits to keep them warm. "I was just thinking about joy. You know, 'Joy to the World,' and all that. Everyone's singing it right now, and I'm wondering if most, or any of the people who are singing it have ever actually really felt it. Or if it's just lyrics. You know, like *the magic of Christmas.* Just words. There's not *actual* magic. Maybe there's not *actual* joy, either. Maybe, deep down, I'm not the only one who thinks the holidays are a crock. Joy to the world, or just joy to the people who lie to themselves? Maybe just joy to the songwriters? What do you think?"

"I don't think you're all right."

"I am. But it's going to be a long night, and I need entertainment. Just answer the question, please."

Another pause. "Okay, um yeah, I felt joy this

morning when I thought you were coming home. I was putting cider in the slow cooker with some cinnamon sticks and making up the guest bed. And the baby was just kicking away, like he was excited, too, and, well, it was joyful. A joyful morning."

"Okay, but this was a special occasion. What about in regular life? Do you ever feel joy?"

"All the time. Johnny makes me joyful. Starting our family makes me joyful. Are you saying you don't experience joy? That's kind of serious, Rowan."

He cupped a hand over his nose, which was starting to get numb. *I'll feel quite joyful if I don't lose my nose to frostbite*, he thought. "No, I experience joy. Sure, I do. But we're not talking about me."

"What exactly are we talking about, then? You keep shifting the conversation."

"What about before you married Johnny? Like when we were kids."

"Oh." Her voice dropped. "I see where this is going. You mean all the fighting and unhappiness and the divorce."

"Yeah. I mean...aren't you afraid of ending up like that?" He paused, unsure what he had been getting at. Why he'd wanted to take his sister into a dark place after she'd obviously had a lovely beginning to her day. "Never mind. I don't know what I mean. I was just thinking, that's all. Trying to occupy myself."

"Rowan, the way we grew up. It wasn't normal. You know that, right?"

Megan had slipped full force into sister mode, and now he was going to have a heck of a time breaking her out of it. He hadn't meant for this to happen. Of all the things Rowan hated, reliving the past was probably something he hated the most. So why had he gone there?

Because it's Christmas, and you always go there at Christmas. Peace and love and joy to the entire world, and a silent night...except for at the Kellys' house.

"Of course I know that." He leaned his head back against the seat and squeezed his eyes shut, using a finger and thumb to press the bridge of his nose. He could feel a headache coming on. "I really was just thinking. Mulling things over."

"Mom and Dad were not good parents, and our holidays were not good holidays. But that doesn't make the holidays themselves bad. And it doesn't make love and marriage and babies bad, either. They were a bad representation of a great thing."

"Right. I know."

"I think they fell down on the job. But that doesn't mean that we should fall down on our jobs, which are to salvage what joy—yes, I said *joy*—that we can out of life. Surely you've felt joy since we were kids, Rowan. I mean, surely you've felt joy today."

Today? Of all days? Definitely not. "Sure. Yeah. Of course I did. And I will. When I get to Des Moines, I'm going to bring so much joy into your house, it's going to need its own guest room. You're going to beg me to leave and take it with me. I'm going to sing all four hundred and seventy-five refrains of 'Joy to the World.' Even the ones nobody knows. I'm going to legally change my middle name to Joy. Rowan Joy Kelly."

Megan giggled, and he smiled. If he'd been pressed, he might have included her giggle as something that brought him joy. When they were kids, he practically lived to make his sister laugh, especially when the atmosphere between their parents was bleak. "Okay, okay. You've made your point. So what's the update? Are you headed to a hotel?"

"Yeah, I'm... I'm back in my car." He eyed the snow that had already covered his windshield. The storm wasn't letting up. If he didn't know better, he would think it had actually gotten worse since he stopped.

"What does that mean, you're back in your car? Are you going to a hotel? Surely you're not sleeping in your car."

He let out a snort that was supposed to be a laugh but was not convincing at all.

"Rowan? You're not sleeping in your car tonight, are you?"

"I'm a firefighter, Megan. I've got this."

"Well, that's just great if your car is on fire," she said. "But given that it's probably exactly the opposite of on fire, I'm going to call the police."

"No. No need to call the police. I'm fine. It's shelter. That's all I need for right now. Tomorrow morning I can worry about other things."

"Like frostbite and hypothermia? I'm calling. Besides, you need food. You need water."

"I'm quite literally surrounded by water. And I just had food. I'm good."

"You need...things. Other people and heat and a pillow. I don't know."

"Megan, stop. Stop. Nobody died from not having a pillow. I'm going to be totally fine. I have all the things I need. I just had a big bowl of soup."

"What do you mean you had soup? In your car? Rowan, are you hallucinating? I think you might be hallucinating. I'm calling."

"No, I'm not hallucinating. I went into a coffee shop on the main street of this town. Haw Springs. And she gave me coffee and soup. On the house."

"She who?"

"She—Ellory McCloud, no, wait, DeCloud—is the owner of the shop. She's this *Alice in Wonderland* kind of woman, who is all about rainbows and unicorns and all that wishy-dreamy hooey, and she has a cat named Cappuccino or Mocha or some nonsense and she..." *is absolutely beautiful*. He sat up with a start.

"And she's staring at me through my window right now."

No sooner had Ellory told Latte that she didn't want Rowan in her shop than she'd wound her scarf around her neck and her pashmina around her shoulders, stepped into her tallest boots, and trudged out into the snow after him.

Oh, how the snow energized her! It was going to be a white Christmas, even if the snow stopped right this minute, and she was so excited by the thought, she could barely contain herself. She had to resist the desire to throw herself down into the middle of Main Street and make a snow angel right then and there.

But, no, she was on a mission to save Mr. Rowan Kelly, the handsome firefighter who'd storm clouded right into her store. Why was she on this mission? She wasn't sure. He was hardly fun to be around. And he was a complete stranger.

He was fine sleeping in his car, so she also

should have been fine with it. Just let him do his thing. Take his anti-cheer attitude into his car and then on to the road to Des Moines.

But no, she couldn't do it.

Partly because she just didn't believe in letting people suffer, even if the suffering was their own doing.

But also partly because she felt a sort of kinship with Mr. Rowan Kelly the Storm Cloud in this very moment. Beneath his closed-off demeanor and his grumpy words and his stated desire to be alone was…pain. She was sure of it. And, from the sound of things, it just might have been holiday pain.

And she could definitely relate to that. Way more than she wanted to. For the first time ever. And it was the worst feeling.

Try as she might, her fa-la-la-la-la had her feeling fa-la-la-la-awful, and it was high time she admitted it to herself.

So why not go out into a blizzard and save a curmudgeon who just might grumble every time Michael Bublé warbled about homemade apple pie, and turn his nose up at Latte's carefully curated Christmas attire? Why not, indeed.

At first, she thought maybe he was asleep, but his eyes were open. He was staring straight up at the covered windshield, and if she didn't know that he'd only been in his car for a few minutes, she would have been afraid that maybe he had already frozen to death. She swiped the snow off the passenger side window with her arm, opened the door, and stuck her face inside the car. It was just as cold as outside, only less windy.

"Hey," she said, as if this was something casual, something they did every day.

"Hey," he answered, dropping his phone into his lap.

"I was thinking. I have plenty of space for you downstairs. Lots of cushions. Lots of blankets. Pillows. Everything."

"Oh."

He seemed to think it over, and she tried not to be offended by that. Would he really rather spend the night out here, possibly freeze to death, rather than join her inside? Here she was, offering a strange man entrance into her coffee shop, which was her *home*, so that he wouldn't turn into a snow mummy, and all he could say was, *Oh?*

She started to back out. "I mean…you don't have to. I just thought I'd offer. It's awfully cold out here."

"No-no-no," he said. "It's just…you're very festive, and I'm not exactly feeling especially festive. I don't want to ruin your Christmas."

She gave a thin smile. "I think you would be surprised by my festivity level," she said. "Besides, maybe you'll start to feel more festive when you're surrounded by it."

She could swear he grimaced.

"Or not," she said. "It's entirely up to you. I can understand your reluctance to experience happiness." She wrinkled her nose and waved her hand as if happiness were stinky.

A gust of wind kicked up and blew snow into the car from behind Ellory. She and Rowan both yelped as she hopped inside next to him and slammed the door shut. The minute she sat down, she felt awkward.

"For what it's worth," she said, "you're not the only one who won't be making it home for Christmas. I'm stuck here, too."

"This isn't home?"

"Well, it is now. But the rest of my family is in New Hampshire. Normally I would be there right now, drinking eggnog and watching a snowy rom-com with my sister. Instead, I'm snowed in here."

"Why didn't you leave before the snow started?"

"Why didn't you?"

"I was dragging my feet."

She paused, unsure what was compelling her to speak. "I was uninvited."

They gazed at each other for a long time. A slight shift caused the seats to squeak. The *tick-*

tick-tick of the snow and ice pellets against the windows remained steady, except when the wind blew.

"Uninvited? By who?"

"By my family."

"Ouch," he said softly.

"Yeah." She shrugged. "It happens." Only it didn't happen to most people. And it didn't happen to other people for the reason it happened to her. She'd done nothing to be cast out. *Ouch* described her feelings perfectly. *Ouch times a million.*

The wind gusted again, rocking the car. But Rowan never broke eye contact with her. It was as if he were trying to figure out a puzzle in her eyes. Finally, she dipped her face, embarrassed and feeling like she'd said too much.

"Are you going to make me sing Christmas carols?"

"Can you sing?"

He shook his head. "Not even a little bit."

"Then definitely not," Ellory said. "But if the Carol Crawl doesn't happen like planned, you may be eating a whole lot of Christmas cookies."

Rowan groaned. "I don't know what a carol crawl is, but okay. If I must."

"Don't let me twist your arm," Ellory said. "You don't have to eat them. All that butter and sugar can't possibly taste good." She pulled her pashmina tighter around herself.

"Okay, okay, they were delicious."

"It's not like I'm asking you to shovel Main Street. I'm offering you a warm place to stay tonight. Take it or leave it, I guess."

"Right. Yes. I know. You're right. Thank you. I'll take it."

"Great." She opened the door. Immediately a gust of wind blew snow over them again. "Let's go. It's cold in here!"

"Okay," he said, opening his door. "But I reserve the right to hate whatever a carol crawl is. Because it really does sound like something I would hate."

"Suit yourself," she said, but she was already trotting through the snow, her voice getting lost in the wind.

Together they trudged back up to Main Street and into the Dreamy Bean. Rowan gave the ceiling another long, weary glare and let out a huge sigh. "No chance we can take some of this down? Just so I don't have nightmares?"

"None whatsoever. I'll go get blankets," Ellory said. "Make yourself at home." Nervously, she made certain that the OPEN sign on the door was flipped to CLOSED and locked the door, then made her way upstairs to her apartment. Once upstairs, she closed and locked her apartment door, pressing her back against it with relief. What was she thinking? What was she doing?

Helping a fellow man enjoy a nice, warm place to stay.

And hoping he doesn't help himself to you, Ell, she thought. She could only imagine what her mother would have to say if Rowan Kelly robbed her blind. Or worse. *This is what happens when you treat the whole world like a friend and keep your head in the clouds, Ellory. You've been asking for this your whole life. It's like I've taught Daphne everything and taught you nothing. Am I right, Danny? See, Ellory, Danny agrees with me.*

No, Rowan didn't seem like that kind of guy. He seemed like he was the one being forced.

Still. She was definitely going to push all of her furniture behind the door when she went to bed tonight. Just in case.

Her phone buzzed. It was her mother. Perfect timing.

"Are you doing all right, Ellory dear?" her mother asked. "Daphne said you sounded morose when she spoke with you earlier. Are you being morose? Are you pouting about your current situation? The one you brought onto yourself, I might add."

"I'm not morose, Mother. I'm just trying to figure out how to celebrate Christmas by myself. Since you chose Danny over me. *I might add.*" She realized she'd adopted a snooty tone with that last bit, but since it exactly matched her mother's constantly snooty tone, she didn't worry about it.

"I did no such thing. I have done nothing differently this year than I have any other year of your life."

"Exactly. You could have done something differently and asked them not to come. Or at least asked him not to come."

"I could never."

"Well, you asked *me* not to come."

"I merely suggested that your presence would be awkward and awful for everyone to endure."

"Thanks for that."

"And since you've been unwilling to even sit down and chat with Danny—"

"Mom, we broke up."

"Correction, *you* broke up. He remains broken."

"Well, that's just sad. He's had a year. More than."

"My point exactly. Maybe it's impossible to repair yourself after losing *the one*."

"He was not *the one*, Mother."

"I'm saying you were. For him. Did you ever think of that?"

Ellory took a deep breath and held it. She had so many things to say, she didn't know where to begin. Or if she even wanted to begin. Going up against her mother was like going up against a very high quality, but very brittle and bitter, brick wall.

"I'm sorry that he feels broken," she said, very measured. "And I'm sorry that I don't get to be with you this Christmas. I will try not to be too morose. Since it's my own doing."

There was a pause, during which Ellory thought maybe her mom might defrost a little bit, maybe ask her to come out anyway. Then she would at least have the satisfaction of turning down the invitation. Instead, her mother switched the subject. "Your father is outside with the snowblower for the third time today. Can you believe it?"

"Yes, I can believe it," Ellory said, pulling off her boots and letting them drop to the floor. Melting snow snaked down the sides of them and pooled on the hardwood beneath them. "It's almost to the tops of my boots."

"What on earth were you doing outside?"

Ellory glanced at her apartment door, wondering if she'd accidentally left the Christmas music going. Would he be trying to locate the source of the music, hoping to turn it off? She grinned just thinking about it.

Part of her felt as though she should tell her mother that she'd taken in a stranger. For safety reasons. But, with her mother, there would be so many questions. So much judgment. So many things that she had done wrong in opening her door to a strange man. And she wasn't sure she had a good argument against it.

The words got stuck in her throat.

"Oh, I was just checking it out. You know I love a white Christmas."

"Yes, you, my Christmas enthusiast. Yet unafraid to ruin it for the rest of us."

Ellory felt a pang of guilt, followed by a pang of indignation. She'd stopped hoping for her family's forgiveness when it came to what happened with Danny. But it still hurt when she was expected to bear full blame. But any attempt to make her mother understand would be pointless. She'd given up on that long ago, pretty much the moment she pulled into Haw Springs, eyed Main Street, and said, *This is the place*.

"Right. Well, I've got cookies in the oven, Mother. Talk to you on Christmas Eve."

"Before four o'clock, of course."

"Of course. Give Daddy my love?"

Her mother made a *mmm* noise that Ellory couldn't quite decipher the meaning of. Her mother had been her biggest critic, but her father was almost worse in his complete silence.

"Mother?" Ellory said at the last minute.

"Yes?"

"Do you think that you might come visit sometime in the New Year? You haven't ever seen the Dreamy Bean or my apartment." The Dreamy

Bean, and Ellory's devotion to following a dream, was the crux of the problem. Yet Ellory somehow still stubbornly held onto a vision that her family—maybe even Danny, if Ellory would let him—would understand the dream if only they saw it in action. "Please?"

There was a long pause. "There's a lot going on in the New Year," was all her mother said. "We'll see."

"Sure. Of course. Yeah." Ellory felt the brush-off all the way to the center of her soul. "I understand." She didn't. She never would.

"I will look at the calendar after things have slowed down," her mother said, the greatest concession Ellory had gotten from her since the whole scandalous betrayal dream of owning a coffee shop had begun.

Ellory smiled, despite herself, mad at herself for allowing it. "Just let me know."

"Well, I suppose I should triple-check that the guest room has clean towels. Chin up. Nobody likes a sad sack at Christmas."

"Got it."

"And maybe consider having a conversation with Danny soon? Then we can put all this ugly business of you breaking his heart behind us and be a family again. Maybe next Christmas we could be celebrating a re-engagement."

Never going to happen. Not in a million years.
"Sure, Mom. Maybe."

Ellory hung up and grabbed an armload of blankets from her closet shelf. She swiped the extra pillow from her bed and changed the pillowcase. In the bathroom cabinet, she found an extra holiday-themed towel, hand towel, and washcloth set. They were all adorned with Rudolph the Red Nosed Reindeer and the words *Be a deer and wash your hands.*

He would hate them. He would have to live with it.

Arms full, she headed back downstairs. The Christmas music, meant to be heartwarming and dear, sounded melancholic. The lights were dim. There didn't seem to be movement going on at all.

She slowed to a creep and spotted him.

He'd pushed two cloud chairs together—the big ones that always seemed to invite giggly, teenage wrestling matches—and was curled up on his side, cramped, but fast asleep. His coat was hung on a nearby chair, his boots and backpack on the floor beneath it. The cuffs of his pants were wet with melting snow.

Ellory stopped and watched as his chest slowly moved up and down. Even in his sleep, he wore the slightest hint of a frown, as if he were troubled by the idea of not being awake.

Lightly and carefully, so as not to wake him, she draped the blankets over him and tucked the pillow into the space between the arm of the chair and his head. She set the towels on a nearby table. She left the kitchen light on, in case he needed to find the restroom later.

And then she turned off the music, silence pressing into the room like a third person. Normally, she found silence to be off-putting. But there was something calming about his slow breathing.

She listened to it for a while before turning and creeping back upstairs.

Maybe he was right. Maybe this year, Christmas was just…too much.

December 23

OVERNIGHT, THE WIND arrived in earnest. It blew and blew, creating mountains out of fence posts and turning dens into enclosed caves.

The animals curled tighter around themselves and their loved ones. They were still not worried, so much as uneasy. They felt confident that their littermates who were not cuddled up next to them were somewhere nearby. Somewhere reachable.

Still the snow fell, dampening their snores and deafening their chatter.

They twitched and huffed in their dreams.

Dreaming of when the snow would stop, and they could take inventory of the ones closest to them.

CHAPTER FOUR

ROWAN SLEPT DEEPLY and dreamlessly, the way he only ever did when he was beyond exhausted. When he finally roused, it was a tickle on his face that drew him out of the darkness of sleep. He swiped at his cheek and blinked awake, only to find himself staring at a soft, gray nose and one golden, unblinking eyeball.

He sat up quickly, confused.

Cat? I don't have a cat. Did we get a cat at the firehouse? He looked down at the pillowy, white fleece that he'd slept on. *This isn't my bed. This isn't the firehouse.*

But then the scent of coffee curled into his nostrils, and his eyes landed on a macramé rainbow wall hanging, a truly awful Christmas elf sitting on top of it like a swing, and the events of the day before snapped into focus.

The stranded car. The coffee shop. The woman who fed him cookies and soup. The cat in pajamas. The blizzard. As much as it may have all seemed like the world's most bizarre dream, it apparently wasn't.

He got up, stretched out his creaking muscles, and padded to the front window, hoping that the snow had slowed. It hadn't. The sky was still gray and heavy. Flakes spiraled their way to the ground, lazy and fat. He squinted against the brightness. His dry throat and foggy brain cried out for coffee.

He heard footsteps descending the stairs. The woman who'd helped him the day before came toward him. He'd joked that she was Ellory of the Clouds but found that he genuinely thought of her that way, both because of her name, but also because there was something about her that was particularly floaty. Something dreamy and buoyant. She was especially festive this morning in a red-and-green argyle sweater dress, with red knee-high socks and shiny patent leather Mary Janes. She'd wound a piece of holly into her hair.

She smiled, and Rowan could have sworn that the sun came out for the briefest moment. The inside of the coffee shop, with that smile, seemed brighter than the snowy sky outside.

"You're awake," she said. "How did you sleep?"

Again, he glanced at the cloud formed by the two chairs he'd pushed together the night before. The cat stretched out regally right in the center of them, his tail swishing. Ownership.

"Surprisingly good," he said.

She beamed. "Comfortable, right? Latte and I may or may not be guilty of dozing in those chairs at night when it gets cozy and quiet. We sit down to read a book with a nice, warm cup of tea and next thing you know, it's morning."

"Latte reads?" Rowan was joking, but she nodded seriously.

"Regency romance is his favorite." She waited a beat and then cracked up. "I mean, I'm not going to say I never read out loud, but Latte's just there for the warm snuggle. And he definitely doesn't mind when a saucy lord gets his lady." Her cheeks instantly flooded with a blush—cute—and she busied herself by shooing the cat away and pushing the chairs apart again, putting them back into their place. Rowan jumped to help her half a second too late and felt his own embarrassment burn, hoping that she didn't notice that he was too rooted in his spot staring at her to actually move.

"I'm sorry if Latte disturbed you this morning," Ellory said. "I told him to let you sleep. He's not always great with boundaries."

"It's okay. I needed to wake up anyway. But waking up to his giant eyeball was a little jarring." He pointed at the horrifying elf he'd spotted earlier. "And that. Jarring to say the least. Maybe more like horrifying."

She gazed at the elf. "You don't like Felix?"

"Felix?"

She pressed her lips together, as if deciding on what to say. "Felix…Navidad. I don't know. I name things. I'll move him." She grabbed the elf, ducked her head, and hurried toward the coffee bar. "Can I get you a coffee?"

Rowan found himself grinning at her embarrassment. "I would love one, thank you."

"Peppermint Mocha? Sugar Cookie Latte? Iced Gingerbread Man?"

"How about just coffee? Black."

She frowned. "That's boring."

He shrugged. "What can I say? I try to avoid drinking my holidays, I guess."

"It's just a name," she said. "It doesn't lock you into celebrating Christmas if you drink something with the word *gingerbread* in the name."

"You make a great point. Coffee is just coffee. I'll have mine black."

"Have it your way," she said, and for the first time, he saw actual gloom beset her and felt horrible for being the reason it happened. He ran his hands through his hair, feeling a little like an unappreciative cad. Was his negativity so ingrained in him that he didn't even realize it anymore? Was it just who he was now? He didn't like to think so, but it was certainly starting to look that way.

"You know what?" he said. "You're right. I'll have one of the gingerbread things. Sure. Thank you."

"Of course," she said, pulling two mugs off the shelf above her. "Two gingerbread things." She glanced up at him and winked. "Also, I'll get some breakfast started, but if you'd like something while you wait…"

"Oh, goodness, no. You're doing so much for me. The coffee will be fine."

"I have cranberry orange scones. They're pretty good. I'm working to perfect the recipe."

"You said that last night about the soup, too. Sounds like you try out a lot of recipes."

"I do. I'd like to turn the Bean into…" She trailed off, let out a breath, waved the thought away.

"Into…?"

She glanced up at him and smiled. "Oh, nothing. Never mind. It's just a silly idea I sometimes have." She pushed a button and the steamer blasted into life. She dipped the end of the wand into a pitcher of milk and held it there with a loud whoosh. There was definitely something more beneath her *silly idea*, but he wasn't sure if he should push it.

He decided against it and again walked to the window. Was this going to be his life until Junior Feeny decided to make his way back to his shop? Arguing over what was festive versus what was annoying, listening to half sentences as she second-guessed everything she said, tormenting himself with wanting to learn about her versus knowing that there was no reason for him to learn, and obsessing at the front window? The very idea seemed almost as bleak as the skies, which were still indiscernible from the ground, everything white as far as he could see.

"Coffee's up," Ellory said from the counter. "And you never answered. About the scones?"

"Oh. Yeah. Um. Sure, I'll have a scone. Thank you."

He retrieved his breakfast and found a table in the back. He bit into the scone as he bent to sit and let out an involuntary groan. "Are you serious?" he said to the scone itself.

"Something's wrong?"

He took another bite and struggled to keep his eyes from rolling back in his head as the layers of orange and cranberry bloomed like fireworks in his mouth. "Definitely not," he said. "It's otherworldly. Let me tell you something, Miss Cloud." He held up the scone as if to toast her with it. "I don't know what you were about to say back there, but I can tell you there is nothing silly about this scone."

She beamed again, and Rowan could envision a world in which making someone's face light up the way hers did when she was happy could be the driving force of a life. "Really? You like it?"

He nodded. "Really. I love it. How many do you have? I'll buy them all."

She let out a laugh. "Stop. You don't have to buy anything. You're my guest. I'll bring you another."

He took another bite, leaned his head back against the chair and smiled. "Nothing silly at all," he repeated.

IF ONLY ROWAN KELLY knew what he was saying.

If only he knew that, in her world, dreams were impractical and indulgent and most definitely silly. Dreams were to be torn apart and laughed at and used to embarrass someone at lofty dinner parties.

Dreams were for people who knew what they were doing.

Dreams weren't for pretty girls who should stick to finding the perfect couch for the media room—one that wouldn't break the bank but would still allow for a gentle, well-placed brag when friends came over.

Dreams aren't for girls like you, Ellory, dear. You've got a pedigree. That's your asset in life. Your father has worked hard to give you that asset, and you shouldn't look a gift horse in the mouth. Now that we think about it, it's downright insulting of you to have dreams, Ellory. It's inconsiderate.

Once upon a time, Ellory had thought she'd been gifted the perfect life. Her mother had given birth to Ellory literally two hours after her lifelong best friend, Amanda Wittfeld, had brought her son Danny into this world. They'd vowed to each other that their babies would grow up to marry, and for all of Ellory's life, she believed it to be true.

Outwardly, Danny was everything a girl could want. He was handsome, charming, intelligent and rich. They grew up side by side. Every vacation, every holiday, every spare moment, they were together. Not that they didn't have their ups and downs. Danny took another girl to the homecoming dance their sophomore year of high school. Ellory spent an entire summer in Colorado dating a river guide during her college internship. But they always came back together. As devoted as life partners could ever be.

Ellory thought she was in love, because that was what everyone told her.

Sometimes love hurt. When Danny would deride her decisions. When he would tell her that her jokes were stupid and refused to laugh at them. When he would instead laugh at her when she was being serious. When he would pat her head like a dog and tell her to *stay pretty* as a way of calling her dumb.

Ellory accepted his behavior. She began to see her gifted life as a little less gift and a little more burden. But who in her life would sympathize with her? Everyone loved and wanted to be with Danny Wittfeld, but he loved and wanted to be with her. She would be rich and coddled, whether she wanted the coddling or not.

Turned out, she didn't.

She wanted to be an entrepreneur. She had a vision for her own life, and that vision included the Dreamy Bean. Danny greeted her vision with encouragement at first, calling it *her little customer service experiment* in front of their friends. But as time wore on, and she didn't stop talking about her little customer service experiment, his patience began to wear thin.

Can't you just let it rest for one day, he'd barked at her when she'd brought it up one day during a double date. She'd burned with mortification and fury, but let it go. He was stressed. He was tired. He didn't understand just how important it was to her, or how serious she was about it.

When they'd gotten engaged, two families rejoiced. What had been decided on a sunny spring day twenty-five years before had come to fruition. At last, the families would be one, everything hinging around the union that would be Ellory and Danny.

At first, Ellory was just as thrilled as the rest of them. And she knew that, now that they were betrothed, he would change his mind about her little customer service experiment. He would welcome her business, because it would be their business.

She was wrong.

And the day that she showed him the space on Water Street where she'd intended to open her shop, she learned just how wrong she'd been.

Her entire world, and everything she believed, had come crashing down on her.

Rowan had called the scones otherworldly. And she had to agree. They were special. She had a talent. She knew it deep within herself, even if it was hard sometimes to hold on to that knowledge when faced with the scorn of people who were supposed to love and support her. Sometimes she wanted to turn back time, back to that day on Water Street when Danny and her mother had ganged up on her. She would love to go back even further, to before the engagement, and stand up for herself. Assert that she could have a pedigree and dreams.

Tell Danny in no uncertain terms that if she had to let one go, it wouldn't be the dreams.

Tell him not to bother with the diamond ring and the proposal.

Ellory gave Rowan the Wi-Fi password and disappeared into the kitchen to whip up breakfast for three. She was hungry, and it would appear that Rowan had awakened hungry as well. She hadn't yet heard from Mr. Crowley, but she'd never known him to not be hungry for breakfast.

The Christmas Eve dinner plans might be in danger, but that didn't mean she couldn't get breakfast to him. It didn't mean she couldn't check on him. She had boots and a coat. Breakfast delivery would be no problem.

"Will bacon, eggs and pancakes be all right?" she called from the kitchen.

"You've really done enough already," he called back.

"That's not what I asked."

A pause, and then, "Sounds great, actually."

She nodded and got to work, lining a baking tray with strips of bacon, and pulling out a whisk for scrambling some eggs. While she waited for the oven to preheat, she thumbed through the news on her phone. Blizzard, blizzard, blizzard. Just about everyone, everywhere was going to be snowed in for the holidays. The roads weren't traversable. The visibility was terrible. The cold was deadly. Rowan's car was but one of thousands abandoned along the sides of highways.

"Fa-la-la-la-la," Ellory said softly. She had better figure out a way to tell Mr. Crowley that he wouldn't be spending Christmas Eve with Mrs. Crowley after all. The thought broke her heart, and she wasn't sure she could do it. But she knew he would ask when she arrived with breakfast.

Her phone rang. Katherine Messing's scowling face appeared on the screen. Ellory let out a long sigh before answering. She supposed she was waiting for this call, even as she hoped she wouldn't receive it.

"Hi, Katherine!" She tried to sound light and upbeat, as if her sunny tone could actualize the sun itself and put an end to this storm. "Merry Christmas Eve Eve."

"Hello," Katherine said. "Yes, merry…things. Do you have a minute?"

Merry…things? Ellory stifled a laugh. She popped the bacon into the oven and set a timer. "Absolutely. What's up?"

"As I'm sure you're aware, the weather forecast is looking perhaps a bit bleak."

"It's going to be a white Christmas, that's for sure," Ellory chirped. "It will make the caroling even more amazing, don't you think? Caroling in the snow on Christmas Eve? So romantic!" She found that she was hugging herself as she spoke, and forced herself to let her arms drop.

"Except nobody can get there," Katherine said. "I hate to do this, but—"

"Then don't," Ellory blurted. "Don't do it."

"Ellory, turn on the news. This snow isn't going anywhere. And neither are any people. I know you're alone down there in that little coffee shop but, generally speaking, allowing people to be home for the holidays is a good thing. There are many songs reflecting that sentiment. You'd be singing those very songs."

"Yes, of course. I know. And I would never want anyone to get hurt trying to get to the Crawl. But...why cancel it? You know? Maybe somebody can get out and walk into town. Those of us who can, will. Those who can't, can stay home. Or...or maybe if a few of us crawl into the neighborhoods, people will come out and walk their own streets. Instead of Main Street being musical and magical, it will be all of Haw Springs, as neighbor after neighbor takes to their own streets to sing." Ellory was finding that she liked this idea even better than the original one to begin with.

"That's a big change. How would we let people know?"

"We don't. We just get out there and start singing. How would you let people know if you canceled it?"

There was a long pause while Katherine thought this over.

"Please, Katherine," Ellory begged. "I think... I need this?"

"There's a lot of work that goes into the Annual Haw Springs Main Street Christmas Carol Crawl. A lot of money."

"Which is why you shouldn't cancel it. I've already done all the work. This way, at least it's not totally wasted."

"I can't be there, Ellory. As you're aware, I live on Evergreen Avenue on the outskirts of Haw Springs. I'm snowed in here."

"I can do it alone," Ellory said. "I'll take full responsibility."

"You've only ever seen one Haw Springs Christmas Carol Crawl before. How can you run one if you've only seen one?"

Just because you've been in a coffee shop doesn't mean you can run one, Ellory. What do you know about running a business?

"I'm smart," Ellory said, channeling the conversation she wished she'd had with her parents and Danny. "I'm totally capable. And I really want this. Maybe it won't look exactly like it always has in the past, but maybe that'll be a good thing. I'll introduce new ideas that people will love. It'll be the dawn of a whole new model for the Haw Springs Carol Crawl."

Katherine hesitated.

Ellory turned so that her back was to the kitchen door. The last thing she wanted was for Rowan to hear her grovel. She already hated for

Katherine to be hearing it. She was not a groveler. She didn't like pity. But sometimes, whether you liked it or not, you just needed it. Ellory suspected that this might be one of those times.

"Katherine, I need this. I'm here alone, and it's Christmas. It can't hurt to try." Her eyes roved to the door. Technically, she wasn't there alone. But she had a feeling that she would be. Rowan was certainly not comfortable being her guest, and besides, if he wanted nothing to do with Christmas, the last thing he was going to want to do was celebrate Christmas with a stranger. She was fairly certain that Rowan Kelly would be looking for the fastest, easiest way back onto the highway at the first possible sign that he could get his car going.

Katherine sighed, the noise of her breath in the phone mimicking the noise of the wind outside, pressing against the side of the shop. "Good luck. It's all you."

Ellory beamed. "Thank you, thank you! I won't let you down. It's going to be spectacular, I promise. Hey, maybe we'll even get as far as Evergreen Avenue."

"If you do, I'll come outside and sing," Katherine said, but she said it with much resignation, and Ellory had a sense that Katherine had only said it because she felt it an impossibility. Ellory decided to let it lift her heart anyway.

"Merry Christmas, Katherine!"

"Yes, of course. You, too."

Ellory ended the call and hugged her phone to her chest, forgetting all about breakfast. Her annoyingly relentless optimism, as Danny had once put it, had been the trait that had gotten her furthest in life.

Or it's the trait that cost you a fiancé and a family, the little voice in the back of her mind tried to remind her.

"Nope," she said aloud. "I gained a dream come true." She nodded once and set to making the pancakes and eggs. Her arms were sore from all the stirring the day before, but for some reason that only made her stir harder. She welcomed the soreness. The soreness meant she was still in there somewhere. She wasn't being morose. "And I'm just going to keep dreaming from here, no matter who doesn't like it."

CHAPTER FIVE

ROWAN WAS JUST about ready to yank the earmuffs off of a stuffed Frosty the Snowman and cram them over his ears when the music mercifully stopped. The relief must have shown on his face, because Ellory, heading toward him with a tray of food, drooped.

"Sorry," he mumbled, feeling caught. Since when did he care if someone knew that listening to the same six holiday songs over and over again in different voices annoyed him? It was practically legendary in the firehouse. Something he was kind of proud of. Only...well, at the moment, he didn't feel so proud. Why be proud over something that makes someone's face fall the way hers just did?

"It's okay." She tossed a smile his way, and for the briefest moment, he thought it might be okay to listen to the same six songs over and over again if you were doing it alongside that smile. *So maybe you ought to smile more, too, Rowan.*

This time it was Megan's voice he heard instead of his own. "Breakfast is served."

Ellory set a platter in front of him, containing a pile of bacon, a steaming bowl of scrambled eggs and a tower of pancakes.

He leaned in and took a big inhale without even thinking about it. "It smells awesome."

She beamed. "Thank you! You might be smelling my homemade syrup. It's pumpkin pecan cinnamon roll flavored. I've been working on a coffee syrup with the same flavor. It's very holiday. Sorry to say."

He aimed his nose toward the syrup, and indeed that was a big part of the alluring scent. Warm and sticky and filled with cinnamon and pumpkin and pecan. It stirred up emotions in him that he didn't care to acknowledge. Yes, they were holiday emotions. It was just that his holiday emotions were rarely good ones.

Still, this smell made him feel cozy inside, as if the potential for holiday warmth was possible. And that was a definite first.

"You shouldn't be sorry about something that smells so amazing," he said. "Truly. It's wonderful, and you don't have to do any of this."

She ducked her head and clasped her hands together. "Except… I sort of do…to repay the favor."

He paused with a fork plunged into the stack

of pancakes, ready to move one onto his plate. "What do you mean? What favor?"

"The one I'm about to ask."

You see, Rowan? No good deed goes unpunished, he could hear his mother say. *You thought she was going to just take you in out of the goodness of her heart? People don't work like that. People expect payback for their good deeds, and you're a fool for not thinking it through before you stayed with her. Now you're going to be fixing a roof or taking care of a baby or who knows what?*

Rowan couldn't count how many times his mother had warned him to close his heart, close himself off from others. She'd done it so often, it was second nature to him now. The thoughts came unbidden. He worried that maybe he followed the advice one too many times, because he most often heard her words in his own voice. Especially when he was being hard-hearted and cynical.

At the same time, it would have been nice of Little Miss Clouds to have let him know up front that she wasn't going to just let him invade her space without expecting something in return. Would it have changed anything? Maybe not. Probably not. The world was what the world was, and there was no changing any of it.

"Are you okay?" Ellory said, lowering herself

into a chair, snapping him out of it. She nodded at his fork. The pancake that he'd stabbed had fallen back onto the stack, and he was simply holding an empty fork in the air.

"What? Yeah. I'm... I was just thinking about...well, about my mom. What do you need?"

Ellory's forehead creased with concern. "Oh, no. Is this keeping you from seeing her for the holidays? I'm so sorry."

"No. Not at all. She's on a cruise. She doesn't even know there's a snowstorm, I'm guessing."

"It must be tough for you to spend the holidays without her, then," Ellory said. "I know it's a bit challenging for me."

He shrugged. This conversation was getting out of hand. Entirely too close for his taste. He didn't talk to his closest friend—if he were to allow himself to have one—about his relationship with his mother. He sure as heck wasn't about to open up and divulge his deepest and darkest to Ellory DeCloud just because she made a syrup that mined some deep-seated nostalgia from a place so hidden within him, he didn't even know it was there. He forced his fork to move, spiked it into the pancake again to scoop it onto the plate. *Syrup is for eating, not waxing poetic*, he thought.

"You said you needed to ask a favor?"

"Oh. Yeah. So I have a regular. Mr. Crowley.

He's a little older and has a hard time getting out and about. He walks here every day for breakfast, and I'm a little worried that he's not going to eat anything with this storm." She gestured helplessly to the front window. Outside, the snow was still coming down in fluffy, oversize flakes. A ledge of snow perched along the outside windowsill and had begun to creep up the corner. "Anyway, I was thinking of taking his breakfast to him. But it's a lot for one person to carry."

Rowan plucked a few pieces of bacon off the tray and put them on his plate, alongside a huge scoop of scrambled eggs. His stomach rumbled, even though it was full of scones and coffee, and he stuffed a piece of bacon in his mouth without thinking about it. "Oh." He chewed, swallowed. "You're wanting me to walk with you and help you carry breakfast to this guy?"

"You don't have to," she said. "I know it's a lot to ask. And I can manage it alone if I make two trips. I'll pack it up in baskets. It's just…"

"You don't want to leave me alone in your store because you don't trust me."

Her eyes grew big. "I didn't mean that at all!"

"But you shouldn't, you know?" He chewed some more, swallowed again. "I mean, you can. I am who I say I am, and I'm not planning to steal anything or do anything weird. I wasn't planning on being here in the first place. But you still shouldn't trust me because I'm a stranger, and I get that totally."

"But I do trust you. I think?" she said.

He pointed at her with his fork and gave a wink. "I think," he repeated. "Like I said, I totally get it. I'll bet you pushed your dresser in front of your door last night."

"I didn't," she said.

"Really? Huh."

"But it's not that I don't trust you to be alone here. It's that I have some bad news to give him, and I guess I'm hoping for moral support. Strength in numbers, and all that. I don't know. It's silly. You can stay. I'll walk there by myself. It's not a long walk. Forget I asked."

She started to get up, but Rowan stopped her. "Wait. You're not going to eat with me?"

She smiled. "I'll eat in the kitchen. It's okay. I'm sure you'd like some time alone."

"No," he blurted, reaching for her arm. He pulled back at the last second. "I mean... I'd like the company."

To his surprise, he realized that he meant it.

To HER OWN SURPRISE, Ellory joined him for breakfast.

Over breakfast, Ellory told Rowan all about Mr. Crowley and her promise to help him with his anniversary dinner that was most certainly not going to happen. She talked and ate around a lump in her throat as she thought about how it must feel to not be able to spend such an important time with the one person in your world who mattered the most.

"If only you had a sleigh," Rowan said. "Then you could get him there."

"And you could get to a bigger city where you could rent a car. Or, even better! Take a plane," Ellory said, nibbling on her last spoonful of eggs. "Alas, we are fresh out of sleighs here in Haw Springs."

He glanced around the shop. "Funny, Haw Springs seems like exactly the kind of town that would have an abundance of sleighs."

Ellory put her spoon down, grinning. "Wait. Are you being serious?"

Rowan nodded. "Yeah. I mean, it seems like the kind of town to at least have an abundance of the ability to have sleighs. Like, *Oh, Old Man Vesper down on Route Triple P could whip us up one right quick.* Or, *We could build our own, using the little Christmas trees out front, some antique tools found in your attic and a good dollop of elbow grease.*" He smiled, then, seeming to realize how flat his joke had fallen, cleared his throat and pointed his face back down toward his plate, chewing.

She gave him a curious glance. "What does any of that mean? Are you making fun of us?"

His face blazed as red as an ornament with his discomfort. "No, of course not. Just, you know, it's the whole small-town vibe thing. It's like a movie here. It's cool. For the record, if we could build a sleigh, I would definitely use it."

Ellory considered this. She wanted to be offended, but if she was being honest with herself, she also felt as though she'd stumbled onto a movie set when she first moved to Haw Springs. It was part of what made the town so charming. And if she thought about it—really thought—she could probably identify a few different ways that they could build a sleigh. Or at least who they could ask to build it for them.

It wasn't so far-fetched.

"I'm sorry," Rowan said. "I was just joking."

"It's okay," she said. "But just so you know, we will not be touching those trees. Except to decorate them."

"All you," he said. "I haven't decorated a Christmas tree since I was a kid, and I don't intend to start now."

"Well, fortunately for you, I don't need any help." Although after her conversation with Katherine, Ellory was feeling a little pressure. Nobody said she had to decorate the trees all along Main Street, but that didn't stop her from feeling like she had to do just that. Call it a gut feeling, but she just had a hunch that people would Crawl their way to Main Street, even if the actual Crawl came to them. "Nobody needs your Scroogey vibes on their tinsel."

Rowan glanced up at her in surprise. She held his gaze, her eyebrows raised in a challenge. He let out a little chuckle and went back to eating. "Fair enough."

They finished their breakfast together, and Ellory set to packing up Mr. Crowley's breakfast into a handful of containers that she loaded into two baskets. She added a couple of sample bags of coffee, some cream, and a bottle of her newest syrup as a personal touch and then wound some leftover pine garland and sprigs of holly around the handle to give it a holiday feel.

She wanted him to feel special, especially since she was going to be immediately letting him down.

Truth be told, Mr. Crowley reminded her a little of her grandfather, who'd passed away when she was a young teenager. Grandpa DeCloud worked hard his whole life and had worked his way up into not just a little bit of money. He'd married into the pedigree but was a self-made man in his own right.

But, unlike her pedigreed grandmother, he was

also kind. Ellory had always been drawn by his smiling eyes and gentle voice.

Grandpa DeCloud believed in make-believe and finding love in small things and following curiosity. He believed in making yourself vulnerable and always told her that good luck was for those who were prepared to receive it.

And he always had a book tucked under his arm, no matter where he went or what he was doing. Ellory's favorite memories were of Christmases spent at the DeCloud estate, where she would inevitably find herself discussing books while wandering her grandpa's study, admiring his treasures, which ranged from miniature WWII battle scenes that he'd constructed and painted himself to a stack of old pop-up books, crunchy and stiff with age. She loved to spin a huge globe with her eyes closed and pointer finger poised and then look up at him for a quick nod or shake of the head, depending on if he'd ever visited the location where she'd randomly stopped the rotation.

Yes, I've been there. Let me tell you, Ell, it's got the greenest trees you've ever seen in your whole life... he would say. Or, *Not yet, Ell, but someday I'll sink my toes right into that white sand. And when I do, I'll find a crab and name it after you.*

Ellory believed that she and Grandpa DeCloud were kindred spirits, and that she even looked more like him than either of her parents. And when she sat with Mr. Crowley every morning at his favorite table right in front of the big window in the back, where he could watch the sun rise, chatting about life and dreams and disappointments, she couldn't shake the nostalgic feeling of being with her grandpa. If Mr. Crowley had ever talked about a pebbled path in the woods in Nova Scotia, she wouldn't have been surprised. She might have looked around for a pop-up book.

She was arranging a snowflake-patterned tea towel over the second basket when she heard a noise behind her. She swiveled to see Rowan standing in the doorway, holding his dirty plates. She realized only then that she hadn't locked the kitchen door behind her.

"Oh! Gosh, you didn't need to bring those in. I would have come for them." She bustled to take them from him, feeling a little caught with him so close in her kitchen space. The whole conversation about not trusting him because he was a stranger came back to her. But, again, her gut told her that Rowan Kelly, grumpy though he may be, was a man of integrity. Someone she could trust. She just felt flustered in such close quarters.

"It's okay. It's the least I could do. Are you okay? You're a little pale."

"You startled me," she said. "You came in very

quietly, and I wasn't expecting you to come into the kitchen at all."

"I'm so sorry. I should have asked. Or knocked. Or...something. I wasn't trying to..."

"No, of course you weren't." She made a concerted effort to let her shoulders relax, let out a breathy laugh. Why was she so tense with Rowan? "I'm just jumpy, I guess. Maybe it's the weather." *The weather? Since when did snow make people jumpy? Come on, Ellory, if you can't say something that makes sense, maybe just stop talking.*

She reached for the final plate, her fingers lightly brushing against his. Suddenly, the entire kitchen was filled with warmth, as their eyes locked. They both seemed to have the words yanked right out of them.

Yet, at the same time, Ellory had a sense that they had communicated something. At least for the briefest moment, she had felt seen, and without the judgment that she was silly or too festive or too effusive or too dreamy or too naive or too gullible or too...Ellory. She took a step back, trying to avoid being bowled over.

She had to have that wrong. There was no way that Rowan Kelly, who seemed to be made out of granite and pragmatism, had seen her for who she really was.

And had stayed standing there.

CHAPTER SIX

CALL HIM CRAZY, but there was a moment in Ellory's kitchen that Rowan felt sure that he'd lifted some sort of veil and peeked beneath to see who Ellory DeCloud really was.

Okay, when he thought of it that way, even he would call himself crazy. She was getting to him. She was making him...poetic. Ha! The guys at the firehouse would bust a gut laughing at the idea.

But there had been a moment between them. That was undeniable. She'd taken the plate out of his hand, and they'd stood there, a zap of something keeping their skin glued to each other for one millisecond too long. He felt the tug of her heart pulling at him. Or maybe it was something deeper than her heart. Maybe something soul level.

Ugh. If he kept this up, he would soon be crooning. And everyone knew there was only a single, snowbound hop, skip and jump between crooning and singing Christmas carols.

When she took a step back, he'd forced himself to move, too. He thrust a thumb over his shoulder awkwardly, as if he were eight years old again, suggesting that they go outside with their sleds.

"I'm sorry. I'll go back. I didn't mean to invade your personal space. I just wanted to help. I could carry something."

"You didn't invade anything," she said, stacking the plate on the others in the crook of her other arm and bustling to a deeper depth of the kitchen. "You didn't at all. I'll get these in the sink, and then we'll go." He heard the plates land somewhere with a small rattle and then she reappeared, pushing loose strands of hair out of her eyes. "If you want to go, of course. Again, you don't have to."

Now, suddenly, they were formal. And Rowan hated it.

Also, he kind of wanted to brush her hand with his again. See if he could recreate the zap of energy.

"I'm happy to help," he said. "I'll just go get my boots on." Again with the ridiculous jabby thumb thing, and then, blessedly, his feet found motion and he lurched out of the kitchen and into the dining room, which felt drafty and empty without her.

They were so awkward together. Yet at the same time, that zap, that moment. If he were forced to put words to what had happened between them, he would say she seemed like the only person in his life that ever made sense.

He remembered when Megan got married. She was so happy she looked like she was lit from within, and while he smiled and said all the hopeful things, on the inside he just didn't get it. Why would anyone ever marry after witnessing the war that was their parents' marriage?

How on earth had Megan found someone she was even willing to get close enough to so she could explore the option?

And now bring a baby into it? No way. He admired his sister for her openness.

But there were times, and he would never tell Megan this, that he wondered if her happiness had lasted. If maybe the reason that it worked was because Johnny traveled every week. If she would admit it even if that was true.

But with the baby coming, it was obvious that she was happy, right?

He decided to check in with her. He pulled his phone out of his back pocket and pulled up his texts. He'd missed six from her.

You okay?

Rowan?

You alive???

Do I need to call someone? Send out a search party???

This isn't funny! If you think you're being funny, you're not.

Rowan, I swear, I'm going to call the police.

He checked the time. It was still early. But Megan was an early riser.

I'm alive. I'm good. Warm and fed. No search party needed.

Her response was immediate.

IT'S ABOUT TIME YOU ANSWERED. I WAS FREAKING OUT.

He scrolled back and indeed could see that the texts had begun at around three in the morning.

Why were you up so late? Or was it so early?

Yes. I couldn't sleep. I was worrying about you. Plus a lot of contractions.

Contractions?!

Don't worry—just the false ones. Practicing for the big day. This kid's gonna be an overachiever.

Like mother, like son.

Ha.

Seriously, Megs, don't worry about me. I slept on a literal cloud last night. Actually, two of them. Pushed together. One big cloud. And I woke up to a cat in pajamas sniffing my face. And bacon and eggs and pancakes.

Are you sure you're not so cold you're hallucinating?

He chuckled. What he was saying did sound a little ridiculous. So why couldn't he stop smiling?

I promise I'm all good. I've got to go deliver breakfast now.

His thumbs hovered over his phone as he considered explaining, but, grinning, he decided to let her wonder. She was an overachiever…and a worrywart. And lots of fun to razz. Something he'd been doing since—he liked to imagine—before they were even born.

Ellory appeared from the kitchen, a large, decorated basket in each mittened hand. She had donned a white, fuzzy coat and a pair of white earmuffs and had wound a bright red scarf around her neck and tucked it into the front of her coat.

"Ready?"

For the briefest moment, Rowan felt frozen in place. She looked as if the snow itself had balled itself up into sheer radiance and plopped itself in the middle of her coffee shop. The most beautiful snowman—er, snowwoman—ever created. As if snowflakes had said, *If you think we're dazzling, you should check this out!* and sent her twirling to earth.

As if maybe you need to get a hold of yourself, Rowan Kelly. Like, now.

She blinked. "What?"

"Huh? Nothing." He hurried for his coat and gloves. "I just...wasn't expecting you to be already in your, uh..." He gestured, trying to find words again.

"My coat?"

"Right." He felt fumbly, his hands and arms flighty and uncooperative. In the end he had no idea how he even managed to get himself ready, but in just moments, there he was, standing in front of her again, his hands held out to take a basket. He was breathing too hard for the minimal effort he'd put in.

Maybe his sister was right. Maybe he was still in his car and was so cold he was acting like someone else entirely.

"Ready," he said. *She's just a woman*, he reminded himself. *And she couldn't be more opposite of you if she tried. You have no reason to be feeling so crushy.*

Crushy? Really? Was that what he was?

She gave him an odd look. "Is everything okay?"

"Huh? Yeah. Of course. I was just texting with my sister and I guess I must have gotten distracted. Sorry to keep you waiting. But I'm ready now." In his mind, the more he talked, the less flustered and weird he sounded, but he knew that in reality he was rambling and sounding very much weird. Probably blinking too much, too. And sweating. Why was he sweating?

"Okay," she said, but she didn't look convinced. "Let's go. He doesn't live far. Thank goodness. It's really coming down out there."

Indeed, the sky had gone from white to grayish again, and was pouring snow, as if someone had knocked a barrel over right at the edge of a cloud.

"There are also going to be some drifts, I'm afraid," she said.

And drifts, there were. Almost immediately after leaving the shop, they were knee-deep in snow, slogging their way, one leaden foot at a time, their heads ducked and eyes squinting. The baskets, steaming when they left the shop, were covered in a layer of snow in no time, the steam squelched. The wind roared in their ears and the flakes made their faces wet.

Also, *doesn't live far* must have been a relative term, Rowan decided, because it felt like they were walking for days before they finally turned down a side street.

"He's the third house on the left," Ellory said, her voice, breathless against the unrelenting wind, still came to him intimately, which was one of the few things he loved about snow. He thought of it as a *quieting*. He paused and lifted his head, listening. If he ignored the wind, there was nothing but silence. Peace. Calm.

He had a moment of understanding.

This was why it was so inviting to sing songs of peace. This was how one could be swept up into a story of a birth. This was why everyone loved their white Christmases.

It was a feeling that he just couldn't remember ever feeling in his life, even as all of his friends and every TV commercial insisted that he should.

Ellory paused and peered out at him from under the fuzzy-ringed hood she'd tossed over her earmuffs. "Something wrong?"

Rowan tipped his face to the sky, let the snowflakes splat against his cheeks. "No," he said. "Just a lot of snow is all. Very quiet. It's peaceful."

Ellory followed his lead in tipping up her face.

"Yeah," she said, then stuck out her tongue to catch a flake. She got one, closed her mouth, and smiled at him. "Catch one."

He wanted to. He started to. But then something familiar washed over him. He feared looking foolish, which often kept him from being spontaneous and playful. And he hated that about himself. Instead of catching snowflakes on his tongue, he shrugged toward a green house ahead. "That one?"

Ellory looked crestfallen. "Yep, we're almost there," she said and went back to trudging through the snow.

Rowan kicked himself the entire way. Would it have killed him to catch one stinking snowflake? No. But that look on her face, man. Maybe not kill him, but sure as heck wound him.

Mr. Crowley's house was tidy and trim, with the look of a home that was well loved for many decades. The old man answered the door in a pair of brown chinos, a tan cardigan buttoned over a plain, white T-shirt, and a pair of brown plaid slippers over white socks. He held a TV remote in one hand and a pipe in the other. He pushed open the door with his elbow.

"Ellory DeCloud, what are you doing on my front porch?" he said, his face filled with glee at seeing her there.

"Well, I couldn't hardly let you starve in this

storm, could I?" she said, pushing her way into the shadows of the living room. "And, besides, I missed you. I need my morning stories."

"Young man," Mr. Crowley said, nodding to Rowan, who gave a single nod back. "Come on in."

"Thank you, sir," Rowan said, and followed Ellory inside.

Mr. Crowley let the door shut behind them, and they all crowded on the throw rug in the entryway, snow scattering on the ground at their feet. Rowan could feel himself being sized up. Mr. Crowley was protective of Ellory. Like a father or grandfather would be.

"I don't believe we've met. You're not from around here."

"Sorry, sorry," Ellory said. "Mr. Crowley, this is Rowan Kelly. He's from Tulsa. His car broke down right outside of town."

"Tulsa, huh?" Mr. Crowley said.

"Yes, sir." Why did Rowan feel like a nervous young suitor?

"What brings you through town?"

"Wrong turn," Rowan said. "Unfortunately, it was the last turn my car wanted to make, apparently."

"He's on his way to visit his sister in Des Moines. She's having a baby."

Mr. Crowley continued to give Rowan the once-over. "And what do you do in Tulsa?"

"I'm a firefighter, sir."

Mr. Crowley's eyebrows lifted and his face lit up. "Firefighter, huh?" He took a puff of his pipe.

"Yes, sir," Rowan repeated.

"Too bad you're not an auto mechanic."

Rowan chuckled. "Truer words have never been spoken, sir. Although I can't complain about where I got stranded. Ellory's been very kind. And the food is out of this world."

"Speaking of," Ellory said, holding up a basket. "I brought you breakfast."

"Well, take your coats off and stay a while," Mr. Crowley said, taking the baskets from each of them and shuffling off to the darkened kitchen. "You can join me."

"We already ate," Ellory called, but she unzipped her coat and shrugged out of it, then slipped out of her boots and padded after him in her stockinged feet, earmuffs still in place. Rowan quickly shed his coat and boots, too. "But we'd love to stay and visit. How are you doing? Staying warm in all this nonsense?"

Ellory's voice faded as she disappeared into the kitchen. Rowan could hear the two of them chatting. The house was cozy, warmed by a fire. *It's a Wonderful Life* played on the TV, the volume so low, Rowan wasn't even sure it was on.

He couldn't help noticing that there wasn't a single Christmas decoration anywhere to be seen.

Strange to be in such plain decor after being in the Dreamy Bean, but not in a bad way. Not at all. Rowan could see himself one day in a house like this. Riding out the storm with a fire and a warm breakfast, something classic playing on TV.

Rowan found himself drawn to the fireplace mantel, a half dozen framed photos lined up like soldiers. He gazed at a grainy black-and-white photo of who Rowan could only guess was Mr. Crowley himself, as a young boy, holding the gloved hand of a petite, smiling woman while standing next to an old Bel Air. Next to that, a photo of a mid-40s Mr. Crowley with a blonde woman smiling so wide her eyes were nearly closed, standing under a hotel carport, flowery leis around their necks, their faces sunburned. Another with the same blonde woman in a frilly gown, a corsage around one wrist. And another of the same woman, much younger, wearing a wedding dress and kissing a tuxedoed Mr. Crowley on the cheek.

"That's my Roberta Ann."

Rowan startled. "She's pretty."

Mr. Crowley nodded. "Just as beautiful today as she was the day we met. Nobody even ever came close."

"His wife," Ellory supplied, picking up a photo

of Mr. and Mrs. Crowley wearing matching cowboy hats and flannel shirts, and handing it to Rowan.

"The love of my life," Mr. Crowley added. "What I wouldn't give to see her today."

"I'm sorry for your loss," Rowan said, studying the photo.

The love between them was so intense you could practically feel it vibrating the picture frame. Their smiles were so natural, the kind of joy that just is, without working for it. For the briefest moment, Rowan was awash with desire for that same kind of love, that same kind of joy and ease.

And in that same moment, he felt certain that he would never have it.

Of course you won't. You'd have to put yourself out there. You'd have to allow yourself to love and be loved. You'd have to convince yourself that you could actually have it, no strings, no tricks, just straightforward love. You can't do that, Rowan. You know you can't.

He cleared his throat uncomfortably and handed the photo back to Ellory.

"Well, thank you, but Ro's not gone. Not yet. She's just got a little of the Alzheimer's."

"He had to move her to a memory care facility on the other side of town last year," Ellory said.

"Thanks to the help of this one here," Mr.

Crowley said, patting Ellory on the shoulder. "We see each other every weekend and talk some between. She's gone above and beyond to help us stay connected."

Ellory shrugged. "What can I say, I'm an old softie for love?" Her eyes lingered a little too long on Rowan's. He looked at his feet to regain ground.

"It's more than that. She's the daughter we never had. A daughter anyone in their right mind would consider themselves lucky to have."

"Stop now. You're embarrassing me," Ellory said. Rowan could tell that she was trying not to catch his eye, ducking and dodging from his line of sight. But he couldn't help looking anyway. This soft, playful side was a side of Ellory he supposed he had seen from the moment he'd laid eyes on her, but didn't realize until just now how beautiful it was.

Mr. Crowley had picked up a photo and set it back on the mantel. He took another puff from his pipe. "Roberta just loves the snow. Always has. That's why we chose a Christmas Eve wedding. She thought snow on Christmas Eve was magical, and if it happened to be the day of celebrating our love for each other, even better. Of course, it never snows on Christmas Eve. Maybe a couple of times in all our years together. And now we have this huge snowstorm and she's not here." He scratched the back of his neck sadly and wandered to the window, which looked out over the street and front lawn, which were nearly indistinguishable from each other at this point. "And every day with this Alzheimer's, we get a day closer to her no longer recognizing me."

Ellory gave Rowan a silent, pained look, chewed her lip nervously, placed the cowboy hat photo back on the mantel, and followed Mr. Crowley to the window. "Um…" she said.

"Oh, I know. You don't have to say it," he said, tearing his eyes away from the snow and turning to pat her shoulder again.

"But I promised I would take you to have a nice dinner with her," Ellory said. "To celebrate your anniversary."

"And I know you would get me there if you could. But you can't control the weather any more than I can. Any more than Roberta could when she so badly wanted us to have a white Christmas Anniversary. It's okay, Ellory. I understand and so will she."

"It's not okay with me," Ellory said. "I feel awful about it."

Mr. Crowley took one long, last look out the window and then sank into his chair, gesturing for Ellory to take a seat on the couch. "Well, it is what it is. It can't be helped. But I will take the opportunity to say this. You should spend every minute with the person you love that you can possibly get. Never take a second together for granted. I sit here all day every day thinking about the times I could have been with Roberta, but I chose not to. Times that we were angry with each other for no real reason. Little things that kept us apart. Wish I could take them all back. I think people spend precious time wondering if they're with the love of their life, but the truth of it is, you know. When you find that person, you know."

Ellory smiled a thin smile. "I definitely knew when I *wasn't* with that person. But it took a while for me to figure it out."

Oof. That had history behind it. And not a good one. But what was worse? Rowan wondered. Investing time in someone and something only to endure the hurt down the line of time and love wasted, or enduring the hurt of never having opened up your time and heart to begin with? After all, he had nothing to add to this conversation, because he'd never allowed himself the closeness with someone to explore the possibility that she could be his someone. A few dates here and there, a couple of kisses with women who would ultimately want more of him than he would ever be willing to give. He'd thought that keeping his course, remaining unattached and unharmed, was the best strategy.

But lately, and he didn't want to admit this to himself until just this very moment, he'd begun to question his course. It was a lonely course. And no matter how he tried to talk his way out of the truth, it was a joyless course.

He found himself staring at Ellory curiously. She led with her heart. That, anyone could see within moments of meeting her. She wore joy on her shirtsleeves and wonder in her eyes. But she'd been harmed in the past. She'd wasted time and love on someone who was not her person. And here she was, just as vibrant and alive as anyone.

She must have felt his stare, because her eyes snapped to him. He felt his face get hot and quickly looked away, his hand flying up to the next photo on the mantel.

"Who's this?" he blurted, only realizing after he'd asked that he was holding a photo of a fireman in gear, looking sweaty and spent, holding his helmet against his hip and squinting into the camera. Rowan knew the look so well, he practically felt the photo rather than saw it.

"That's me," Mr. Crowley answered.

Rowan looked closer at the photo. Sure enough, he could see the shadows of the old man in this young firefighter's face.

"How long were you on the job?" Rowan asked.

"Twenty-seven years," Mr. Crowley said.

"Coulda retired earlier than I did, but I wasn't ready. Best job in the world."

"Only job in the world," Rowan said. "Only one I can imagine doing, anyway."

"You said you're down in Tulsa?"

"Yep."

"You know Captain Sebelius?"

Rowan lit up. "Frankie? Well, yeah, of course I know Frankie!"

"I went to firefighter academy with his dad. We were the best of friends and we were co-workers. Hoo-boy, do I have stories about Lyle Sebelius. And about little Frankie, too."

Rowan replaced the photo on the mantel and sat on the couch next to Ellory. "Oh, I would love to hear some of these."

Ellory touched him on the shoulder. "How about I'll put together a plate for Mr. Crowley while you two catch up on firefighter news."

Rowan offered her a thankful smile, and in that moment, her hand felt warm and perfect on his shoulder. As if he wasn't here by accident but was meant to be here. With Mr. Crowley.

And with her.

ELLORY DIDN'T KNOW quite what to make of all that had transpired between her and Rowan in there. First, there was the look after she revealed that she'd been burned by love. It wasn't pity. It was more…incredulity.

As if he didn't quite believe that she'd had a relationship that didn't work out?

Or as if he didn't quite believe that someone would be in a relationship with her?

She didn't want to think it was the latter. She was hardly an ogre, after all, and she tried really hard to be agreeable and friendly. But you never knew with some people. Even people you knew really well could surprise you with their innermost thoughts. Danny Wittfeld, for instance. But when it was someone you didn't know well, it was even easier for them to surprise you.

But then, soon after, when she'd put her hand on his shoulder, she was pretty sure she felt something rush between them. And she was even more certain that he'd leaned into her.

He's a stranger, Ellory, she tried to remind herself. *Then why does he feel so familiar?* she argued.

Secretly, she was thrilled that this stranger was getting along so swimmingly with Mr. Crowley. She wanted Mr. Crowley's approval. She also wanted Rowan to approve of Mr. Crowley, but again, couldn't quite pinpoint why it mattered to her. In two days, the snow would stop, Junior would get back to Haw Springs, and Rowan would get back on the road. He'd head on up to Des Moines and she would never see him again.

She would never see him again. The thought brought a lump to her throat, but it was a lump that she cast away immediately. She'd only just met him—his absence will be nothing to her. Right?

Right?

"Hmm, I don't know," she murmured out loud as she crisped up Mr. Crowley's bacon in his microwave, then artfully arranged it on a small plate. "I think it's quite possible that I'm losing it. All that cookie-dough stirring I did yesterday. Oh, no!" The Christmas cookies. She'd forgotten to bring them.

"What?" she heard from the other room. She'd forgotten that she'd been talking aloud; this last bit was probably louder than she'd realized.

"Nothing," she called. "Never mind."

But Rowan came into the kitchen all the same.

"Everything's okay?" he asked.

"Yeah. Yes, of course." She scooped some eggs onto the plate. "I just realized that I forgot to bring Christmas cookies for Mr. Crowley is all."

"I'll go get them," he said.

"No. You don't need to do that. I'll bring them later. He'll understand. He'll be happy with bacon and eggs and pancakes."

"Really, it's no big deal. I can follow our footsteps back, and I'll have them here before he even takes a bite of pancake." He held out a hand for keys, but Ellory continued to hesitate.

If Rowan started doing little favors for her, memorized the path between her shop and Mr. Crowley's house, used the key to unlock the Dreamy Bean, searched through her pantry for a container for the cookies, the closeness she was trying to pretend she didn't feel would press in on her even harder. It would become impossible not to feel it. And then what?

What would she do with those feelings once he left?

She let out a breath and pulled the key out of her pocket. "Thank you," she said. "There are empty Christmas containers in the pantry on the left side, second shelf down. Just fill it up. You don't have to do this, though. It's awfully cold out there."

He smiled. "Makes me feel like I'm earning my keep. I won't even feel the cold."

"Thank you. Oh, and make sure Latte doesn't escape," she said to his back as he practically sprinted out of the house, still zipping his coat as he walked across Mr. Crowley's lawn, following the quickly filling footsteps they'd left behind on their way here.

She put the finishing touches on Mr. Crowley's plate and took it out to him, setting it on the little table next to his chair, where his daily newspaper and crossword puzzle book and readers lived. "Bon appétit!" she said. "Breakfast is served."

Mr. Crowley inhaled deeply through his nose and let out a satisfied sigh. "I'm starving, and it smells like heaven." Ellory went back into the kitchen and poured him a cup of coffee out of the thermos she'd brought. "Mmm-mmm-mmm," he said, taking the cup from her. "You are simply amazing, Ellory DeCloud. What would I do without you?"

"Eat cold cereal, probably," she said, sinking back into the sofa.

He chuckled around a huge bite of bacon. "A fate worse than death. Why don't you get some for yourself?"

She waved him away. "Oh, I'm not hungry. I ate with Rowan this morning."

He lifted one eyebrow and smiled as he took another bite of bacon.

"It's not like that. He's far away from home and having to sleep on two chairs pushed together in a drafty old coffee shop and put up with Latte waking him up with tickly whiskers. I figured he could use some company."

"I see. Well, I misread things, then."

"What do you mean?"

He took a bite of eggs. "You two just seem very comfortable together. I figured maybe he was someone you knew and that's why he came to you when he was stranded."

"Nope. Complete stranger. I feel bad for him is all. Away from his family at Christmas."

Mr. Crowley slurped his coffee and silently studied the photo of Mrs. Crowley in her nursing uniform that resided on the table next to him. Ellory felt washed over with shame.

"I'm so sorry. I'm sure you know exactly how that feels."

He nodded. "As do you."

Ellory opened her mouth to argue but found that she couldn't. She, too, was alone for the holidays. In this way, they were quite the trio.

"Have you talked to your family?" he asked.

Ellory nodded, fiddling with the hem of her shirt. "Unfortunately, I have. They still insist that I'm being difficult and that I could still come to Christmas if only I would stop being obstinate and get back with Danny."

Mr. Crowley made a disapproving noise. "They don't know you at all, do they?"

She peeked at him. "What do you mean?"

He swallowed the pancake he was chewing and took a sip of coffee. "Everywhere you go, your heart gets there a day and a half ahead of you."

She shook her head, confused. "I still don't understand."

"What I mean is, you follow your heart. You

lead with your heart. You are guided by your heart. Now, I don't know the fella, but I know that if there was any chance whatsoever that Danny Wittfeld was at the other end of your heart's path, they wouldn't have to talk you into anything. You'd already be there. So if they don't know that, they don't know you at all. Why would you spend Christmas with strangers? You belong here, where we all know and love you, Ell."

Ellory felt tears form in her eyes. "Thank you, Mr. Crowley."

"Anyway," Mr. Crowley said. "Nothing to be done about my situation with Mrs. Crowley. I'll get to her as soon as I can get to her. Junior will come get me himself in that tow truck of his if he has to. And Rowan will get to his people up in Iowa. It'll all be okay."

"Doesn't feel okay to me," Ellory said, realizing that she sounded pouty. She forced herself out of it and curled her legs up beneath her as he poured syrup over his pancakes. "So tell me a story about your days as a firefighter," she said.

This was something she did every morning—ask for him to regale her with a story about his past. She would hang on his every word, living in his past, imagining herself there, just as she had done with Grandpa DeCloud.

These were moments that she wished she had with her father. Stories that she wished he would tell. Her father was well-known in business, a regular in Wall Street circles, wealthy from the moment he opened his eyes onto the world. He'd lived a life filled with luxury and adventure. She knew he had stories. Incredible stories.

He just never seemed to have the desire to take the time to tell them.

Where Grandpa DeCloud's study was a wonderland of books and miniatures to explore, her father's study was an uninviting slew of papers and decor that held meaning only for him. If someone happened to tread over the threshold of his doorway, they felt instant regret. At best, his disinterest in fraternizing rolled off him in unwelcome waves. At worst, you might find yourself at the receiving end of a flung pencil or a booming *I'm working, here!*

Mr. Crowley had been right. Those were not her people. They were not who she belonged with.

Mr. Crowley quickly finished his pancakes, then sank back in his chair, holding his coffee cup, his eyes taking on the faraway look of memory. He thought it over for a moment and then launched into a story.

"I've got an even better one for you. Did I ever tell you about the time that Mrs. Crowley and I went parasailing over water that was so full of jellyfish, it looked like you could walk across the top of them? It was the captain's first day on the job."

And they were off, Ellory laughing at Mr. Crowley's zany descriptions of even zanier stories.

Soon, she saw a familiar figure treading back over the lawn, and next thing she knew, Rowan was standing in the living room, holding a plastic container stamped with Santas.

"Cookies," he said breathlessly. His face was red from the wind, the shoulders of his coat covered with snowflakes. He handed the cookies to Mr. Crowley and held the key out to Ellory. "I locked up after myself, and Latte was very cozy on the cloud chair, watching me leave."

"Thank you," Ellory said. "You have officially earned your keep."

"I doubt that, but I'll keep trying," he said.

"And you touched Christmas cookies and put them in a Santa tin and you didn't even die of icky Christmas," she teased.

He placed one hand on his throat. "It's a slow death."

"Well, if you manage to survive the next few minutes, I have something to show you." She stood. "Mr. Crowley, is it okay if I show him your project?"

Rowan glanced back and forth between them. "Project?"

"Sure," Mr. Crowley said, easing himself out of his chair.

Ellory held out a hand for Rowan, excitement welling up inside of her the way it always did when she was about to get a chance to explore Mr. Crowley's lifelong passion project. "Come with me," she said. "You're going to love it."

Hesitantly, Rowan took her hand and followed as she pulled him out of the living room and down the hall to a small den.

When she flipped on the light, he let out a childlike whisper.

"Whoa."

CHAPTER SEVEN

Rowan could hardly believe what he was seeing. In the center of the den—taking up the whole den, really—was a table. On top of the table was a tiny, bustling town. Rowan leaned over the table to study it. The detail was intricate and mind-blowing. A tidy Main Street dominated the center of the town, with side roads leading all directions to little subdivisions. Houses dotted the streets and cul-de-sacs. A mobile home park sat sentry on one end of town. A small warehouse district. And rolling hills on all sides, the houses climbing up and up, getting sparser and sparser until just a couple of farms stood king of the hill, looking down over the bowl of houses and shops.

One was clearly a horse ranch, with children sitting atop the horses, wearing pinpoint-sized helmets. Three tiny children rolled a snowman into being on the grass.

Another appeared to be a working farm with alpacas and geese and miniscule kittens pouncing over each other outside the barn. A tiny couple sat in rocking chairs on the front porch, their laps covered with thick blankets, a little wavy-furred dog curled up at their feet.

"This is astonishing," Rowan said.

"It's Haw Springs," Ellory said proudly. "Here's the house that we're standing in right now." She pointed to a matchbox-sized house with neat little shrubs lining the front. Indeed, it did look identical to Mr. Crowley's house.

He pointed. "Look. There's the coffeeshop. And you're standing out in front of it. At least I think that's you? You're pretty bundled up." But the hair color was right, and the white coat with the red scarf and earmuffs.

Ellory leaned in and gasped. "You decorated for the Crawl!"

"I did," Mr. Crowley said.

"Katherine Messing wants to cancel it," she said. "I begged her to let me do it anyway. Even if it's only me."

"Well, I'll join you," Mr. Crowley said. "So it won't be only you."

"And me," Rowan said. "For what it's worth, I'll still be around."

"See, Katherine Messing may not want to have the Carol Crawl, but that doesn't mean my Haw Springs won't. Lookie here." Mr. Crowley reached over to the corner of the table and flipped a switch. Hundreds of tiny, blinking lights came to life, and the miniature people began to sway all over Main Street. Choir music echoed from a little box under the table. Christmas carols.

But they weren't obnoxious and overdone. They somehow...worked.

Ellory gave a little squeal and hopped on her toes, clapping. Rowan smiled. Who could resist smiling in this close proximity with such joy?

"Look," she said, leaning over the town again and pointing. "Marlee's flower shop. Junior's garage. Fox's Drugstore. Donnelly's Honey Shop. It's all there. And everyone's out singing." Her finger bounced from figurine to figurine. "Marlee, Morgan, Ben and Annie, David, Decker, everyone. Look, Rowan! That one could even be you! The coat is the same color and it looks kind of like you."

Rowan leaned over the table in awe. It wasn't just that the coat was the right color. The figurine struck an uncanny resemblance to him. "How?"

Mr. Crowley shrugged. "Coincidence."

Rowan squinted at the character. "That's one heck of a coincidence."

"Oh, Mr. Crowley, you've really outdone yourself," Ellory said.

Mr. Crowley beamed. "I only paint the figurines."

"You shouldn't sell yourself short," Ellory said. "These aren't just painted, they're perfect. Why, look, you even have Latte's little pajamas correct."

Indeed, there was a cat in the front window of The Dreamy Bean, wearing pajamas that looked strikingly similar to the ones he'd seen the cat in that very morning.

"Well, I couldn't leave Latte out, could I?" Mr. Crowley said.

"What do you think, Rowan?" Ellory asked. "Isn't it the absolute best thing you've ever seen?"

Rowan nodded, unable to tear his eyes away from the table. They were drawn again and again to the Rowan figurine. A part of him wondered again if he was in his frozen car, hallucinating just as Megan had suggested. "It's really something," he managed at last. "This took a ton of work. I've never seen anything like it before."

Mr. Crowley shrugged and gazed forlornly at the table. "I'm an old man with lots of time on his hands."

Ellory followed Mr. Crowley's gaze and put her hand on top of his. Rowan could see that they were both focused on a building just outside of town—a squat, nondescript, L-shaped building, all beige, except for the tufts of cotton snow he'd temporary affixed along the roofline and gutters. One of the windows was lit, and a woman sat on the other side of it, looking out toward them. Rowan didn't need to look any closer to guess that this was Mrs. Crowley in the memory care facility.

"What about a video call?" he asked, the words

coming out before he'd even fully registered that he'd had the idea. He gazed around at Mr. Crowley and Ellory. "Do you have a laptop? Does she? Or even a cell phone?"

"Oh, I don't think that would work," Mr. Crowley said, waving Rowan away.

"Wait, I think that's a great idea," Ellory said. "I could call the center and see if they could set her up with a laptop."

"Great for her, but I don't have one of those blasted things. Why would I?"

"You can borrow mine," Ellory said. "I can bring it when I bring dinner. I'll get you all set up. I'll have the center get her all set up. And then I'll skedaddle until you're ready for me to come back for it."

"Oh, I don't know."

"Why not?" Ellory cried. "It's worth a try. It's better than nothing."

"I'll help however I can," Rowan said, unsure why he was inserting himself into this problem, but he was. He shouldn't care. But he did. *Just like in a sappy Christmas movie*, he thought. *The outsider suddenly cares a great deal about the townies. Something I would have always laughed at in the past. Called cliché. Groaned, rolled my eyes. But here I am. A human cliché.*

Mr. Crowley made another noncommittal noise

and left the room. Ellory bit her lower lip as she looked up at Rowan.

"I should have stayed out of it, I know," Rowan said. "I got caught up in this." He gestured at the table. "And I guess it made me feel part of something I'm not really part of."

"It's okay," she said. "It was a great idea. And we're going to try it. He may not like the idea now, but he'll get there when he sees Roberta's face on his screen. I think he's just afraid."

"Afraid of what?"

She shrugged. "Afraid that it won't work?"

"Then we need to make it work."

She gave him a quizzical look.

"What?" he asked.

"Nothing," she said, but he could tell it wasn't nothing. Something was grinding the gears in the back of her brain, and he was afraid it was him. *I know*, he wanted to tell her. *I'm not sure who I am, either, so I can't blame you for being confused.*

He opened his mouth to press her, but decided against it, turning back instead to continue studying the little town. "It really is so impressive, isn't it? Not just that he could do that, but that he did do it. That he wanted to, because the little town inspired him to do it."

"That's Haw Springs." Ellory reached down and delicately straightened a wreath the size of a peanut that was affixed to the front door of a store on Main Street. "Do you know why I came here?"

"No. Why?"

She fiddled with a Christmas tree, smoothed some snow, wiped a smudge off of a skating pond. Satisfied, she straightened and turned so that her back was against the table and she was facing Rowan. She smiled. "Neither do I."

"I don't get it."

She shrugged. "When I left home, I was headed to Kansas City. That was where my future belonged. I was sure of it. I was used to a lifestyle that was more…I don't know, urban? Modern?"

"Wealthy?"

She squinted at him. "How did you know?"

Now it was his turn to shrug. "Just a guess. You seem refined."

She arched an eyebrow. "Haw Springians can be refined."

"I'm not saying they can't. I'm just saying you are, and when you were just now struggling to describe what sort of lifestyle you come from, it clicked into place. You're used to something a little posher than the Dreamy Bean. Maybe too posh for your taste?"

She chuckled, once again looking at him as if she didn't quite believe he existed, or maybe believed it, but didn't trust it entirely. "Fair enough," she said. "Anyway, I was looking for something different from what I'd grown up with, that was for sure, but not *that* different, you know?"

He thought about his own life in Tulsa, fully devoted to his work, and how he'd escaped Des Moines to escape any notion of familial obligation. Sometimes you didn't need to run away so much as you needed to think. And sometimes, in order to think, you just needed to get some space around your head. He nodded. "I actually do."

"Anyway, I got to Kansas City, and it just didn't seem right. So I kept driving. I didn't know where I was driving to, only that I needed to keep going. And this is kind of embarrassing, because I started to cry. I think maybe I thought I was just going to end up turning around and going home. And I didn't want that. But, I thought, maybe a part of me did. I don't know. But I kept driving and driving and then I saw the exit for Haw Springs and I took it. I have no idea why." She turned back to the table and traced her finger along the road coming into town. "So I pulled in, and I stopped right…here."

To Rowan's surprise, she wasn't in front of one of the charming little stores downtown, or even the building where her coffee shop came to be, but out in the middle of nowhere, halfway down one of the rolling hills.

"I got out of my car and it just smelled right. Leafy and clean, and if hope had a smell, it was there, too. It was summer, and you could hear the clicking of grasshopper wings and the buzzing of bees, and the wind softly blew, and far-off in the distance I heard the whinny of a horse. I looked down into the valley at the little Main Street and I thought, *How safe it must feel to wake up to this every morning.* I felt like I had stepped into a dream."

"And you had a dream to fulfill."

She searched him with her eyes. He felt as if she were seeing him all the way to his core. "I did."

"And the rest is history."

"The rest is history and present and future. I've never for one second regretted driving right through Kansas City. I've never thought, *What if I had stopped there?* This was where I was supposed to stop." She bent to fiddle with the town again. "Who knows, maybe you were meant to stop here, too, and you just don't know it yet."

Rowan chuckled. "My situation is a little different. I wasn't moving."

He was struck with the truth of what he'd just said. He wasn't moving. But not in the sense of packing up your things into boxes and bags and relocating your life, but in the sense of progressing. Taking life to a new step. The next step. Going forward.

No. He wasn't going anywhere.

And when he got right down to it, that was the problem, wasn't it?

ELLORY KEPT TELLING herself that she should feel embarrassed after telling Rowan her whole story. Maybe *embarrassed* wasn't the right word? Exposed. Yes, *exposed* was a better word.

After all, she'd so far told nobody in Haw Springs, not even Marlee West, her closest friend in town, her story of how or why she came to be there. She'd dodged any and all questions about her past. She'd channeled all of her feelings into hard work and told herself that she didn't need to spill her guts to anyone.

Until Rowan Kelly came along.

Now, all of a sudden, she wanted to spill everything.

What was up with that?

She excused herself, left Rowan to continue to admire Mr. Crowley's mini town on his own while she padded off to the bathroom to collect herself and her thoughts. When she got there, she was shocked to find a text. From Danny.

Are you not even coming home for Christmas?

Ellory read the text and sank down on the closed toilet lid, letting her phone fall into her lap. So her family hadn't even told Danny the truth of why she wasn't there. They were, undoubtedly, letting him hold on to hope, just as they were doing.

Well, that was cruel and unfair.

She was unsure how much to divulge.
Not this time, she typed.
It's not the same without you, he responded.

We did the whole Wassail thing. Nobody knew the lyrics.

Ellory smiled, remembering how much fun they had every year, driving out into the country to a roadside orchard, bundled up and eager to buy soaps and ornaments and knitted blankets from local vendors. As children, she and Danny raced through the trees, playing hide-and-seek. As they grew older, they would purchase mugs of hot cider and wander out into the trees, singing "Here We Come A-Wassailing" to ensure a fruitful crop come spring. Ellory was the only one who knew the words to the song, and every year they all nearly doubled over with laughter at everyone's attempt to sing along.

To keep the joke going, Danny made up different lyrics every year, just to confuse things as Ellory struggled, to no avail, to get everyone on the same page. It had become their big, family inside joke.

And she'd missed out on it this year. Her heart felt so heavy.

Surely you know them by now.

I've sang something different every single year. I have no idea what the real lyrics are.

Before she could respond, he sent another text.

We all miss you terribly, Ell. Christmas isn't the same without you.

This was classic Danny manipulation. Make her feel guilty in hopes of getting what he wanted. She'd fallen for it so many times, she'd started to question her own sanity or intelligence every time it happened. Surely she should have caught on by now.

"Fool me once," she said aloud.

You don't miss me. You miss the idea of me.

I think I would know the difference.

The Ellory that learns all the lyrics to the Wassailing song is the "dreamer" that you laughed at.

You're still not over that?

She stared at her phone in disbelief. *Still not over that?* After the way that it ended, she would never be *over that*.

It was her life, her dream, and he still didn't get it. None of them did. They were still hoping for her to come to her senses.

"My senses are just fine," she said.

Learn the lyrics, she typed. It's not that hard. She paused for the briefest moment, her thumb hovering over the send button. He would certainly pass this on to her family. Did she want to invite the criticism that would surely follow?

"They will criticize anyway," she said, and hit Send.

She got up, wiped the corners of her eyes with toilet paper, put her phone back in her pocket, and stepped out into Mr. Crowley's hallway.

"So," she said, trying to muster a can-do energy that she didn't quite feel. "I also included some lunch in the basket. But I'll be back with dinner."

"Oh, sweetheart, you don't need to do all that," Mr. Crowley said. "I've got cans of soup in the pantry. I'll be just fine."

"It's really no big deal. I have to make dinner anyway. I have a guest."

Rowan came out of the bedroom and stood behind her. She edged to the side to let him by, but he didn't move. She liked him there. How quickly she'd gotten used to having him near her.

"Yes, well, I've been thinking about that," Mr. Crowley said. "Why don't you stay here, Rowan?"

She felt Rowan shift behind her.

"Oh," she said, surprised. She had not been expecting this at all, and would never have thought to ask.

"I couldn't impose," Rowan said.

Mr. Crowley waved him away. "It's not an imposition. I'm here alone. You're sleeping in chairs. I have an extra room. It makes perfect sense."

"I don't know. I hate to put you out."

"Bah," Mr. Crowley said, pulling himself to standing. "One brother putting up another. What kind of firefighter would I be if I didn't have you here?"

Rowan ducked his head, deferential, then gave a single nod. "Yes, sir. Thank you, sir."

Mr. Crowley clapped once and hitched up the sides of his pants. "It's settled, then. Go get your things and we'll get you all set up in the back bedroom."

Ellory smiled and glanced back and forth between them. "How wonderful," she said. "Thank you, Mr. Crowley!"

She only wished she felt as happy as she was pretending to be.

CHAPTER EIGHT

THEY WALKED BACK to the Dreamy Bean in silence, the snow feeling much less energizing as it pelted Ellory's face than it had felt on the way there. What once filled her with the excitement and awe of a child now just annoyed her.

"Everything okay?" Rowan asked as they entered the shop. If Ellory didn't know better, she would have thought he sounded as deflated as she felt.

You're imagining things. Trying to read someone you don't even know.

"Everything's great," she said, pasting on that ridiculous smile once again. "I have so much to do. The Crawl is tomorrow. This is good. If you stuck around here, I'd probably just put you to work." She let out a gusty, hollow laugh.

"So do it," he said.

She paused. "What?"

"Put me to work." If she didn't know better, he seemed eager.

"I couldn't. Mr. Crowley is expecting you."

"I'll go over there, but nobody said I have to go over there right now," he said. "What do you need? I'm happy to help."

"You're definitely not happy to help with this," she said. "I have a dozen little Christmas trees to decorate. I don't even know if I have enough decor."

He glanced around the shop, amused. "You definitely have enough decor. This place is nothing but decor. You could get a hundred tacky trees out of this decor."

He was joking, but this rankled her. She knew that part of him really did find her aesthetic tacky, and she was feeling out of sorts to begin with. "I wouldn't want you to subject yourself to *tacky trees*," she said.

He frowned. "I was just teasing. It's not you that's tacky. Your vibe is…interesting and unique. You know I'm just not a Christmas person."

Interesting and unique. Or…ridiculous?

You can't be serious about this dream of yours, Ellory. It's ridiculous. This whole dreamer thing you've got going on. It was cute in high school, but you're not in high school anymore. Now it's just…well, it's ridiculous. And if you expect us to be together—if you expect to be my wife— you'll have to, you know, conform a little. Be like the other wives. Set your sights on things you can achieve. Do a little fundraising like our moms do. Volunteer. And if you just have to let your little freak flag fly, get on the arts council or something.

"What? What did I say?" Rowan asked, following as Ellory hung up her coat in a huff.

"Nothing. You didn't say anything." And he didn't. She knew he didn't. It was Danny she was mad at. It was her parents. It was herself. Why did she have to be born with a little freak flag to fly anyway?

Suddenly, Ellory felt very bare. Exposed. She was a success. The Dreamy Bean was a success. But what if she was the only one who saw it that way? What if even the Haw Springians were chuckling about her behind her back? *Oh, that Ellory. Yes, she's sweet, and she can make coffee. But does she have to wear overalls and hang puppets from her ceiling? Does she have to paint poetry on the walls? And what's with all the colors, anyway? She's unique and interesting...and utterly ridiculous.*

She took a breath and steadied herself, eyes closed. Then opened them and pasted on that pleasant, everything's-fine-and-dandy expression she'd perfected by the time she was seven. "I know you're not a Christmas person. It's okay. You can get your things together and go on over. I've got things under control here."

"I'm sorry. I didn't mean to insult you."

Flatten, flatten, flatten your face, Ellory. Everything is fine. Everything is perfect. So fine and perfect even Danny and your mother would approve. "I'm not insulted."

She began pulling garland and lights off the wall around the window, plucking off ornaments that hung across the top of the window as she went. She had a box full of empty creamer packets that she'd painstakingly glued green and red and gold sequins on and a long string of glittered stir straw garland for her own tree, but the other trees would need ornaments and garland, too. She had work to do and did not have time for any sort of distraction.

In fact, she thought, his leaving to stay with Mr. Crowley was going to take care of this distraction nicely. It was fun while it lasted, but she needed to get back to business.

"Well, here, let me at least help with this." Rowan began rolling the lights she'd let fall in a heap on the floor into a much more manageable strand.

Ellory paused, ready to tell him to just leave it to her, but she let him keep going. After finishing with the lights, he did the same for the garland. And then followed her to the windows in the back of the store, doing the same. They worked together, side by side, without a word, and then he followed her outside. She'd brought a tote filled with the glittery coffee-themed decorations and set it on the ground beside her tree, which was covered with snow.

She began knocking the snow off the tree on her side, and to her surprise, Rowan began knocking it off the other side.

"That was a great idea, by the way," she said. "The video call tomorrow night."

"Hopefully we can pull it off. He didn't seem so sold on it."

"We'll pull it off. Mr. Crowley is definitely not computer savvy, but once it sinks in with him that he'll be able to see Roberta and she'll be able to see him, he'll be on board. He'll do whatever it takes." They worked in silence for a moment, brushing, brushing, brushing the snow with their hands. "It's so romantic. Inspiring."

Rowan peered at her over the top of the tree. "What is?"

"Their love for each other. Do you think you'll ever find that kind of love?" Ellory had no idea why she was asking him this, and even as the words were leaving her lips, she wanted to slurp them right back in. What was she thinking?

"Oh. Uh. I don't know." He'd gotten flushed, the redness in his face blinking bright as a neon sign against all the whiteness around them. Why was he so red? And why did she ask him that question to begin with? "I guess I never thought about it."

"You've never thought about falling in love?" *Ellory! Stop talking!*

"I mean, of course I've thought about it. I just...it just...it never..." He cleared his throat. "What about you?"

"I thought I'd found it, but I was wrong," she said.

Rowan paused and gazed at her over the tree. The snow that he'd been brushing away had sifted up into his hair, his eyebrows and eyelashes. "Can I ask you a personal question?"

Ellory paused, too, suddenly feeling icy inside. She nodded, although she wasn't so sure she was prepared to answer. "Okay."

"What happened?" Ellory didn't answer, wasn't sure what exactly he was referring to. "You've hinted around at it. You thought you found love. You were with someone. Clearly there was a difference of opinion somewhere. You were uninvited from Christmas. And when I called you interesting and unique, it triggered something in you. I could tell. So what happened?"

Ellory felt her mouth go dry. She hadn't talked about what happened since that last day with Danny.

The day she decided to pack up everything and simply...leave.

She hesitated for so long, Rowan tried to back out. "You know what? Never mind. You don't need to tell me anything. I shouldn't have asked. I had no right."

"He lost it," she blurted. She blinked. If it hadn't been for the puff of breath hanging in front of her mouth, she might not have believed that she'd said anything at all. But now, knowing that it was out there, she wasn't sure if she could stop herself from continuing if she tried. "He completely lost it. He didn't believe in it. In my dream. He tried everything he could think of. He called it stupid and useless, he said it wasn't sustainable. He tried to scare me out of it, saying I would go broke and take my parents' money with me. He tried to tantalize me with the promise of a lazy, luxury life that I didn't want. He appealed to my parents, my grandparents. Everything. And then...he lost it."

"What do you mean?"

She took a deep breath, flicked her eyes to the sky, as if trying to summon a memory. Or maybe as if finally allowing in a memory that she'd long ago pushed into hiding. "I decided to surprise him. I didn't need anyone to do it for me. I was more than capable of making my own dream come true. All by myself."

"Clearly," Rowan said, glancing toward the Dreamy Bean. Latte, just like in Mr. Crowley's miniature, was sitting in the window, watching the snow fall.

"And I guess I thought maybe if I just rented the space and surprised him with it, he would see the vision. He would get it and it would make sense to him and he would be on board. So I found a place, got a lease, the whole bit. I even decorated." She chuckled. "I mean, of course I did, right?"

Rowan smiled. "I wasn't going to say it."

"Anyway, I chose a date night and took him to the space I'd rented to surprise him."

"And?"

"And...he was surprised."

Surprised wasn't the half of it. Danny had been infuriated. For months after they broke up, every time Ellory closed her eyes, all she could see was the look on Danny's face as they walked into her brand-new space. His expression went from curious to incredulous to angry in a matter of seconds.

What do you think? she'd asked, trying to appease him, or at least get a feel for where he was at.

What is this? he'd asked, but the way his lips were pulled back from his teeth told her that he knew exactly what it was. He'd plucked the handmade sign off the wall. *Ellspresso? What on earth is Ellspresso?* And he'd done the last thing she'd expected him to do: he shattered it against the wall.

She'd let out a terrified squeak and jumped back. *You broke it!* Even as she said it, she knew what she was saying was obvious and pointless. But a part of her just couldn't believe that he'd done it. Even though she'd long known that he was capable.

"He pulled every single thing off the wall and smashed it," she said. "And he told me in no uncertain terms that Ellspresso wasn't ever going to be a thing and that I needed to get it out of my silly, brainless head immediately before he got really mad about it. So I went to my parents' house for support."

"And they didn't support you?"

She smiled a thin smile. "I'm uninvited from Christmas, remember? No, they absolutely did not support me. Which I probably should have seen coming. But I didn't. I was naive, and I went to my parents for help. My father was silent, as always. And my mother agreed with Danny. Told me that my dreams were a waste of time and derided me for wasting money on a lease that she was going to have to spend more money to break. Nobody asked if I wanted to break the lease. They just…did it."

"I'm so sorry, Ellory," Rowan said.

"Anyway, I realized then that Danny had sort

of always been that way. Even as children, when we played games together, we always had to play by his rules. And they changed to suit him whenever he was losing. He always had to have the upper hand. I loved him dearly. As a friend. But I mistook those feelings for real love. And he literally smashed them to bits."

"And so you played by your own rules."

She went back to brushing the snow off her side of the tree. "Something like that. Maybe a little bit more like…I decided to stop playing at all."

She felt good, having told someone the story. Clean. As she worked the words around in her mouth, she realized that they tasted different. Gone was the coppery flavor of shame and disappointment, replaced by a cleaner, sharper feeling.

His hand found hers through the tree and stopped it from its movement. She glanced up. Rowan was gazing at her intently from over the top of the tree.

"Thank you for telling me," he said. "For what it's worth, you were right. The shop is a success. You're a success. And, for what it's worth, I like the name Dreamy Bean better, anyway."

A little laugh escaped Ellory. "I like it better, too."

He let go of her hand. "And if anyone understands getting out of the game, it's me. In some ways, I never even bothered to get in. Honestly, most days I don't understand why anyone would ever want to play."

"I don't know," Ellory said. "When I look at Mr. Crowley and he's still so in love, even after all this time, I think, *Wow, Ell, maybe you're really missing out. They've probably decorated fifty Christmas trees together, and here I am, decorating mine alone.*"

Rowan cleared his throat and bent back a limb to slingshot a shower of snow onto Ellory. "What am I, chopped liver?"

She giggled as the snow trickled down the collar of her shirt. "Okay, maybe not technically alone, but with a stranger who is also a Scrooge."

"Ouch."

"Untrue?" He shook his head, looking ashamed. Ellory couldn't tell if it was playful shame or the real thing. "Even if you're not a Scrooge, this is hardly the same as Mr. and Mrs. Crowley decorating their tree together, in love and excited about the holiday." She bent back a limb to slingshot Rowan, but it didn't work. The snow simply drifted to the ground.

Rowan laughed triumphantly, but Ellory came around the tree so fast, he didn't even have a chance to move. "Not fair!" she shouted, lunging into him with all her might.

Could she shove him to the ground, even using every reserve of strength she had? No, not likely.

But could she knock him off-balance so that his boots slipped and slid and ultimately he ended up on his back in the snow anyway?

Absolutely.

And she landed on her belly next to him.

"That's what you get for firing the first shot." She picked up a handful of snow and tossed it at his chest.

"Is that so?" He grabbed his own handful of snow and smashed it over the top of her head.

"Oh, that's it," she said. The two of them pulled fistfuls of snow and rapid-fired them at each other from only inches apart, laughing and panting like children. Finally, Ellory called for a ceasefire and rolled onto her back. "When was the last time you made a snow angel?" she asked.

"I don't know. I was probably seven."

"That is way too long ago. Get to swiping, sir."

To her surprise, he began dragging and pushing his arms and legs through the snow, his angel and hers so close their wings were nearly touching.

When they were done, he got up and held out his hands. Ellory took them and let him pull her to standing. "We still have so much decorating to do," she said. But the stress was gone. Replaced with something lighter. Something more hopeful.

They fell into silence as they wrapped lights and then garland around the tree. Ellory found herself sneaking glances at Rowan, peeking at the angel shapes they'd left in the snow.

She found herself fighting to keep from imagining that this was something more than it was.

ROWAN WOULD NEVER admit this out loud to anyone, not even as a deathbed confession. Wild horses couldn't pull it out of him. If he was being interrogated with toothpicks under his fingernails, he wouldn't admit it. But...

He didn't hate decorating that tree.

In fact, he didn't hate it so much, he helped her decorate three more. And then three more after that.

And they would have kept going, except it was getting really cold and their clothes were wet from all the rolling around in the snow and their fingers were numb and Ellory had begun to insist that he learn lyrics to Christmas songs—*After all, you'll be here for the caroling*—and he had to draw the line somewhere.

He wouldn't admit this to Ellory, for obvious reasons, but he already knew the lyrics to those songs. How could you not? If you were alive during even one holiday season, it was all you heard, everywhere you went. Grocery stores, restaurants, even in the firehouse, they insisted on playing them. Just because he didn't want to sing them didn't mean he couldn't sing them.

One more thing he would never in a million years admit?

Decorating the trees, alone with Ellory, in the snow, on December 23 was…nice. He could have been talked into singing those carols if only she'd tried just a tiny bit harder.

But, he supposed, they were both distracted by all that talk of love. Lost love, future love, forever love. Did he think he would ever find the sort of lifelong love that Mr. and Mrs. Crowley had found, she'd asked.

He was being truthful when he said he hadn't thought about it. But that was only partially the truth. Because when it came to relationships, he shut his brain down. When it came to the word *forever*, he just didn't believe in it. When it came to the possibility of him ever even being able to find something like the Crowleys had—much less keeping it—he had never allowed himself the luxury of dreaming. Fantasizing was an indulgence, wasn't it? An indulgence he hadn't grown up with. He was so sure, he didn't need to think about. Why think about something that will never, ever happen?

If he were to force his brain in that direction, what did he think?

He just didn't know. That part was also the truth.

None of this was new to him. The only thing that was new was that it bothered him now. He never would have guessed that he would find himself so confused and confounded by the subject. Ellory was getting under his skin. He knew that much. But why and how far under? Well, that was another subject he didn't want to think about.

After all, as soon as the snow melted, he would be leaving.

When they came back inside, Ellory made them both hot chocolates and then took hers with her as she disappeared into the kitchen to start dinner for Mr. Crowley, leaving Rowan to gather his belongings. The problem was, he didn't really have that many belongings—everything was still in his backpack—and so he was left to contemplate all the things he didn't want to contemplate over the creamiest, sweetest hot cocoa he'd ever tasted.

He began to smell food and wandered to the kitchen.

He stood in the doorway for a good long while, watching her bustle from refrigerator to pantry to counter to stove, as light and lovely and mysterious as a moth, softly humming to herself. He finally caught in her periphery and she startled, then went back to work, smiling to herself.

"Can I help?" he asked from the doorway. It smelled like sage and butter and garlic. His stomach rumbled.

She regarded him for a moment as she turned a ball of dough out on the counter, then nodded and stepped aside. "Do you know how to knead dough?"

He rolled up his sleeves. "Do I know how to knead dough? Do I know how to knead dough?" He bellied up to the counter. "Actually, no, I don't. How do I knead dough? Is it something more complex than...well, kneading dough?"

Ellory, stirring something on the stove, laughed as she came back to him. "Why do I have a feeling that you make everything more complex than it needs to be?" she asked.

"Like what?"

"Like making snow angels and singing songs."

"Hey," he said. "I did it, didn't I? And I decorated trees. What more do you want from me, woman? You know what? Forget it." He held her at bay with one outstretched hand. "Keep your help. I'm going to knead the heck out of this dough. It can't be that hard, right?"

She put her hands on her hips and raised her eyebrows. "Knock yourself out. I can't wait to watch this."

He gathered the dough in his hands and turned it a few times, appreciating its heft. It was cool and smooth to the touch, and he wondered how on earth he would even know if it was done being kneaded. He set it back on the counter.

"Okay, I'm full of bluster. I have no idea what I'm doing. I mean, I guess first, I shame it? Maybe yell at it a little bit? Call it a few names? Try to antagonize it into a fight? Otherwise, it sort of seems like a sucker punch."

"I said knead it, not give it a beatdown. I thought firefighters could cook."

"Some can, but not all of us. And some are better than others. I'm proud to say I fall in the mediocre category of firefighter cooks. There are worse, but there are definitely better. I'm not a making-dough-related-things-from-scratch chef so much as a make-a-boxed-dinner-but-add-broccoli-to-it-for-pizazz chef. And I don't do sucker punches on innocent dough."

Ellory took the dough from him and bumped him out of the way with her hip. "Well, there's a lot to be said for pizazz."

"I agree," Rowan said, trying to think of his next punch line. When Ellory smiled and laughed, it was as if the whole entire world lit up. He could imagine a world where making Ellory DeCloud smile and laugh would be the most important item on someone's daily agenda—the payoff was that good. In fact, he might already be living in that imaginary world, if only temporarily.

"So you just use your palms like this. And then fold and go this way with it. And then fold and so on. Got it?" She gazed up at him with those big blue eyes, her floury palms turned upward.

"Got it," Rowan said, feeling a lump in his throat. She stepped out of his way and maneuvered to the sink to wash her hands. Rowan began kneading the dough, tentatively at first, but then with more confidence as he realized how much he loved the silky feeling of the dough in his hands. He began to hum while he worked, then realized with alarm that he was humming a Christmas song. He stopped, but when he looked sideways at Ellory, he could see that she was grinning. He was never going to hear the end of this.

"It's not what you think it is," he said.

"I didn't say anything."

"It's a rock song. A hard rock song. All about hating Christmas songs."

She raised her eyebrows and laughed out loud. "Is that so? What's it called?"

He thought about it for a second. "The Anti-Christmas Song Christmas Song. It starts with *Chestnuts roasting on an open fire created out of piles of burning tinsel...*"

She glanced up. "Hey, you can sing."

"No, I can't. That's what you got out of that? You are impossible."

"Why, thank you. And you know what I think? I think Christmas music has kind of started to grow on you a little since you got here."

"Like mold."

"Like you like it. I think, by the time you leave here, you're going to be singing the real thing at the top of your lungs."

"Oh, is there a lyric that goes, *Get me out of here*?"

Okay. That one fell flat. Ellory let out a low chuckle, but it was obviously forced.

"I'm sorry, Ellory. I didn't mean that."

"Oh, I know," she said. "I'm not upset by it. I've just enjoyed having the company, that's all."

"Me, too," he said.

They worked in silence for a few moments, Rowan kicking himself the entire time for killing the mood. They'd been having so much fun. Why did he always have to say the wrong thing at the wrong time? He didn't want to ruin the closeness he'd been feeling with Ellory. And he didn't want to stand there ruminating over what that closeness with her meant to begin with.

"So," he said, breaking the tension. "Tell me your favorite Mr. Crowley moment. What is it about him that gives you such a soft spot for him?"

"Well," Ellory said, back to stirring the roux that she was making. "In order to tell you that, I have to tell you another story."

"Oh. Well, I don't know if we have time for that. Hang on." He trotted to the kitchen door, where he could look out the big front window and then came back. "Nope. Still stranded by a blizzard. I have nothing but time. Go for it."

"Okay. First you need to know that my Grandpa DeCloud was a lot like me."

"Blonde? Blue-eyed? Wore Mary Jane shoes with knee socks? Obsessed with festively decorated confections and creepy elf puppets?"

Ellory leaned over, grabbed three fingerfuls of flour, and flicked it at Rowan. "You know, you're a lot more of a jokester today than you were yesterday."

Rowan shrugged. "What can I say? You got your wish. I'm having fun." He brushed his forefinger through a small pile of flour and swiped it over her nose. She squealed and turned away.

"Do you want to hear this story or not?" She rubbed the flour off her nose.

"I do," he said. "If you'd ever get around to telling it. I feel like you're needlessly wasting time. Is that what you and your grandpa had in common? Both needless time wasters?"

"*Anyway*," she said, giving him a fake glare.

"Anyway," he repeated. "I'm waiting. So far, this story is slow."

"I had a grandpa who thought about things very similarly to the way I think. We had comparable worldviews." She paused to let Rowan interject more nonsense, but he didn't, so she continued. "I spent a lot of really great moments with that grandpa, in his office, talking and reading and exploring. He was the person in my life I felt actually got me. He understood me because he was just like me. Or I was just like him. Same difference. And I always felt most accepted by him. I could talk about whatever I wanted to talk about, because he was interested in whatever I had to say. Or at least he pretended to be, even if he wasn't actually interested. Did you have anyone like that in your life? The person who just made you feel safe?"

Rowan's thoughts immediately turned to Megan. Even when their parents were at their worst, Megan was there for him. She cared about what he was going through, no matter what she was going through. She wanted to make his life better. She put in effort. Maybe it was a twin thing. Maybe it was a sibling thing. Maybe it was just a Megan thing. Regardless, it was an important thing. Some days, the most important thing in his life.

He nodded. "My sister."

"The one who's having the baby?" Ellory asked.

"Yeah, I only have one. We're twins, actually."

Ellory looked delighted. "You have a twin?"

"I do."

"There's another you out there?"

"That explains why she's so great." He winked.

"Is she also a big old Scrooge?"

"Actually, no. She does have her drawbacks, I guess."

Truthfully, if Megan had drawbacks, Rowan didn't know what they were. Of course they'd had their sibling moments—someone not wanting to share, someone chewing loudly, someone tattling—but for the most part, she was…well, Megan was just perfect.

Many times over the course of his life, Rowan had thought that he really needed to thank Megan for all that she'd done and all that she'd been for him throughout their lives. He'd never shown her the appreciation that he actually felt. He'd never let her know how great he thought she was. He hadn't taken her for granted, but he feared that she felt as if he had. It would be just like Megan to be too kind to complain if she did feel that way.

He made a mental note to check in with her as soon as he was done with the dough.

Ellory cut through his thoughts. "Well, the first time Mr. Crowley came into the Dreamy Bean, I just had a feeling about him. He was so polite and sweet and happy, and when he would ask about my day, I felt like he really meant it and wanted to know. So then I would start asking him about his day, and he would talk about his mini town project—which, by the way, he updates for all of the holidays, not just Christmas, and also other town gatherings and such—and he would regale me with all these stories about Haw Springs and he would do it in such a way that I could really see it happening in my mind's eye, you know? The people he talked about, even if they were no longer here in Haw Springs, were so real to me, I could envision them perfectly. There are people he's talked about who have been dead for forty years that I feel like I know. Like, if they were to walk through the front door, I would recognize them and feel like we were old friends. That's what Grandpa DeCloud was like. And that's why I'm so attached to Mr. Crowley. He's like the father I never had."

"How interesting that you've had not one, but two people like that come into your life," Rowan said.

Ellory stopped stirring and looked him directly in the eye. "That's the thing. I think people come into your life for a reason, and it's a mistake to ignore that. I don't think I really realized that until Mr. Crowley, though. I'd already followed my gut and come to Haw Springs instead of what my original plan had been. And it had worked out so great, I decided to follow my gut again. And my gut told me that I needed to spend time with this person. To really listen to what he had to say. To invest in the relationship with my full self, even if investing in relationships in the past had turned out really badly for me.

"So the next time Mr. Crowley came in, I stopped what I was doing and just talked to him for a few minutes. And then a few minutes turned into an hour, which turned into two hours. I would have to stop every now and then to greet a customer, make some coffee, whatever, but when I came back to him, the conversation picked up like it had never paused."

"And a friendship was born," Rowan said.

"Roberta had just been diagnosed at that time, and he needed a friend. I was new here and I needed a friend. It was perfect timing. I started cooking him real breakfasts, and the first time I brought it over to his house, he showed me the miniature project and I could have sworn I'd time traveled back to my grandpa's den. At least that was how it felt. We spent hours looking over it, with him telling me story after story about Haw Springs history. I left there feeling like I'd lived here my whole life. That's probably ready to go."

She edged over to take over the dough, but

Rowan didn't step aside. She'd woven him so completely into her story, he couldn't move. He wanted to be standing near her, feeling her warmth, smelling her shampoo, their hands brushing and twining together as they kneaded dough forever and ever.

She paused, gazed up at him, her hand hovering over the dough. "Everything okay?"

That was all it took to snap the fantasy. He lurched away as if she were on fire. "Yeah. Sorry. I was sort of mesmerized for a minute there." He let out a croaky laugh. "I guess you're one heck of a storyteller, huh?"

"Hmm," she said, working the dough one last time before shaping it into a ball and placing it back into the bowl she'd turned it out of. "I think kneading dough is really meditative. I find my mind wandering all the time while I'm baking. Sometimes it's when I do my best thinking. I figure out lots of problems while baking."

"I definitely need to take up baking, then," he said.

"What problems can we solve for you?" She covered the bowl, brushed her hands off, and turned to face him with an expectant smile, leaning back against the counter, her hands on the countertop behind her. She looked so open and vulnerable and available, and even though Rowan was feet away from her now, he still felt the pull.

His mind flashed with images of going to her, sweeping his arm around her waist, pulling her to him.

He cleared his throat. "Boredom. What else can I do to help?"

She arched one eyebrow. "Oh, you're bored now, are you? I'm a dull host?"

He ducked his head, afraid that his attraction was still showing on his face. "Anything but," he said. "I just want to be helpful. Pay my dues and all that."

Ellory popped the bowl into a drawer under the oven, then stood and turned to him again. "You've been so kind and helpful already. Really, you don't need to do anything. I've got it from here. You can just relax."

Her smile was so brilliant, her presence so soft and light, he didn't want to go.

Which meant he definitely needed to. *This is your out, Rowan. Break the spell while you still can. Don't make the one time you open yourself up to someone be someone who is one hundred percent a transient person in your life. What is wrong with you? Singing, playing in the snow, acting like you're in love. Get. Out. Now.*

"Actually," he said. "I think I'll go on over to Mr. Crowley's and get out of your hair."

He could have sworn he saw actual alarm and regret wash over her. He was sure that she was going to argue. Maybe assure him that he wasn't an inconvenience for her. Ask him to stay until dinner was finished. And, had she done that, he wasn't sure he would have had the strength to resist.

Instead, she lowered her shoulders and went back to stirring, stirring, stirring. All that endless stirring.

And, thank goodness for that endless stirring, the little voice in the back of his mind said. If it weren't for that endless stirring, he might do something rash. Something he would definitely regret later, when he held his heart in his hand as he drove away.

"Okay," she said. "Thank you again for everything."

"Oh, I'm the one who should be thanking you."

"It was really my pleasure, Rowan Kelly. I hope you get your car up and running soon." She held out one hand. It took Rowan a beat to realize that she intended to shake his hand. And even though it felt silly and over-the-top formal, he took it and gave it two solid pumps.

"Me, too, Ellory of the Clouds. I hope you have a really pleasant, you know…" He mouthed *that insufferable holiday*.

"You, too," she said. "I hope your insufferable holiday is the pleasantest. And that maybe you suffer the joy of it for just the tiniest bit."

"Thanks a lot," he said. "You've just cursed me with a loop of 'Santa Baby.'"

"*Hurry down the chimney tonight...*" Ellory crooned and then laughed as he put his hands over his ears and left the room, yelling, "Lala-lala I can't hear you!"

Two minutes later, he was ruining the whispers of the footsteps they'd left earlier that morning as he plugged along through the snowstorm toward Mr. Crowley's house.

He felt as if he could breathe much better, now that he was away from her.

But, at the same time, without Ellory beside him, the snow felt so much colder.

CHAPTER NINE

LATTE TWINED BETWEEN Ellory's ankles, mewing for his dinner. She didn't normally let him in the kitchen—his fur had a way of getting into anything and everything he touched, and even most things that he didn't touch—so he must have come in with Rowan.

"Hey, buddy, you looking for something to eat? It's a little early for your dinner, isn't it?"

The cat blinked up at her with his huge, gold eyes and let out a plaintive meow.

"Okay, okay, you make an excellent argument." She always had a hard time saying no to that sweet kitty face.

She took the pot she was stirring off the heat and wiped her hands on a tea towel, then padded to the pantry, with Latte following after her. He crowded into the pantry behind her and let out a wail as she reached for the can of cat food.

"My goodness, you're being impatient," she said. "Let's go, before you starve to death."

She grabbed his food dish out of the dish rack

and led the cat out of the kitchen and upstairs to her apartment. Latte's cries grew louder and louder as he followed her up. At last, she placed his food dish on her bedroom floor and dumped the food into it. Latte scrambled to gobble it up. She gave him a long pat down the length of his back and tail, then sank onto her bed with a sigh.

It seemed so quiet without Rowan there.

"That Christmas crankypants sure did grow on us fast, didn't he, buddy?"

She wasn't quite sure how that had happened. It had only been yesterday that she had rescued Rowan from his car and then blocked her bedroom door with furniture. She couldn't even blame the romance of Christmas, although things had felt a little more…intimate…between them when they were talking in the kitchen and discovering the miniatures in Mr. Crowley's house. And especially when they were outside decorating the trees. He'd gone from hating the very idea of Christmas to standing in the snow with her, garland in hand, earnestly helping her and even having a little bit of snow angel fun in the process.

She flopped back on the bed and grabbed a unicorn pillow, hugging it to her chest. "Oh, Latte, why do I have to go and make some big deal out of a small thing? So what that he helped me decorate trees? What does that really mean?

Nothing. I should be concentrating on how I'm going to start the Carol Crawl all by myself, not how Rowan Kelly might have revised his feelings about Christmas. What was I thinking, saying that I could do it all alone? I should have let Katherine cancel it. I should, at the very least, be thinking about how I'm going to help Mr. and Mrs. Crowley spend their anniversary together. Even if it's just on video, there needs to be a plan."

She tossed the pillow back onto the bed and dug her phone out of her pocket. She looked up her friend, Tena, who stopped in for a large caramel macchiato every day on her way to work at the memory care center. Ellory and Tena had gone out for lunch a few times and had become fast friends.

"Hey, Ellory! Merry Christmas!" Ellory could hear revelry going on in the background behind Tena.

"Merry Christmas," Ellory said. "Are you at a party?"

"Yes and no. I'm at work. We're sort of all stranded here. Junior's stuck in Riverside, so nobody's getting in or out of Haw Springs until someone gets some plowing done. Which isn't happening until it stops snowing. Which…" She paused, and Ellory imagined her looking out the window. "…just isn't happening. So we decided to keep it festive while we're here. Making due, and all that. How are you doing? Is Main Street a ghost town?"

"Kind of," Ellory said. "So you'll be there tomorrow night? Christmas Eve?"

Tena's voice lowered, as if she were trying not to be heard by the people around her. "It's not ideal, I know, but things happen. Some people are pretty unhappy about it, and we're getting tons of calls from people who are afraid their loved ones are going to…I don't know…stay snowed in forever? All day long, I'm repeating that we're making sure everyone is safe and warm, we will reopen when the plows come through, et cetera, et cetera."

"I'm sorry. I'm sure you're sad to be celebrating the holidays without your family," Ellory said.

Tena got louder again. "Hey, it's okay. I'm not with my family, but I'm with my work family, right?" There were cheers in the background. "Everything will be okay."

"It's perfect, actually," Ellory said. "I mean, I hate that you're away from your family on Christmas Eve, but it's a little perfect for me. I need your help."

"My help? How?"

"Roberta Crowley," Ellory said. "Can you set her up on a video call tomorrow night during dinner? It's her anniversary. I had promised to get them together for the occasion, but the snow has sort of made that impossible. But if you have a laptop or a phone that she can use, I'll take mine to Mr. Crowley's, and they can at least see each other that way."

"Oh, gosh, yes, of course! I would be happy to. We can use a staff computer. We have loads of them. It'll be great. Now that you say that, I can think of a few other residents who could use a little virtual face to face time tomorrow and the next day. Maybe we'll get a whole rotation going. What a great idea."

"Really?" Ellory asked. "You're the best. Truly. You have no idea what this will mean to them. Thank you, thank you."

"Of course," Tena said. "Send me a text when you're about an hour away from wanting the call. That'll give us plenty of time to get things ready."

"Great. You'll hear from me tomorrow."

Ellory hung up and hugged her phone to her chest. If nothing else, they could definitely connect the Crowleys with a video call. At least all was not totally lost. She needed to let Mr. Crowley and Rowan know as soon as possible.

Her phone rang. She answered quickly.

It was Marlee. "Are you hanging in there, Ellory? You're not a frozen block, are you?"

"I'm all good. Better than good, actually. I just

found a way for Mr. and Mrs. Crowley to spend Christmas Eve together. How about you? Did you make it home last night?"

"Better. I actually made it all the way up to Morgan's house." Morgan was Marlee's sister who lived with her husband, Decker, and her son, Archer, on a horse ranch that overlooked Haw Springs. Decker's ranch hand, Ben, also lived in a small house on the ranch, and Ben's girlfriend, Annie, was frequently there as well. Getting up there must have been a challenge, but if there was a place to ride out a storm, it was Decker McBride's ranch. It would be beautiful and peaceful. How lovely it would be to sit atop the town and look down at the lights as Christmas Eve turned into Christmas morning, listening to the horses whinny inside the barn. "We're having Christmas up here. I wish I had thought to invite you. It was really insensitive of me. That's why I'm calling to check on you. I hate that you're all alone down there. Well, you and little Latte."

"Oh, we haven't been alone," Ellory blurted without thinking. She squeezed her eyes closed and hoped that Marlee hadn't heard her and would blow right past what she'd just said. Unfortunately, Marlee heard her loud and clear.

"You're not? Who's down there with you? Surely not Katherine."

Ellory felt her face get hot. She wished she

hadn't said anything. Or that she hadn't sounded so hopeful. Or...something. She actually didn't know what she wished anymore. She had so many wishes, they were all getting confused.

Maybe, Ellory, your life is too full of wishes and dreams and not full enough of actual things. Maybe you're missing something and you know it.

"There was a traveler who got stranded outside of town is all."

"A traveler? What kind of traveler?"

Ellory paused. "A...man."

"You've been stranded down there all by yourself with some strange man? Are you okay? Say the word *nutcracker* if you need help. We'll slide down on a sled to rescue you if we have to."

"I'm all good. Really." Marlee's words, *We'll slide down on a sled to rescue you if we have to* rang the tiniest bell in the back of Ellory's mind. "Hey...Marlee? Speaking of sleds. I don't suppose Decker and Morgan have a sleigh up there, do they?"

Marlee laughed. "A sleigh? Like what Santa drives?"

"Sort of? Only, you know...with horses instead of reindeer."

"No. I don't think so. At least I've never seen one. Not sure where they would hide one. But I'll ask Ben. Maybe there's one hiding in the barn or the cellar." She paused. "Why would you be asking about a sleigh anyway? Say *eggnog* if you're being held against your will."

"I promise, I'm all good. I'm not being held against my will."

"Which is exactly what someone who was being held against their will would say if the perpetrator was standing right there. Is your stranger standing right there?"

Ellory laughed. "He left a while ago. It's just Latte and me now. And a whole lot of snow."

Marlee let out a skeptical noise. "Just let the record show that I don't like it."

"Record shown."

"And that I think it's slightly weird that you're randomly asking about a sleigh and thus I have expressed my worry that you might have fallen into a snowdrift and frozen your head."

Ellory laughed out loud. "Hey, are you saying my brain is frozen?"

"Just voicing my concern is all."

"Okay, okay, concern voiced. However, I promise it makes sense. I'm just trying to get Mr. and Mrs. Crowley together for their anniversary dinner tomorrow night, and even you have to admit that a sleigh would come in really handy for that right about now." She heard Rowan's voice echo in her mind, and it made her smile. "Haw Springs seems like exactly the kind of town that would have an abundance of sleighs. Or at least an abundance of the ability to have sleighs."

"Yeah. It does," Marlee said. "You're right. And if there were two potential sleigh builders in all of Haw Springs, Decker and Ben would be those builders. You know what else there's an abundance of in Haw Springs?"

"What?"

Marlee let out a soft groan. "Poinsettias. You still have that extra key?"

Not long after Ellory had moved into the Dreamy Bean and struck a friendship with the flower shop owner next door, they'd decided to give each other extra keys to their shops. You never knew when you might need someone to turn off an emergency water valve or gift you a roll of toilet paper if you ran out after the grocery store was closed. "I do."

Marlee sighed. "Go help yourself. Christmas it up, girl."

"Ho, Ho, Ho!" Ellory said.

Rowan returned just as Ellory was packing the basket with Mr. Crowley's dinner, surprising her with a soft knock on the front window. The snow had started to let up the tiniest bit, but his shoulders and beanie were still covered.

His knock had startled her, causing her to whip around, nearly knocking the entire basket onto the floor. Her heart pounded wildly, and she wasn't sure how much of that was from the scare, and how much was the simple fact that he was there, a presence that had gotten familiar all too fast. Maybe the romance of Christmas was getting to her after all. She didn't know Rowan Kelly. She couldn't possibly be feeling for him what she thought she might be feeling for him.

Nutcracker, she thought. *Eggnog! Eggnog! I'm being held against my will, not by him, but by myself!*

She waved him inside. "Missed me already, huh?" she teased, and then instantly felt regret. *Flirting?! Now you're flirting?! Maybe Marlee was right and you do have brain freeze.*

Latte jumped from a stool at the bar and trotted to greet Rowan with a warble. Rowan scooped him up and began petting the top of his head. "Weirdest thing. I was sitting there by the cozy fire, drinking a warm brandy, listening to an incredibly interesting story about Mr. Crowley's childhood on the heels of World War II—which, by the way, his father fought in—and I thought to myself, *Rowan, what you really need in this moment is a cat in pajamas. In fact, you need it so badly, you should put on your coat and walk what will seem like a million miles through knee-high snow and bitter cold to get to said cat.*" He held Latte up so that they were looking into each other's eyes, Latte's little legs dangling in a full display of trust. "Right, Mr. Coffeecat? Right. So here I am. And while I'm here, I might as well take the dinner basket so you don't have to get back out in the knee-high snow and bitter cold."

Ellory cocked a hip. "Latte, I would be insulted if I were you. Mr. Coffeecat? Really? That's almost as bad as Ellory of the Clouds." Although, secretly, she didn't exactly hate Ellory of the Clouds all that much. Or maybe not at all.

"My nicknaming skills are perhaps not the stuff legends are made of." Rowan bent to let Latte down, but Latte snuggled up closer, and he stood, hugging the cat to his chest. Seeing Latte trust Rowan so completely warmed Ellory through and through.

"Never underestimate Mr. Coffeecat's desire to cuddle," Ellory said. "He is, above all else, a little space heater."

Rowan stroked Latte's ears. "I don't mind. He's not a cozy fire, but he's kind of close to one. After being out there, I'll take all the space heating I can get."

"I'm just about finished packing the basket. You definitely didn't have to come get it, though. I would have brought it."

Truth be told, Ellory was a little disappointed that she wouldn't be bringing it. Part of her really wanted to be part of the stories-by-the-fire club, too.

"Oh, and by the way, your homemade bread came out perfect. You're going to love it."

He raised his eyebrows. "My homemade bread? You mean the busywork you put me to while you did the real cooking?"

"Kneading is a very important step in the process. If you do it wrong, the whole loaf fails. If that happens, you've wasted your time and a whole lot of flour. So, well done on the kneading!"

"You're just being nice. If I recall, you literally stepped in to take over the kneading process."

Ellory ducked her face to the floor. She could feel herself blushing, just thinking about their closeness as she took the dough from him. Even in the memory, she could feel his presence all the way to her soul. It had unsettled her, unseated her. But in a good, warm way. In a way that let her know that she wasn't imagining things. There was a connection between her and this so-called stranger.

"I'm sorry about that. I can be a little bossy in the kitchen, I guess."

He finally extricated himself from Latte. "I assure you, the end result will wash away any feelings of being slighted."

She picked up the packed basket and held it

out to him. "There's a thermos of decaf in there, along with some brownies for dessert. I figure you're probably sick of Christmas cookies by now."

"Oddly, I'm not," he said. "But I love a good, warm brownie, too." He took the basket. "Do you want to join us? I'll share my portion. Except the brownie. And the bread. Actually, now that I think about it, I'm probably not willing to share. I don't know why I even said it. Maybe Mr. Crowley will share with you. Or…you could come watch us eat?"

"I thought you came down here so I wouldn't have to get out in the cold."

He shrugged. "Turns out, I was wrong about that. I enjoy eating with you. I just don't like to admit it when I enjoy things."

Ellory laughed. "Good thing I always pack extra food. Let me get my coat."

THEY ATE AND talked for so long, they lost track of time.

They didn't even bother to turn on the lights and instead ate by the light of the fire alone.

Rowan had never felt woven into the fabric of someone else's life before, and here he was, so entangled with these two people, it was as if he didn't know where his experience ended and theirs began. He felt enchanted by Mr. Crowley's tales, as if he'd lived in Haw Springs his whole life.

As if his DNA existed there before him.

He started feeling as if his apartment in Tulsa was somehow less real than this place—this home, this town—his brothers in the fire department less real than this grandfather figure, this woman.

This woman...

This woman.

The orange of the flames danced across her face, pulling tiny flecks of light out of her eyes, giving the impression that she was constantly moving, constantly dancing. He imagined that Ellory DeCloud danced often, and sometimes for no reason at all, and that was why he couldn't stop looking at her. He wanted to be there to witness her dancing. He wanted to dance with her.

When they finished eating, he walked her home and found himself wishing that he was still staying at the Dreamy Bean. He wasn't sure how or when it happened, but at some point he created the desire to sleep in two pushed-together cloud chairs rather than an actual bed. He stalled saying good night and found himself standing side by side with her as the clouds dissipated for the slightest moment, allowing the moon to scatter glitter over every surface.

"It's beautiful." Ellory breathed in the still night air, her breath coming out in a little puff.

"Yes, it is," Rowan said, trying to make the direction of his own gaze less obvious.

She began to sing a song he'd never heard before.

"What's that?" he asked.

"It's called 'The Wexford Carol,'" she said. "It's an ancient Irish carol, I think. I've just always loved it. I'll teach it to you, if you want."

"Sure," he said, mostly because what he didn't want was for this night to end. For the next twenty minutes, she taught him the song.

"Do you think this means the snow is over?" she asked.

"I hope not."

She gazed at him, the moon reflecting in her eyes. "Why not?"

He shrugged, tore his eyes away from her. "I don't know. I kind of like it. If I'm going to be snowed in anyway, it might as well keep coming."

"But the more snow we get, the harder it will be for you to get out."

He shrugged. "I stopped being in such a hurry about that."

"Why?" He expected a cocky grin from her, or maybe a hip bump, forcing him to admit that Christmas wasn't as bad as he made it out to be.

But instead what he saw was softness, her lips slightly parted, her face open and wondering.

He saw...a reflection. Not of the moon, but of his own desires.

"You know when you talked about finding Haw Springs? How you drove through the city and kept going until you found yourself in this tiny town?"

She nodded.

"And you said you just knew that it was the right place. The sights, the sounds, they just felt right to you."

"Yes," she said. "I've never looked back."

"What did that feel like, exactly?" His hand twitched toward hers, but he forced himself not to clutch it.

"It felt like...homecoming."

"I don't know if I've ever had a home," he said. "Not in the truest sense."

"Well." She licked her lips, thinking, and turned her face to the moon, this time closing her eyes as she turned in a full circle, as if she could feel the moonlight bathing her face. "It felt like slipping into cool, cotton sheets at the end of a long, hot day. And it felt like melted marshmallows against your upper lip on top of a mug of hot chocolate. And it felt like the fur on Latte's chest, right under his neck." She gestured toward her own neck, but still kept turning, kept her eyes closed. "And it felt like sinking into a warm bath and coming up from the deep end of a cool, refreshing pool and being held when you have really, really good news to share." She crossed her hands over her chest and opened her eyes. "It felt like...longing. And *be*longing." She turned her face to the sky. "This is what perfection looks like."

But Rowan wasn't looking at the snow; he was looking at her.

"I agree," he said, taking in the soft upward slope of her nose, the length of her eyelashes, the curve of her lips. "You are so..." he breathed, the words coming up from the very depths of him, so big and full he couldn't get the rest of them out.

"So...?"

He reached out and gently pushed a strand of her hair away from her face. He could feel the vibration of her, as if she'd spun him into a web with her slow twirl, had wrapped him up. He was in her orbit now. Her gravitational pull. If he didn't break the spell, he knew he was going to kiss her.

He forced himself to step away. "We should call it a night."

"Oh. Yeah. Okay. You're right. It's getting late."

He saw her inside and walked back through the moonlight on his own. Mr. Crowley was already in bed when he arrived, so he quietly saw himself to the guest room and lay back on the bed, feeling full and satisfied in a way that he hadn't felt in…well, maybe forever.

Yet, at the same time, he felt empty. Longing. The snow would stop. It would melt. He would be on his way. If he didn't stop this now, he would break his own heart as he left.

He slept deeply, dreaming of the moon and of the fire and of little puffs of condensation hanging around a Christmas bow of a mouth. Lips that he wanted to stare at and stare at. Lips that he wanted to graze with his own.

December 24

SOMETIME IN THE NIGHT, the snow stopped. The animals began poking their heads out of their dens, their little noses wiggling, their feet trembling as they pushed warm prints into the snow. Some—the coyotes, the rabbits—played in the white powdery drifts, pushing their noses down for a quick, cold snuffle and then pouncing to another location, and then another, their tracks turning circles.

If the moon had scattered glitter into the night, the sun polished diamonds into the day, and as the sun rose, it became almost too bright to see.

Still, the animals stayed close to their hiding places.

More snow was on the way.

It would find them soon.

CHAPTER TEN

WHEN ROWAN WOKE UP, he saw that he'd missed half a dozen texts and calls from Megan. He blinked twice at his phone and then sat straight up, his heart in his throat.

9-1-1.

Rowan I need you!

I need you NOW!

Answer your texts

Pick up your phone!

With shaking hands, he thumbed on his voicemail. It started with a lot of heavy breathing, which sent chills down his spine.

"Row? Um, I sort of have a situation here?" A pause, followed by the release of breath. "Oh. That one was strong." More breathing, some bumping and fumbling around. "Okay. Okay. I'm in labor. Like, actual labor. My water broke. Huge mess." She let loose a high-pitched, maniacal-sounding string of giggles. "My water broke. This is happening. This is happening. Okay-okay-okay. Um, this is happening, Rowan, and you're wherever you are, and I don't really know what to do here. Anyway, so like call me back. Right now? Thanks."

He checked the time that she'd left the voicemail. It had been a couple hours.

He called, and she picked up on the first ring.

"Thank God. I started to think you were dead and didn't even have the decency to let me know." She sounded totally calm now, the complete opposite of her voicemail. "Where have you been?"

"I was sleeping. It doesn't matter. I'm here now. But you sound calm. So you're not in labor?"

"Oh, I'm definitely in labor," she said. "I'm actually at the hospital right now." Her voice broke on the word *now*. He heard her take some slow, deep breaths and let out a little cry. He realized that there was something—or, rather, someone—missing from this conversation. Her breathing slowed and she whispered. "Okay. Okay. That one was okay."

"Megs? Why didn't Johnny call me?"

"Funny thing, Rowan," she said, tears in her voice. "The blizzard is stretching all the way to Newark, where he is currently stuck in an airport. All flights have been grounded, all of the rental car companies out of cars. He literally can't get home. He says he's working on it, but it's not looking good."

"How did you get to the hospital?"

"I flagged down a passing plow."

She let out a bark of a laugh, and Rowan joined her. Leave it to his sister to be resourceful enough to heave her laboring self out into the street to find one of the only reliable vehicles sort of able to get around in the snow.

"You should have seen the guy's face. He was so sure he was going to have to deliver a baby on the side of the road. He couldn't get here fast enough. He was probably faster than an ambulance would have been." Her laughs turned to sobs. "I'm having a baby, Rowan. By myself. I'm all alone here. Can you come?"

"I know, Megs. I'm so sorry. I can't even flag down a plow."

"So you're still stuck in that coffee shop?"

"No, I'm at a house now. A friend of the shop owner. It's hard to explain. Regardless, I walked here from the coffee shop. My car is still stuck on the side of the road outside of town. I haven't even tried to start it again since I got here. I know it's dead as a doornail."

"I understand," Megan said. She paused for another contraction. "I'll just have to suck it up and be brave. I wish you could be here, though. Or Johnny. I really wish he could be here."

"I'm sorry, sis. I really am."

"Oof, here comes another... I need to go..." Megan's phone went silent. Rowan held his phone in his lap and stared at it for a long moment, feeling terrible. His sister was having a baby alone. She deserved better than that. She put so much good out into the world, she deserved nothing but great and happy things.

It would be bad enough that he and Johnny were both stuck, unable to get to her for Christmas. But now the baby, too? It was unfair.

He would have to get his car working and get up there. That was all there was to it.

"Stop playing around with this pretend life and get where you need to go, Rowan," he said aloud.

He quickly dressed and made his way into the living room, where Mr. Crowley was already standing in front of the fledgling fire, gazing at the orange flames while he puffed on his pipe. "Mornin'," he said around the pipe stem clenched in his teeth.

"Good morning," Rowan said.

"Sleep okay?" Mr. Crowley turned away from the fire and sank into his chair.

"I did," Rowan said, sitting on the couch across from him. "Got some much-needed rest, thank you."

Mr. Crowley nodded. "Of course, of course. Snow stopped for a while, but now it's comin' down to beat the band again."

It was hazy gray outside again, a curtain of snow blotting out the sun. The snow was finer now, more like powder than flakes, and it had accumulated another inch, at least, overnight. Rowan felt ashamed that he'd been enjoying this time with Ellory—in fact, until he'd looked at his phone this morning, the only thought he'd had was that he was looking forward to seeing Ellory again today—while his sister was alone, in pain, and scared.

Just as they'd grown up.

This was the time of year. Every year. Neither parent loved Christmas, but his father loved celebrating. Not with them, of course, but with every stranger he could find in random bars around the city. As the celebrations grew, their mother grew more silent and broody and angry. The littlest bit of excitement seemed to set her off, and Rowan and Megan learned that, of all the times that they needed to be seen and not heard, Christmas was, for sure, that time.

They also knew instinctively to go play in their rooms after dinner. Because the moment their father would return home, jovial-with-an-edge, the fighting would begin. Things would break. The tree would get knocked over so many times, they would eventually just put it away before Christmas Day even arrived. And usually, they would go their separate ways—their father back out for more celebrating, and their mom into her bedroom to cry.

And in all of his years living at home, Rowan could only remember one Christmas morning when their dad was at home.

Megan didn't like to talk about their childhood.

But he knew that, right now, she had to be thinking about it. How sometimes things don't change down the generations and no matter how hard you try, in the end you very well could end up alone.

"You're anxious to get back on the road, son?" Mr. Crowley asked.

I was. And then I wasn't. And now I am again. Funny how quickly things change, over and over and over again. Shift, move, spin, repeat. "I am," he said. "My sister sort of needs me."

"I understand. It's tough being away from family over the holidays."

"Not normally, for me," Rowan said. But a colorful movement outside caught his eye. Ellory was traipsing through the snow, carrying those baskets again—one over each arm—and he forgot that he was speaking at all.

He got up and went outside to greet her, the snow instantly soaking his stocking feet.

"You're going to catch your death coming out here like that," Ellory said.

"You should have told me you were coming. I would have come and helped you all the way." He took both baskets from her and hightailed it back toward the house. She was right—his feet were already growing numb.

"So much for that beautiful pause in the storm last night, huh?" she asked, trailing behind him. "It seems even colder today than it was yesterday. And so much snow. I almost couldn't push my door open to get out."

Mr. Crowley, waiting at the door for them, pushed it open and held it until they were both inside, stomping. Rowan took the baskets straight to the kitchen and dropped them on the table, then wasted no time peeling off his socks. He hurried into the bedroom to put on a clean, dry pair and draped the wet ones over the heat register to dry.

He paused to text his sister. How's it going?

Slow and steady, she responded. But I haven't heard from Johnny in over an hour. I'm worried!

I'll see what I can do.

But what exactly could he do? It was the most frustrating feeling in the world, not being able to help.

He pulled up Johnny's number and sent a text.

You good, man? This storm is insane. Meg's worried.

Nothing right away. Johnny wasn't a sit-on-your-phone kind of guy. *But when his wife is having a baby?* Rowan wondered.

Ellory appeared in his doorway, pulling the gloves off of her hands one finger at a time. "Are you okay?" she asked, then scrunched her eyebrows in concern. "What's wrong?"

Rowan wasn't sure how she could already tell by looking at him that something had gone sideways, but he kind of liked it. And at the same time, hated it.

"My sister," he said. "She's in labor."

"Oh, no!" Ellory cried. "You're going to miss it. I'm so sorry!"

"I can't miss it."

"You won't miss it by much. As soon as it stops snowing, Junior will come through, and you can head up and meet your niece or nephew. A little late, but he won't know the difference."

"It's not that," Rowan said. "Her husband, Johnny, is stuck at an airport in New Jersey."

Ellory placed a hand over her mouth. "She's all alone."

Rowan nodded slowly, feeling like the worst brother in the world. All she'd wanted was for some company over the holidays and he'd resisted her. He'd waited too long to leave. He'd selfishly only considered his own desires. He'd acted, as Ellory put it, Scroogey, and now look what had happened.

He peeked at his phone to see if Johnny had responded yet. Nothing. He hung his head.

Ellory came to him, sat on the bed next to him. "I'm so sorry, Rowan. This must be really hard for you. But you know it's not your fault. Nobody could have seen this coming." Her closeness felt warm and safe next to him, her forgiveness of him so generous, but he couldn't let himself off the hook.

"That's the thing. People who were paying attention prepared for the storm." He gestured at the window. "She's early, but not that early, and babies get born when they get born. And Christmas comes on the same day every year. I literally should have seen this coming. All of it. But I was too busy thinking about myself."

"You left a little late is all. It's forgivable."

Rowan turned to look at her. She was so radiant, he was reminded of the moon reflecting off of the snow the night before. Everything about her was soft and glowing, as if she herself were lit from within. It terrified him. "I wish I had your positivity," he said.

"I can offer it to other people, but it's hard to give it to myself," she said. "So I understand."

You understand me. I've never felt so under-

stood in all my life. The urge to let the words out was so strong, his mouth opened, but he shut it again. *You're being swept away in the moment, Rowan,* he thought. *Get your head together. Stop being selfish for once in your life. Is the lesson you're learning right now not big enough?*

"This is temporary." His voice came out in a whisper so soft, he wasn't certain that she'd even heard him. He raised it. "We are temporary. You know that, right? I'll leave as soon as my car is working, and we won't see each other again."

Ellory recoiled, pulling away from him in every way. "Why are you...yes, of course I know that." She gave a breathy little laugh, but her hands knotted together nervously as she did so. "I don't know why you're saying that."

"Ellory... I know you felt it last night, too. I know you've been feeling what I've been feeling. But this isn't real. It's...Christmas romance."

She stood, yanking at the connection between them. But at this point, in this moment, it was so present, it was impossible for her to break. "I think you must have misread things," she said. "I'm not...we're not..." She took little nervous steps toward the door as she talked. "I don't know what you think you felt."

"Ellory, stop." He went to her, but she was turning away, heading toward the kitchen before he could reach her.

"We should probably eat breakfast before it gets cold," she said, raising her voice so Mr. Crowley could hear. "I brought biscuits and gravy."

"My favorite," Mr. Crowley said from the living room.

"They're all your favorite," Ellory said. And that was that. The subject was closed. Rowan felt like a fool.

At the same time, she wasn't fooling him. He knew he'd been right.

She could try to hide and deny it, but a connection this strong couldn't be felt by just one person.

It had to be felt both ways.

ELLORY BUSTLED INTO the kitchen and began pulling things out of the baskets like her life depended on it. Warm biscuits, a still-steaming tub of gravy, a plastic tub filled with fruit, pumpkin muffins with a cinnamon streusel top that floated warm holiday memories around the room like an excited child. She loudly opened and shut cabinets and drawers, hunting for plates, silverware, glasses.

"Coffee, Mr. Crowley?" she called.

"Don't mind if I do."

She supposed she was trying to get Rowan to stop talking, to stop saying the things she knew but didn't want to hear. At the same time, she was a flutter of nervous energy, unsure what had just transpired between them.

This was temporary. Of course it was. She had always known that.

Except at some point, she must have begun allowing herself to pretend that maybe there was a world where it wasn't. *A world where, what happens exactly, Ellory?* she asked herself. *Where it never stops snowing? You'll be literally buried. A world where he chooses to just stay? With nothing but a few items of clothing in a backpack and an incapacitated car? Why would he do that?*

Because, a tiny voice tried to answer. *Because that moonlight...the sparkles...the cooking and the tree decorating...it all felt so good. It all felt... right.* And he had been correct—she had felt it, too. Of course she had. She had been certain that he was about to kiss her last night, and she'd been certain that she would let him.

When she was describing what it felt like to just know that Haw Springs was where she belonged, it had taken everything she had not to say, *It felt like being with you, Rowan.*

Well, thank goodness she hadn't said it.

Because it isn't right, no matter how it feels. And the minute he can get out of here, he will, and that's why it's temporary. Case closed.

"Hey." Rowan ducked into her view, leaning

against the table so that she couldn't get to the food she'd just unloaded without acknowledging him. "Are you okay?"

She pasted on the biggest, fakest smile she could muster. Tried to channel her inner holiday cheer. "Of course. Why do you ask?"

He tipped his head to one side, his arms crossed over his chest. "You know why."

She moved so that she could reach around him, making him move a step to the side. "Oh, that? You didn't even need to say it. Of course I know this is temporary. What else could it even be?"

"I just..." He cleared his throat. "I guess I thought I felt something that you also felt. In the moonlight. Well, in a lot of things yesterday, I guess."

She gave her head a brisk shake. "Nope. I'm not sure what you even mean by that."

He scratched the back of his neck, which had begun to turn red. "I must have misread things. I'm sorry. Never mind."

He started to walk away, but Ellory put a shaky hand on his arm to stop him. She felt terrible gaslighting him this way.

She let out a breath. "You didn't misread things," she said. "I felt them, too. But, you're right, we were just getting caught up in Christmas romance." Her voice cracked at the end. She hoped he didn't notice. "Hard not to. We probably aren't even that compatible, and a day or two of space will show us that."

He moved so that her hand fell away. "Yes," he said. "I'm sure that's it."

But she knew for a fact that he didn't really believe what he was saying. Rowan Kelly didn't believe in Christmas romance. He didn't find the holidays to be romantic or magical in the least.

Still, she was grateful to end the subject and get on with breakfast, even though she ached on the inside and wanted to just go home and curl up with Latte and *White Christmas*.

"What do I smell?" Mr. Crowley had appeared in the doorway, his morning pipe left behind. He patted his stomach with both hands. "Are those Ellory's famous homemade biscuits?"

Grateful for the interruption, Ellory beamed and handed him a plate. "You know they are. Everything's still warm. Go ahead and get yourself some."

"Did you know, my grammy used to make homemade biscuits on Christmas, too?" Mr. Crowley asked, loading his plate with three biscuits and heaping ladles full of gravy on top.

"I didn't know that," Ellory said. She handed Rowan a plate while trying not to look directly at him.

"Of course, back then, we didn't have boxed biscuit mix, and we certainly didn't have those biscuits in a can. It was her only choice. But she knew how to make these fluffy biscuits that I swear were the size of your head. And she would fry bacon, and we would dip the biscuits right in the grease. I didn't even know about cream gravy until I joined the service. Let's eat in here. Did you bring enough to join us, Ellory?"

Ellory took a deep, steadying breath. She wanted to forget that her conversation with Rowan had ever happened. She wanted to go back to the Dreamy Bean and let Rowan go. She didn't need to say any formal goodbyes. She didn't want to. She wanted to pretend he had never stopped in Haw Springs in the first place.

But they had a breakfast to eat. And a dinner to plan. And they hadn't even talked about Christmas Day yet.

"I would love to join you," she said.

She waited until they had each taken a seat and then purposely sat closer to Mr. Crowley than to Rowan. And then, in seeing the look on his face, instantly felt guilty.

"How is she doing, Rowan?" she asked as she smoothed a napkin over her lap. "Your sister?"

He checked his phone, scrolled a little bit, winced. "She's okay. The labor has kind of stalled a little, I think. Which could be good, except..." He scrolled some more, then shrugged. "Except Johnny isn't responding to either one of us. So it's looking like, unless it's stalled for a good long while, she's going to be having this baby alone."

"What's going on? Who are we talking about?" Mr. Crowley asked.

Rowan told him about his sister and the baby and this being the year he finally went home for the holidays. Then he launched into the story of leaving Tulsa too late and not realizing there was going to be a blizzard until he was right in the middle of it.

"And Ellory was kind enough to take me in. Even though it was pretty much the last place someone would want to be if they were trying to escape Christmas." He winked, making an effort to appear jovial. Ellory burned all the way to her toes.

"He didn't care for Latte's Christmas pajamas," Ellory said. "And whatever you do, don't play Christmas music."

"Speaking of Christmas music," Mr. Crowley said. "What's happening with the Carol Crawl tonight?"

Ellory drew her lips down in a sad frown.

"Ah. I'm sorry, darlin'. I know you were looking forward to it."

"I was," she said. "I still am. I'm planning to take the Crawl to the side streets and see if I can get anyone to come out. But I'll be honest, I haven't seen hide nor hair of anyone since the snow started falling. I think everyone is afraid to come outside. And it's just me. Not much of a crawl."

"Old Junior's in Riverside with his truck," Mr. Crowley said. "Otherwise, I'd say he'd plow a street for you. And then you could have your carols, and you could get up to see your sister."

Rowan looked at his phone again. "I would try to get through the snow anyway, plow or no plow, if my car was working. But it's dead on the side of the road. I'm quite literally stranded here until Junior comes back from Riverside."

"Which probably won't be until after Christmas," Ellory said softly. She didn't want to dishearten him, not to mention remind him that his temporary status in Haw Springs was still days away from coming to an end, but she wanted him to be realistic.

"Well, we ought to see what Lindsay is doing," Mr. Crowley said.

Ellory wondered what that meant, and then a memory wiggled out of hiding in the back of her mind and came to the forefront. "Oh, my gosh, I totally forgot!" she cried. "Yes! Of course!" She turned to Rowan. "Mr. Crowley's neighbor Lindsay works at Junior's garage. She knows how to fix cars. I'll bet she could fix yours. If she could get to it."

Rowan raised his eyebrows and turned to Mr.

Crowley. "Really? You think she could at least look at it?"

"Tell you what," Mr. Crowley said. "As soon as I finish this here biscuit, I'll give her a call. See if she's around."

"That would be amazing," Rowan said.

He and Ellory caught each other's glance, and if Ellory didn't know any better, there was an apologetic look in his eyes that matched exactly how she felt. It would be amazing to get him on the road.

And it would also be terrible.

CHAPTER ELEVEN

Turned out, Lindsay was home and not busy. In fact, she was thrilled to have something to do, after being cooped up for days.

She came to Mr. Crowley's door geared up from head to toe in Carhartt and wool.

"Come in, come in," Ellory said, holding the door open for her.

Lindsay lumbered in, seeming huge, when in reality she was no bigger than Ellory. She took one look at Mr. Crowley and flung her arms wide. "Merry Christmas, Will, you old coot."

Will, Ellory thought. In all this time, she had never even considered Mr. Crowley's first name. She felt a pang of jealousy that Lindsay's relationship with him was Will-level close, while her own was on a last name basis. *Maybe*, she thought, *just maybe, you have a problem with letting people in, Ellory. Maybe you're all about the beauty of love and being in touch with the universe, but when it comes to people, there's noth-*

ing but brick walls. Huh. Maybe you should ask Rowan his thoughts on the matter.

"Merry Christmas, you whippersnapper," Mr. Crowley said, and gave Lindsay a big, back-slapping hug. "You doing good?"

"Eh, other than a little cabin fever, I'm okay, I guess." She stepped back. "It was my year to host for the holidays, so my whole family was supposed to come in from KC. All of my sisters, their husbands and kids, everybody. But obviously, now they're not coming, so it's just me. And my parents of course. And a huge turkey dinner that was meant to serve nine. You wanna come eat tomorrow?"

"Oh, I don't know," he said. "I don't really celebrate much anymore without Roberta here."

"I get it," she said. "But ya gotta eat, and we've got so much food. The offer stands if you change your mind." She turned to Ellory. "You, too, by the way."

"Thanks," Ellory said, and left it at that. The idea of spending Christmas with someone else's family hurt too much right now. She'd been so caught up in having Rowan around, trying to keep the Christmas Carol Crawl going, and figuring out a way for the Crowleys to have dinner together, she hadn't really even considered the fact that she would be alone on Christmas Day.

Totally alone.

For the first time, ever.

She didn't even have a turkey.

Where was the celebration in that?

Lindsay turned to Rowan. "So your car is stranded on the side of the road?"

Rowan had already donned his coat, hat, gloves, scarf, boots. He was ready to go, leaning forward on his toes anxiously. He pointed. "That way just outside of town."

"Okay, let's go look at it," she said. "I loaded up my nephew's sled with some tools. Hopefully we can figure out the problem."

"If anyone can, you can," Mr. Crowley said, slapping her on the back, a muffled whump through the coveralls. "Junior trained her himself. And he can fix anything."

She pointed a gloved finger at Mr. Crowley. "See you tomorrow around two for dinner. Don't let me down."

He chuckled. "Yes, ma'am. I'll give you a call."

Lindsay and Rowan headed out into the snow, their boots leaving fresh tracks as they sank in. It was going to be a long, exhausting walk to his car, and a part of Ellory wanted to go, too, but she knew she had no real reason to. After all, she was temporary.

"Thank you for getting her over here to help," she said, once they'd gotten out of sight and she'd shut the door. "Would you like a pumpkin muffin?"

"I'm pretty full," Mr. Crowley said, patting his stomach as he lowered back into his chair. "But never too full for an Ellory DeCloud confection. I'll have one."

"I'll get it for you." She hurried into the kitchen and paused at the counter to let herself breathe a little. So much had transpired this morning, her head was spinning. She didn't quite know what she'd been expecting out of her morning, but it certainly hadn't been this. She took a deep breath, steadied herself, then set about putting a muffin on a plate and getting a napkin.

She brought both into the living room and handed them to Mr. Crowley.

"You didn't get one for yourself?"

"I don't have the appetite for it," she said. "Plus, I have more at the shop. These are for you."

He took a bite, closed his eyes, laying his head back against his chair, and smiled. "You sure have a gift," he said. "I wish I could share these with Roberta. Pumpkin was her favorite."

Guilt panged around behind Ellory's ribs. "I'm so sorry," she said. "I wish she could have one, too."

"Well, I may think you hung the moon," Mr. Crowley said. "But I'm certain that you don't control the weather."

"Still…" Ellory said, looking down at her shoes.

"Still…you don't control the weather," he repeated. "Just like you can't control that he's here while his sister is having a baby in Iowa. Things happen that are out of our control all the time."

"Well," Ellory said. "For the record, I don't like it when things are out of my control."

"I understand completely," he said. "Anything else you want to put on record?"

Ellory adjusted so that she was sinking back farther in her chair. Letting the morning go. Letting the stress drain. "For the record," she said. "I plan to get the whole town of Haw Springs singing tonight."

"Now that's a tall order," he said.

"I'm up for a challenge."

He took another bite, chewed, thought it over. "If anyone is," he finally said, "it's you. What else?"

She thought. "For the record, I'm going to add a food menu to the Dreamy Bean next year. It's my New Year goal."

He held up his half-eaten muffin. "Now that, I very much believe you can do."

"Thank you. And I'm going to go for it no matter who thinks it's a silly dream."

"I don't know why anyone would think it's a silly dream," he said. "But, regardless, it's your dream, and if you don't think it's silly, then it's not."

"Exactly."

He smiled. "This is fun. What else?"

She chewed the inside of her cheek, thinking. "Um...for the record...I think Latte needs a friend. A cat friend. I'm going to ask David McBride if he knows anyone looking to home one. I'll name her Cappuccino."

Mr. Crowley laughed. "Well, I can't wait to see what her pajamas look like."

Ellory beamed. She was proud of herself for shifting out of the panic mode she'd been in earlier. All it ever took for her was a little dreaming, a little planning, a little belief in herself and in her path, and she felt right. Or righted. Or maybe both.

"Now it's your turn," she said. "What would you like to put on the record?"

"Oh. Me?"

"Yes, you. This is an open record."

"Okay, let me think." He stroked his chin with one hand. "For the record," he said slowly, going from stroking his chin to wiping crumbs from the corners of his mouth. "I plan to eat all of the pumpkin muffins before the end of today. Maybe I'm a bad host, but Rowan gets none."

Ellory laughed out loud. "Well, with a little luck, he should be on the road before the end of the day today, anyway. I'll pack him up a care package and include all the leftover pumpkin muffins."

"Good. Now I don't feel guilty. Although those are so good they can wipe the guilt right out of a guy, anyway. I would have muddled through just fine."

"What else?"

"For the record. Hmm..." He rubbed his chin again, gazing into the fire. "I would like to see Roberta every day next year. No matter what. Even if I have to rent an apartment next door to the care center."

"I'll help you however I can."

"For the record," he said. "I'll spend every minute of every day that I'm not with her, missing her."

Ellory felt tears well up in her eyes. "Your love for her is so beautiful," she said. "I've never seen anything like it."

And she hadn't. To call her parents' relationship cold was the understatement of the century. But her relationship with Danny had only been marginally less chilly. It was like they were afraid that falling in love and showing it would be undignified.

How much of that had she absorbed, she wondered. *How much of the way she'd just acted with Rowan reflected that fear of showing vul-*

nerability? How much was she waiting for him to rip pictures from the walls and smash them on the floor?

"You're young yet," Mr. Crowley said. "You just haven't had a chance to experience it. But you will. When you find the other half of your beautiful thing, you'll know it."

"I'm not sure if I'll find it. But I'm also okay if I don't, you know? I'm not really interested in love."

"For the record," Mr. Crowley said. "I don't believe that."

Ellory blinked at him in surprise. He turned up his palms and cocked his head to the side as if to say, *What can you do?*

"You're a daydreamer and a romantic. Anyone who has stepped foot into the Dreamy Bean knows this. Half of the people who walk in, literally hit their heads on clouds hanging from your ceiling."

"They do not," Ellory said. "Just that one really tall guy. And I knew I would regret you witnessing that."

"Regardless," Mr. Crowley said. "I've spent enough time with you to know that love matters to you a great deal. So much so, you're tearing yourself into pieces over not being able to get me through a blizzard to have dinner with my wife."

"That's different."

"It's not. It's love. You said it yourself—you think it's beautiful. People who don't care about love don't think love looks beautiful on other people." He sat forward, resting his forearms on his legs and tenting his fingers together. "And, for the record, I know what's happening between the two of you."

"Nothing's happening," Ellory protested.

He pointed at her. "And that's the problem. You know what I just said about knowing when you're with the one who makes it beautiful for you? You are seeing it when you're with him. You're feeling it. And you're fighting it. You both are."

"We barely know each other."

"Which is irrelevant to what I'm saying."

"Mr. Crowley, with all due respect, you're wrong."

He shrugged. "Maybe. But for the record, I don't think I am."

"Well, but for the record, even if you weren't wrong—and you are—he is leaving as soon as he can."

"And, goodness knows, he can't return."

"He won't return," she said. "He said it himself—this is temporary."

Mr. Crowley held his hands up, palms out, as if in surrender, and shook his head slowly. "Then I stand corrected. How about another muffin? You say there's more in there?"

"Yes, of course," Ellory said. Her voice felt tiny and defeated. She didn't want him to be wrong. But she didn't want him to be right, either. She didn't want any of this.

She brought him another muffin and then went for the coat closet, where she'd hung her coat when she'd arrived. "If you're all set, I think I'll go home and get started on the dinner menu."

"You're doing too much," he said. "You don't have to make me a special dinner."

"Of course I do," she said. "It's your special day. And it's no big deal."

"Why do I have a feeling you're going to make it a big deal?"

"Because that's what I do." She wound herself into her coat and bundled up with her scarf and gloves, then turned around and put a hand on his shoulder. "For the record, you can't stop me."

"You didn't need to go on record with that one. I already knew."

Ellory smiled and allowed herself to feel the warmth of her relationship with Mr. Crowley seep in. He was an excellent man, the father she always wanted, the grandfather she missed dearly.

"See you this evening. I'll bring my computer, so dress nice. And no pipe. Mrs. Crowley hates that pipe."

"For the record, I wish I hadn't told you that," he said, staring forlornly at the pipe in his hand.

Ellory raised up on her toes and kissed him on the cheek. "Dress nice," she repeated. She patted his shoulder twice and plunged back out into the unrelenting snow.

"This snow is too much," Rowan panted. His legs, at first warm and taut from the work of walking through the snow, had begun to tire, get cold.

"Looks like it's slowing down, though," Lindsay said. She stopped short, peered out from under her hood at him. "Are you sure you want to try to drive through this?"

"I'm sure I have to," he said. "My sister is counting on me." He'd already told Lindsay all about his sister's labor, all the while trying unsuccessfully to reach Johnny. He'd started to worry about something altogether different. It wasn't like his brother-in-law to ghost anyone. He hoped everything was okay.

When they reached Rowan's car, it was hardly visible. It seemed to be a white, snow lump just like all the others he had seen as he was driving into town. Rowan had no idea how Lindsay was going to do anything under all that snow. But she didn't seem the least bit fazed. Together, they brushed the snow away from the hood, using their whole arms, snow mist blowing back in their faces. Rowan produced his key and, with a lot more brushing, and quite a bit of tugging, managed to pull open the driver's side door.

It was like being inside an icicle.

"Hey, buddy," he said, patting the steering wheel. "I told you I wouldn't forget you. Thanks for hanging in there. We're gonna get you all fixed up."

He stuck the key in the ignition and...nothing.

"Pop the hood?" Lindsay called from the front of the car. He did, and she set to work tinkering around on things. Every so often, she would call out, "Try it again," and he would turn the key, only for nothing to happen.

Every time he tried and failed, his heart sank deeper into the pit of his stomach. There was no way he would get to Megan on time—he recognized that—but he'd begun to worry that there was no way he would get to her at all.

"Try again!"

He turned the key, and this time heard the tiniest click and whir.

"Okay," Lindsay said. "Okay. I think I know what's going on here." She shut the hood and came around to the open door. "I need to get some things from the shop. Go with?"

"Sure," he said. "Where is the shop?"

She indicated a building that was no more than a hundred yards away. He couldn't help thinking that if Junior had just remained in town, his entire journey might have been different. He would have gotten his car fixed right away, the Main Street might have been plowed, and...

Well, and he might have never met Ellory.

Which would have been a horrible thing.

But also might have been a good thing.

Then he wouldn't have had any idea what he was actually missing out on when he inevitably went on his way.

He and Lindsay walked to the auto shop. She immediately fired up the coffee maker when they arrived, their noses and the tips of their ears red, their fingers numb and then aching.

"Let's warm up for just a few, and then we'll get back out there. Feel free to have a seat."

She gestured to a gritty, grimy waiting area, which consisted of three rusty-legged chairs with cracked upholstery, fluff poking through the cracks like tiny snowdrifts. Someone had strung Christmas lights and an old Merry Christmas banner across the front of the counter, the bottom of the *y* torn off, so that it read *Merrv Christmas*. Rowan chuckled. He imagined himself telling Ellory to have a *Merrv Christmas* and watching her head explode with the very idea of him not saying it the right way.

Maybe I should buy her a banner and rip off the bottom of the y *so she can string a Merrv Christmas banner across her counter, too*, he thought and then realized that he was future planning with someone he didn't have a future with.

This is temporary.

We are temporary.

Why did his brain keep insisting that they would have something?

Lindsay had laid her coat across the counter; it dripped melted snow onto the floor. He sat in one of the chairs and watched the puddle grow, watched the water ripple every time a new drip hit it. He imagined the puddle as Haw Springs, and every drip as another person dropping in to change it, make it bigger, make it fuller. He imagined himself as one of those drops, swimming around, trying to get his bearings, trying to understand this place, all the while changing it himself.

This was how the world worked, wasn't it? You dropped in somewhere, morphed it into something else, and then every time you did something new, it was another drop, another change. And another, and another.

And then someone else dropped in next to you, and that, too, changed your world. And the change was sweeping or it was subtle, but either way, it moved you. It moved your world.

And sometimes you moved with it.

And sometimes you didn't, and the puddle grew without you.

And you were comfortable in your old side of the puddle, but at the same time, you wished to see the other side. The new side. The side that had blown you to bits with its exciting newness.

And sometimes, if you thought about it really hard, you could imagine an even newer puddle somewhere down the road, with all kinds of newness dropped in, and it was the most alluring puddle of all. But the jump to get there seemed impossible.

You were living in a world that was no longer the one you entered. And you didn't know what to do about it. You weren't prepared for life in this puddle. You weren't prepared for life in any puddle.

And so you floated, floated.

Because floating was something you could do. You've been floating your whole life. Floating was boring and dull and made you feel itchy with restlessness. But it was safe.

In the end, you didn't like safe, but you chose it every single time. So why not this time, too?

He tore his eyes away from the puddle and called Megan.

A nurse answered. "Hang on, she's in the middle of a contraction, but she wants to talk to you," she said. He could hear Megan letting out a long moan in the background. All the information he needed. The moaning was replaced with panting and then fumbling.

"Rowan?" Megan sounded tired. Upset. "Have you heard from him?"

"I haven't. I'm sorry."

Her voice filled with tears. He could only imagine what panicked thoughts she could be thinking at this point. "Do you think he's okay?"

"Yes," Rowan said, without hesitation. Truthfully, he wasn't sure what was going on with his brother-in-law, but he knew that, in that moment, his sister needed comfort. She needed validation and confirmation. She needed him to tell her that everything was fine. That everything would be okay. If it turned out not to be, they would deal with that down the road. But today, right now, fine was the only option. "I think he's trying to figure out how to get to you, and it's making it hard for him to call."

"If he's okay… I'm going to…" she paused, panted. "Murder…him…when he…gets here."

Rowan laughed. "That's the spirit. Let the murder of your child's father bolster your birth experience."

"You know what I mean," she said. "Why isn't he calling me? I need him."

"Megs, listen to me. I think we've figured out what's wrong with my car. We're working on it right now."

"Really? Do you think you can get here?"

"If we can get it running, I'm sure going to try. It might take me a few hours longer. But I'll do my best. I think the snow is about to stop. So all I'll need to do is get past this, and a few other, small towns. Once I'm in Kansas City, I think it'll improve."

"Please be careful. I don't want you driving all that way in this. But I'm so glad you're coming. Please hurry. But don't."

Rowan laughed. "I'm not sure I understood all of the directives, but I'll do my best, okay? I'll text you when we get the car going. Watch your phone."

"Oh, sure, in the middle of doing nothing at all."

"That's the spirit. Also, hold the baby in until I get there. Is that a big ask? I don't know."

"Rowan?"

"Yeah?"

"I don't know if I can do this by myself."

He turned to watch Lindsay through the window into the garage. She sipped a cup of coffee as she pulled what seemed like random things off shelves and dropped them into a backpack. He was grateful for what she was doing. But he wanted her to do it faster.

"Megan, do you remember when Dad left and Mom just basically checked out on us?"

"Zombie Mom? Yeah, I remember."

"We were just kids. But you gave her about a week, and then you took charge. You made our breakfasts, you packed our lunches, you figured out how to do the laundry. Do you remember this?"

"Of course I do."

"I do, too. You became the mom when you were still in elementary school. And you did it with kindness and intention. You helped me with my math homework."

She chuckled. "You failed the test."

He laughed. He remembered the feeling of failing that test. He'd been so angry at himself, so angry at his parents, so angry at his teacher. But when he'd shown Megan the test, she'd cried and apologized to him, and he'd been so awash with a feeling of solidarity with his sister, his test no longer mattered. "I did fail it. You're terrible at math."

"And I married an accountant."

"That was probably wise on your part." They laughed a little more.

"Well, he's terrible at making pancakes," she said. "We all have our strengths and we all have our weaknesses."

"That's what I was getting at," Rowan said, growing serious again. "It's because of that time, and because of that test, that I know you can one hundred percent do this. It's not ideal, and I don't blame you at all for being upset. But I know my sister, and my sister can handle this. No problem. So, whoever you are, if you're thinking you can't do it, you need to get out of her way."

She paused, sniffled. "Thanks, Row."

"You're doing great. I'll call you when I'm on my way."

"Okay. Oh, no, here comes another one." She paused, let out another groan. "Hey, Row?"

"Yeah, I know, I'll let you go."

"No…" Another groan. "I was going to say… your strength…"

"Yeah?"

This time she moaned with such force, he actually pulled his phone away from his ear and stared at it. Hearing his tough-as-nails sister suffer so loudly rattled him.

"She needs another moment," the nurse said.

"It's okay," Rowan said. "She can finish the thought when she sees me."

He hung up just as Megan's cries ratcheted up a notch. Lindsay had come back into the waiting area.

"I think I've got what we need. You ready to get back out there?" She pulled on her coat.

"Definitely," Rowan said. "More than ready."

CHAPTER TWELVE

LINDSAY WORKED HARD into the afternoon. The sky cleared and then raged again. And then cleared again, the haze darkening as evening pressed in upon them. Rowan had stood next to Lindsay, digging things out of the backpack and handing them to her, only to drop them back inside moments later. Twice, they went back to the shop to get more tools and drink more coffee. Twice she called Junior for advice.

Three times, Rowan texted Johnny and got no answer. He still hadn't even opened a single one of Rowan's texts.

He'd begun to lose hope.

And just as the situation seemed at peak hopelessness, just as he was fixing to suggest to Lindsay that they just go back to Mr. Crowley's house and wait for Junior to return and maybe even for the snow to thaw, she cried out, "Try it again!" and it worked.

They both let out yelps of joy and triumph and high-fived in the dimming light.

The car was purring like a kitten. The best it had sounded in years.

Lindsay let the hood drop shut and Rowan turned on his wipers and cranked the heat to full blast.

The last time they'd stopped at the shop, they'd come back with a snow shovel, which Rowan had used to clear the area immediately around the car's tires, on the off chance that she would be able to get the car going.

"Can I give you a ride back home?" he asked.

"Sure!" Lindsay hopped in next to him. "I'll be honest," she said, once she was inside. There were icicles on her eyelashes and she rubbed them away. "I was starting to get a little worried."

"Not me," he said. "I believed in you the whole time." They traded glances and laughed.

He expected whirring engine and spinning tires, but it seemed the car was as ready to go as he was. He crept forward and then they were off, Rowan giving his best guess where the road was.

When they reached Lindsay's house, he left the car running. He shook her hand.

"What do I owe you?"

She waved him away. "Nah. Nothing."

"Are you kidding me? You were out there for the whole day. You've gotta let me pay you something."

She shook her head. "You gave me something

to do in the middle of a blizzard, and you let me prove to myself that I can do the job even without Junior. And I got to be part of helping your sister in her time of need. That's payment enough."

"Are you sure?" he asked.

"Positive. Just...you know...maybe give Junior's shop a shout-out on YELP or something."

"Will do." He held out a hand for a handshake. She shook it.

"Merry Christmas, Uncle Rowan," she said.

He perked up. "Hey! Uncle Rowan! I like the sound of it. Merry Christmas," he responded without so much as a pause.

A part of him hoped that Ellory would still be around when he raced into Mr. Crowley's house next door. But she was gone.

"You get her fixed?" Mr. Crowley asked from his chair.

"She sure did!" Rowan said.

"I expect you'll be on your way, then."

"I will. Thank you for everything, sir. The kindness in this town is really something."

Mr. Crowley nodded, looked up from his newspaper, and pulled the pipe out of his mouth. "You're welcome to stay on through the holiday, of course."

"I wish I could," Rowan said. "But my sister is waiting."

"Yes, yes, of course."

Rowan ran into his bedroom and crammed his things into his duffel bag, then stripped the sheets and blankets off the bed and left them in a pile.

Mr. Crowley was standing at the door when he emerged. Rowan stuck out his hand for another shake. "Thank you again, sir."

Mr. Crowley gave him a hearty shake. "You're always welcome here."

"I appreciate that."

"Stop on by and say hi when you come back through."

"Oh. I don't know if I'll be coming back through," Rowan said. "I'm here because I took a wrong turn. Normally, the highway wouldn't bring me through here."

"I know," Mr. Crowley said. "But when you come back, stop on by. I'll be happy to see you." He gave a wink and opened the door.

What was that about? Rowan wondered as he got back into the car. But then, as he drove down Main Street, craning his neck as he passed the Dreamy Bean, looking for Ellory in the dim and honey-colored lighting inside, hoping that he would have an excuse to stop and say goodbye, it dawned on him.

He knew exactly what Mr. Crowley was saying.

The hole in his gut as he kept driving said exactly the same thing.

But that was exactly why he knew he wouldn't be coming back.

He had to let her go.

There were tire tracks in the snow outside the coffee shop.

Ellory followed them with her eyes all the way until they disappeared out of town. She knew what this meant. Rowan was gone.

She hadn't even said goodbye.

But, then again, she supposed that they'd said goodbye that morning. *This is temporary. We are temporary.*

Right.

She tried to let the excitement of helping the Crowleys with their anniversary dinner, combined with the excitement of tonight's Crawl bolster her spirits. But the truth was, she had begun to envision those things happening with Rowan at her side.

How quickly she'd begun to depend on his presence.

She'd gone all-out for dinner, having procured the ingredients before the storm had hit. It was a proper Christmas Eve dinner, the kind she'd grown used to as a child. Beef Wellington, mashed potatoes and gravy, steamed green beans, caramelized yams, a glistening cheesecake for dessert. She'd spent all day in the kitchen, and she was tired.

And while a part of her knew that Mr. Crowley would appreciate the meal, she also knew that it would be bittersweet for him, watching his beautiful bride eat something bland and boring on the other side of town. As she packed the food into her baskets, she tried not to focus on such things.

They were doing the best they could do under the circumstances.

Her phone rang.

"Merry Christmas Eve, sis," Daphne whispered.

"Merry Christmas Eve." Ellory could hear voices and laughter in the background. She closed her eyes, envisioning exactly what was happening. The Wittfelds and the DeClouds were settling in with cocktails and appetizers and an annual game of Christmas charades that decides who hosts the New Year's Eve gathering (spoiler: it is always and will always be the DeClouds, because nobody but nobody would ever wrestle that kind of social power away from Angeline DeCloud).

Ellory could see the tree, with its all-white-and-rhinestone decorations, dominating the corner of the living room, the tasteful pine boughs marching up the stair rail, the distressed metal lanterns on the front porch. The fire, modernly tucked into the half wall that marked the space between dining room and living room, would be filled with modest flames quietly licking the glass that held them inside. No warmth, just flicker. All visual with no real feeling.

There would be gifts under the tree—boxes that were uniform in shape and size, in matching silver and white paper and adorned with rattan bows and frost-tipped holly sprigs. These, too, were empty, the real gifts hidden from sight until tomorrow morning, not to keep a surprise intact, but to keep guests from the unsightly vision of things that aren't symmetrical and uniform.

Jazz renditions of traditional Christmas Carols would be piping throughout the house over a system of speakers that were so well hidden, guests would sometimes wonder if they were hearing a sound at all, or if maybe they were so joyful and so filled with beautiful and tasteful Christmas revelry, they were simply imagining it.

This was all the doing of Angeline DeCloud, whose finger was so firmly on the pulse of the appearances behind elite pleasure, she practically oozed it.

Even the scent of Christmas spirit was released on a carefully calibrated timer from unseen corners of just about every room in the expansive home. If Ellory breathed in long enough, she could just about smell it now—a generic, unpinpointable mix of berry and green and fresh and wood.

It was no wonder to Ellory that she grew to love Christmas, having grown with such holiday perfection. It was like living in a movie. Even if none of it was real, it was such a good fake, it felt real.

"Why are you whispering?" Ellory asked.

"I'm not," Daphne whispered. The voices drew farther away and she repeated herself, full volume. "I'm not whispering."

Ellory stopped what she was doing to focus on the conversation. "Wait a minute. Are you whispering so nobody hears you talking to me? Seriously?"

"No." Daphne's tone was too defensive to be real. "Nobody said I couldn't talk to you."

"That's not what I just asked, though. You're whispering so nobody can hear you talk to me, and that's because you don't want to have to answer to anyone about having talked to me. Nobody said you can't, but that doesn't mean they won't be mad that you did." Ellory placed hands on hips, indignant, but at the same time, she felt tears welling in her eyes. "Take me into the living room and put me on speaker," she said.

"I'm sorry," Daphne said. "I didn't mean to upset you by calling. I can let you go."

"Take me into the room where our parents are. I have something to say."

"Ellory, it's Christmas Eve." Her sister's voice was plaintive, regretful.

"Exactly. Let me talk to everyone." Daphne was silent. "I'm serious, Daph."

Ellory heard her sister sigh, and then some rustled walking that brought the background voices and laughter louder. Finally, Ellory could tell that she was in the same room with the rest of them.

"Well, there you are, Daphne," Ellory heard her mother say. "We've been waiting for you so we can start our game."

"Sorry, I was on the phone," Daphne said.

"Who could you be calling that's more important than Christmas Charades? Nothing is more important than Christmas Charades. Christmas Charades is life." That was Mr. Wittfeld's voice. Jovial and joking, just like always. Mr. Wittfeld was, generally speaking, a good guy. A much better guy than the son he raised. "We've been practicing all year for this. Let's go."

"Put me on speaker, Daphne," Ellory said, recognizing that her moment might be slipping away. "Daphne? Put me on speaker."

She heard her sister sigh again and then the room got the tinny sound of a phone on speaker. "Go ahead," she said.

"Merry Christmas, everyone," Ellory said. She tried to make her voice light, but knew that it fell flat, with a tinge of sarcasm. The room grew silent.

"Is that Ellory?" she heard her mom whisper,

and knew that she'd gotten Daphne in trouble with what their parents would undoubtedly call *a stunt*. She felt the tiniest twinge of guilt, but drew herself taller and pushed her chest out, pressed her phone harder to her ear.

"Yes, Mom, it's Ellory. Don't punish Daphne. She didn't do anything wrong. I'm the one who called her and insisted she bring me into the room." It was a lie, but not a big one, and it would shield Daphne from their mother's wrath.

"This is hardly the time, Ellory."

"Really? Because it seems like exactly the time to wish your *family* a Merry Christmas. It's Christmas Eve, Mother."

"What is this stunt you're pulling?" There it was. Her father, just as expected.

"It's not a stunt, Daddy. It's your daughter wishing you a Merry Christmas on Christmas Eve. Aren't you going to say it back?"

Her mother's voice grew closer, as if she were about to confiscate the phone. "She's throwing a temper tantrum because she's not here."

"No. Mom. I'm not throwing a temper tantrum. I'm justifiably upset because my own family told me I couldn't come to Christmas this year unless I planned to patch things up with Danny."

"Wait, is that true?" she heard Danny say, and then someone shushed him.

"So...for the record..." Ellory's voice caught.

She would need to thank Mr. Crowley for this strength that she was finding in this moment. Clearly it was inspired by him. She cleared her throat and forged on. "For the record, I will not be patching things up with Danny. Not this year or next, or the one after that. I don't want to patch things up with someone who literally shattered my dreams."

"Oh, well now you're just being dramatic," her mother said, and then louder, as if a proclamation, "And if you're going to be dramatic, then I'm afraid we'll have to hang up and talk to you later. This is Christmas Eve, and we're not going to have it ruined."

"I think we should listen." Daphne sounded uneasy and frightened, but strong. Ellory's heart warmed. Her sister wasn't totally lost to her. Not yet.

"Your opinion doesn't factor into anything at this time," her father said, but she didn't wait for him to continue.

"I think we should hear her out, Daddy. Go ahead, Ellory."

"Also, for the record, my ridiculous little dream has been such a smashing success, I'm dreaming even bigger."

She heard a dismissive *pssh*, the origins of which she couldn't quite pinpoint, and then Danny. "I hardly think your tiny little hole-in-the-wall coffee shop is such a rousing success. There's no way it's bringing in the kind of money my career as a day trader is bringing in."

"There's more to success than money," Daphne said, her confidence betrayed by the tiniest quiver in her voice.

"Oh, really, Daph? Because I can't help noticing that your boyfriend over there is filled with loads and loads of money. He's like a cash piñata."

"You know what?" Ellory cut in, realizing only just now the full extent of the dysfunction she'd grown up with. Her idyllic Christmas was, in fact, filled with pretentiousness, lies, and a seriously malignant lack of actual connection. "Maybe someday you'll make it down to that tiny little hole-in-the-wall coffee shop and see for yourself. We'll be adding made-to-order crepes to the menu next month. Yours will be on the house."

"Spiteful," Mrs. Wittfeld said in a singsongy voice.

Ellory laughed. Of course her family and their best friends would see a kind gesture as something spiteful. Because that was how they operated. Spite and jealousy and one-upmanship.

"Not spite, Mrs. Wittfeld, just an invitation and a really good crepe. I hope you make it down sometime."

There was silence all around now, and she could envision the scene once again. Her mother with her arms crossed, her jaw set in fury. Her father idly toeing the foot of a chair, whiskey sloshing around in a highball glass in his hand. The Wittfelds sitting one-two-three on the couch, Mr. Wittfeld fiddling with his whiskey glass in his lap, Mrs. Wittfeld with legs crossed at the knee and perfect, indignant posture. And Danny, loungy and disinterested, practically sprawled, as if he owned the place.

As if he once almost did.

In this moment, Ellory was extremely grateful for what Danny did. For the laughter and ridicule and for constructing an army against her, a family united in their disbelief. She was grateful for the opportunity to leave it all behind. To leave them, and their cynicism and doubt. To make something of herself.

"Merry Christmas, everyone," she said. "I mean it."

And she did.

THE DRIVING WAS way worse than Rowan expected. He puttered along down what he figured to be the exact center of every road he took, praying not to get swept into a ditch or a drift. Praying to get back to the highway.

He backtracked through Haw Springs and

through the outskirts, his car valiantly trying to stay alive in the snow, the tires desperately working to keep their footing. Occasionally, he lost control, but then regained it just when he thought he was going to be headed down a more hopeless path than before.

Eventually, he found his way to the highway, and—luck of all lucks!—a plow had been through. Maybe just once, but once was enough. His putter turned to a slow drive and then to a medium-paced drive as he left the sticks behind and got closer to the city.

With any luck, he would be in Iowa in just over three hours.

EVENING FELL.

The snow stopped. The stars came out, crisp and blinking in the night sky.

Christmas Eve was, by far, Ellory's favorite time of the entire holiday season. It always seemed so peaceful and anticipatory, as if the whole world was holding its breath, readying to shout in celebration.

Surprise!

Dinner was ready and packed. Her laptop was tucked into the basket alongside the beef and potatoes. She'd texted Tena, who assured her that Roberta was on her way down to dinner as they spoke.

Everything was a go.

Ellory, decked out in a pair of green snow pants and a long Christmas sweater with about three shirts underneath it, put her head down and followed Rowan's tire tracks to Mr. Crowley's house, the baskets dangling from her arms.

There was a spring in her step she might not have expected to ever have again, a year ago.

She was just about to turn onto Mr. Crowley's street when she heard bells behind her and someone calling her name.

She stopped and turned, just in time to see two horses coming toward her, and Marlee West waving frantically at her from behind them.

"What the...is that a sleigh?" Ellory said aloud and then laughed and called it out. "You brought a sleigh?"

"I brought a sleigh!" Marlee yelled, continuing to wave.

Ellory waited while Ben Werth, Decker McBride's ranch hand, steered the sleigh toward her. They reached her and stopped, the horses snorting and stomping. Ben tipped his cowboy hat, calm and collected, as if he navigated a horse-drawn sleigh into town on a daily basis.

"Ma'am."

"Oh...my... I can't believe you did this," Ellory said, reaching to pat one of the horses on the side. The sleigh was truly not much more than a wooden box on a pair of skis, but to her, it represented the impossible. "Ben! You made a sleigh."

"Mr. Decker and I did it together," Ben said. "Miss Marlee said you needed one and we didn't have anything else to do, due to the blizzard and all."

"So you made *a sleigh*." Ellory was still filled with awe. "Who does that?"

Ben looked confused. "I just told you that Mr. Decker and I did that."

Funny, Haw Springs seems like exactly the kind of town that would have an abundance of sleighs. Or at least an abundance of the ability to have sleighs. Like, Oh, Old Man Vesper down on Route Triple P could whip us up one right quick. Or we could build our own, using the little Christmas trees out front, some antique tools found in your attic, and a good dollop of elbow grease.

"Rowan was right," she said. "We are that kind of town. He would just die if he saw this."

"Who?" Marlee asked.

At the same time Ben, who was on the autism spectrum and was as pragmatic as the day was long, said, "We made sure it's extra safe so no one will die, barring some unforeseen tragedy. But unforeseen tragedies are impossible to plan for, as they are unforeseen."

"I've got to admit," Marlee said, hopping out

of the sleigh. "It's fun to ride in. You want to take it for a spin?"

Ben held out a protective hand. "With all due respect, Miss Marlee, I don't think we should spin the horses. It might make them dizzy and sometimes when I get dizzy I get sick to my stomach. That doesn't seem fair to do to Tango and Queenie, what with them not having any say in the matter."

"You're so right, Ben, my apologies. I just meant maybe we can take Ellory for a ride. Where was it you wanted to go?"

Ellory shook her head. "Not me. Mr. Crowley. Give me five minutes." She shoved the baskets at Marlee and took off.

She didn't even notice her boots sliding in the snow as she sprinted to Mr. Crowley's house and didn't stomp to rid them of the snow when she landed in his entryway, excited and out of breath. Mr. Crowley was waiting for her to arrive, wearing a suit coat and tie, his hair slicked down perfectly. Thank goodness he'd taken her directive to dress nice.

"Well, that was an entrance," he said. "Is everything okay?"

"You won't believe it," she said, grabbing him by the elbows. "It's so much better than okay. Ben Werth made a sleigh. They came all the way down from the McBride Ranch."

"You don't say," Mr. Crowley said. But he didn't seem to understand what she was getting at. He brushed at some invisible lint on the front of his shirt. "That Ben Werth is quite handy."

"It's right outside," she said.

He leaned toward the door to take a look. "Well, I'll be. There it is."

"You've got to get your coat, Mr. Crowley," she said, pulling at his elbows.

He moved his arms out of her hands and then patted one of her hands. "Oh, sweetheart, I don't think I'm up to caroling tonight. I thought maybe we would go ahead and just get to having dinner." He smiled sadly.

"No, you don't understand," she said. "We've got a sleigh. We're going to take you to have dinner with Mrs. Crowley. Face-to-face."

She watched his face as the realization slowly dawned on him. His eyes lit up with excitement. "We can get there?"

Ellory nodded excitedly. "Let's leave now!"

She helped him into his hat, coat, scarf, and gloves, and waited while he stuffed his feet into a pair of galoshes. Ben and Marlee had moved the sleigh in front of Mr. Crowley's house and were waiting for them.

They climbed inside and sat on the crudely built bench across from Marlee. A heap of blankets were piled on the floor at their feet. Ellory picked up one and spread it over them.

"I wish I had known," Mr. Crowley said. "I would have gotten Roberta a gift."

"I've got you covered," Marlee said. "Ben, do you mind stopping at the flower shop?"

Ben nodded, secured his hat onto his head, and used the reins to get the horses moving. They trotted down Main Street, pausing only long enough for Marlee to duck into her store. When she came back out, she held a bouquet of red roses in one arm and a potted poinsettia in the other.

"Hope she likes red," she said, climbing back into the sleigh.

"Oh, this is wonderful," Mr. Crowley said, wiping first one eye and then the other. Maybe the wind, Ellory thought. But more likely the gesture. "She's just going to love it."

The ride to the care center was brisk and breezy, and Ellory loved the rhythmic tinkling of the bells that the horses wore. She watched as children peered out of their windows, cupping their hands around their eyes, to see if the sleigh rushing down their street might have been Santa, and waved at the people who took to their yards to witness the passing spectacle.

She yelled *Merry Christmas* to friends and regulars, to children she recognized and moms whose coffee orders she had memorized. There were no Christmas Charades, no white-and-rhinestone trees, no scent of holiday on the air or saxophones and horns playing "Here Comes Santa Claus."

This was better. On just about every single level.

CHAPTER THIRTEEN

"She's having a really good day," Tena said when they arrived in the lobby of the memory care center. "She's been really excited about seeing her Billy."

Ellory grinned at Mr. Crowley. "Billy?"

He shook a finger at her. "Now, she's the only one who can get away with it. Don't get any ideas."

Ellory nodded very seriously. "Of course. Billy."

They unwrapped themselves from their winter wear and helped themselves to a carafe of hot apple cider on the front desk.

"She's waiting in the dining room. We haven't told her yet that you're coming in person. She's going to be so surprised."

"She loves surprises," Mr. Crowley said. "How's my hair?" He stood before Ellory with the nervous air of a teenager about to attend his first dance with a real date. She smoothed a few wisps that his hat had displaced and stood back to admire him.

"You look perfect. She's going to be so happy."

"Are you ready?" Tena asked.

Mr. Crowley picked up the flowers that he had momentarily laid on the desk and nodded. He took a deep breath and let it out. "I think so."

"Well, then, let's go have an anniversary dinner."

Ellory watched as Tena led Mr. Crowley through a door into a candlelit room. Seated at the only table in the room was an elegant, elderly lady wearing a maroon chiffon gown, her hair swept up and dotted with little gems that glinted in the candlelight. She was peering uncomfortably at an open laptop, her hands in her lap.

When the door opened, she looked up, then did a double take. She stood, her hands going to her mouth.

"Billy?"

He went to her and held out the bouquet of roses. "Happy anniversary, my love."

She took the roses and buried her nose deep into the bouquet. "How did you get here?"

"You wouldn't believe me even if I told you." He set the poinsettias on the table and then wrapped his arms around his wife, letting out a cry that came from somewhere so deep, Ellory felt it in her bones.

What must it feel like to hold on to that one person? she wondered. *To finally feel them in your arms after you thought you might not get to?*

Unbidden, she thought about Rowan, and what it would feel like to be wrapped in his arms. She would never know. But a part of her wondered if he, too, would cry out in that moment. A cry of love felt so deep it was indistinguishable from anguish.

Tena left them and came back through the door, shutting it behind her. She took hold of the basket that Ellory had brought. "I'll make sure to get these reheated. They'll be eating in no time. Do you want to stick around while they eat?"

"Nah," Marlee said. "We've got something to do. We'll come back."

Ellory, surprised, followed Marlee as she rebundled herself and took a cup of hot cider for the road. Marlee tugged Ellory outside and looped an arm around her neck.

"You do amazing things for people, did you know that?" Marlee said.

"I just have a soft spot for him is all," Ellory said. "Besides you, he was kind of my first friend here. We both understood what it was like to miss someone."

Marlee bumped her with her hip. "You can pretend it's a one-off kind of thing that you don't normally do, but we both know the truth. You have a soft heart for everyone. You even took in a stranger because he needed a place to stay. A total stranger, Ellory. I think that's the definition of philanthropy. Is he going to go caroling with us tonight?"

"He left," Ellory said.

Marlee stopped walking. "He left? Those tire tracks…?"

Ellory nodded. "They're his. His sister was in labor. He had to go."

"Oh." Marlee looked closer at her friend. "*Oh.* And you're sad about it."

"I'm not. I mean, maybe just a little. He was nice."

"I thought he was a grumpy Scrooge."

Ellory let out a laugh. "He was, at first. But… I don't know. He got used to it? Or he changed his mind, maybe? Or maybe I just got used to him? He had good reasons for the way that he felt about things. He came around. We had a good time."

Marlee put her arm around Ellory's shoulders again and continued walking toward the sleigh. "I'm sorry. But, hey, maybe he'll come back!"

Ellory would be lying if she said she hadn't already thought of this. That he would have to pass through Missouri again on his way back down to Tulsa. But the truth was, he was here on a wrong turn, and to come back, he would have to purposely veer off his path. And, well, she didn't know Rowan all that well, but he just didn't seem like the veer off a path kind of person. But Marlee was trying to be hopeful and positive on her behalf, and who was she to rain on that parade.

"Maybe," she said. Just as they swung open the sleigh door, she stopped. "Wait. Did you say caroling with us?"

Marlee smiled wide. "You don't think I'd come all the way down here and not participate in the Annual Haw Springs Main Street Christmas Carol Crawl, did you? Or should I say the First Annual Haw Springs Off–Main Street Christmas Carol Sleigh Ride? I hear we're doing the crawling. And what more festive way than in a handbuilt sleigh?" She got into the sleigh and held out her arms for Ellory to join her. "Ben, I don't suppose you know all the words to 'Silent Night'?"

"Of course I do," he said. "All three verses."

"Excellent," Marlee said. "We have a tenor. Into the neighborhood, Ben! Nice and slow!"

ONCE ROWAN GOT through the city, the highway was clear. Nice and fast. He even began to see other cars on the highway. The snow barely slowed them down. The plows seemed to have gotten the better of the storm the farther north he went. There were fewer cars abandoned on the side of the road, fewer accidents, and much more salt ticking up against the bottom of his car.

He was home free.

But it had been a long day, and a long, boring drive. He turned on the radio to keep himself company. And then, despite himself, flipped through the stations until he found what he was looking for.

It was Christmas Eve, after all.

And "Silent Night" was on the radio.

He thought about Ellory, wondered how her Crawl was going—if she'd managed to get anyone on board, or if she was out there singing by herself.

He chuckled to himself. She probably wouldn't care, even if she was out there by herself. She sure did love those Christmas carols. She loved to sing along.

"For you, Ellory of the Clouds," he said. He turned up the song.

And sang along.

IT STARTED WITH a group of children, who raced out into their yard, curious about the singing and the bells. Ellory and Marlee let them hop into the sleigh which Ben kept at a slow walk. Soon their parents joined and walked beside the sleigh. And then more kids and more parents.

And more. And more again.

Ellory and Marlee got out so the sleigh wouldn't get too heavy. But they didn't mind.

Soon there was an entourage, walking through the snow under the blazing Christmas star, their voices raised, some carrying lit candles, others looking up lyrics on their phones. It was exactly as Ellory had imagined.

Okay, maybe not exactly as she'd imagined when she'd taken on the job of organizing the Carol Crawl. But it was a good compromise, and something approximating what she'd been thinking when she'd convinced Katherine not to cancel.

"We're going to continue this on Main Street," she said every time someone left the sleigh. "Come on down if you can. Tell your friends. There are cookies. Loads and loads of them. If you can't come down, just keep on singing. We'll still hear you. All of Haw Springs will be singing tonight!"

They'd gone three, four, five streets, and finally Mr. Crowley emerged from the memory care center. His cheeks were pink, his eyes sparkling, and he had an easiness about his step that Ellory had never seen before. Ben directed the horses to him.

The crowd of singers swelled around him.

Tena brought Mrs. Crowley to the door, a blanket hastily wrapped around her. She, too, was singing, and when Mr. Crowley realized she was there, his hand momentarily went to his heart and then reached out to her, as if of its own volition.

They sang "Away in a Manger," "O Holy

Night," and "Joy to the World," the Crowleys holding hands and belting out the lyrics louder than anyone.

It was getting late, and Ben was worried that the horses were getting tired. He wanted to get them back up to the ranch before it got too late. He also missed Annie, he said. And he wanted some eggnog.

The Crowleys said their goodbyes, the crowd dispersed to their homes, and Marlee, Ellory, and Mr. Crowley rode in the sleigh through the crisp Christmas Eve air back into town.

"Well, how was it?" Marlee asked as they pulled away. "She sure seemed surprised."

He nodded. He hadn't stopped grinning since he stepped outside. "She was surprised, that's for sure. It was…miraculous. She was the most like herself I've seen in a year. They played our song, and we danced to it. Oh, and the food, Ellory." He kissed his fingertips. "Out of this world. And she got to sing Christmas carols, her absolute favorite." He leaned back, relaxing on the sleigh seat. "The Christmas Carol Crawl used to be her favorite Haw Springs tradition. We did it every single year. There were some years we were the first two people there. She would look forward to it for months. I don't know if she remembers those years or not."

"She definitely remembered the songs," Marlee said.

"That, she did. Did you see the look on her face?"

"She glowed," Ellory said. "I saw it. She was glowing."

He closed his eyes. "My bride. She looked like she'd drunk from the moon on our wedding night, and she looked like she'd nibbled a star tonight."

Marlee snuggled closer to Ellory. "A Christmas Eve wedding. Can you imagine the romance?"

Ellory laid her head on her friend's shoulder. "Mrs. Crowley is one lucky girl." She closed her eyes to try and imagine it. "You know what I would have at my wedding? All the poinsettias in your shop."

Marlee groaned. "Don't remind me. I should have grabbed more than one while I was in there. I would have given them away like parade candy."

Ellory opened her eyes, then sat up and gasped. "You may still get the chance. Look!"

Nearly every store on Main Street was lit up. The trees that Ellory and Rowan hadn't gotten to were hastily decorated. Shop owners were standing at their front windows and front doors, holding platters of cookies. The street was milling with people, bundled in their winter coats. Ellory could hear their voices all the way to the sleigh.

"People really did tell their friends," Marlee said. "They're singing! Listen!" Not only could they hear the voices of the people on Main Street, but voices echoed all around the Haw Springs valley.

Ellory was too choked up to respond. She could hardly believe what she was seeing and hearing. The whole town of Haw Springs, it seemed, had found a way to the Carol Crawl, one way or another. Turned out, they didn't even need her. They just needed the idea. The belief.

Ben had barely brought the horses to a stop in front of Mr. Crowley's house before Ellory was out of the sleigh and running toward Main Street, Marlee running behind her yelling, "Wait up! Ell! Hang on!"

But Ellory couldn't stop. It was the most beautiful sight she'd ever seen.

She opened her shop and flipped on the lights. The little tree outside her shop lit up. She fired up her machines and rushed to the kitchen to plate up a massive mound of cookies. *Hot chocolate*, she thought. *We need all the hot chocolate.* On her way back to the counter, she stopped to flip on the music, smiling to herself as she thought about Rowan's reaction to the music when he'd first arrived here.

Oh, how he'd hated it. But he'd grown not to hate it, and in the end, she was pretty sure he actually liked it a little.

Singing swelled outside her door—"O Come All Ye Faithful"—and she raced to greet the carolers.

"Come on in, get some hot chocolate," she said. "Welcome, welcome! Merry Christmas!"

"Oh, thank goodness you're open," she heard someone say from Marlee's shop next door. "I was afraid I wouldn't get my poinsettias this year!"

"Me, too!" someone else cried.

"I got mine!" One of the carolers standing before Ellory held a potted poinsettia over her head.

Over time, the cookies dwindled, and Ellory ran out of hot chocolate. But the people lingered. She stepped outside and joined in the singing, high-stepping through the snow to the middle of the street.

Last year, she'd been new and shy during the Christmas Carol Crawl, but had sung along from her bedroom window, feeling the warmth of community from a distance. She'd eventually gone out and joined in, watching neighbors greet neighbors, family greet family, and longing for the day that she felt like she truly belonged.

That day was already here. Haw Springs had a way of folding people into the family that quickly.

It was one thing to sing along to the music from behind a pane of glass; it was another thing entirely to be in the middle of Main Street, singing with your whole heart under the Christmas star. An entire town—hundreds of people—lifting their voices. The song had become its own entity. You could feel it vibrating your bones. You could feel it coiling its arms around you. You could feel it snaking through your body, wrapping its fingers around your heart.

So why did she still feel like something was missing? Something that was keeping her from being fully in the moment.

Maybe you're the problem, Ellory. Maybe your mom is right and you are just incapable of being happy and satisfied. Maybe it's you.

Maybe you don't actually like Christmas anymore. Maybe Danny ruined that for you forever, and you're just pretending.

It was getting late. The carolers had begun to say their goodbyes, give their final Christmas hugs and handshakes, and disperse into the streets they'd come from. Ellory went back inside and began to clean up, her limbs so tired they felt leaden.

The shop door opened and Katherine stepped inside. "You were right," she said.

Ellory gave a smile from behind the counter. "You made it. Coffee?"

"No, thank you." Katherine sank wearily into a chair at a nearby table. "I think this may have been the most attended Crawl I've ever seen. And I've been coming every year since as far back as I can remember. What do you think that's about?"

"Haw Springs shows up," Ellory said. "It's what they do. I can't take any credit."

"They wouldn't have had anything to show up to if you hadn't insisted on having the Crawl," Katherine said. "Plus you had the cookies and hot chocolate. Both of which people were raving about, by the way. You should add more food to your menu. People love your cooking."

"That's the plan. Call it a New Year's resolution."

"Well, I, for one, look forward to you completing your resolution. Anyway, good job tonight."

"Thanks," Ellory said.

"You okay?" Katherine asked. "Just…in general? You seem a little off for someone who was a major success today. On Christmas Eve, to boot!"

Ellory's cheeks started to quiver trying to hold up that smile, but she gutted it out. "I'm good. Just tired, I think. A lot going on."

"Well." Katherine gathered her things. "If you'd like someone else to cook for you for a change, come on over tomorrow. You can have dinner with my family."

"Oh. Thank you. I think I'll probably spend

some time by myself tomorrow. Like I said, a lot going on."

"Okay. But if you change your mind, the offer stands. You don't even have to let me know. Just show up. We'll be there."

"Thank you, Katherine. And thank you for letting me push forward with this."

"Thank you. And Merry Christmas, Ellory."

"Merry Christmas."

Ellory was tired. She did have a lot going on. Most of it going on inside her head and inside her heart. No matter how hard she tried to forget that Rowan Kelly had ever been there, she just couldn't shake him. She wanted to stand under the moon with him again, tell him every detail of what had happened tonight.

But that wasn't going to happen. Ever. And she needed to let it go.

She rushed through cleaning up, then locked up and trudged upstairs for bed.

She left her phone downstairs.

She didn't see it light up with a message.

Merry Christmas! It's a boy!

CHAPTER FOURTEEN

Megan looked like she'd been through the wringer. By the time Rowan arrived, she was asleep sitting up, her head slumped to the side, her sweaty hair plastered to her forehead. Her familiar rosy cheeks were now pale, and even in the dark, he could see faint mascara stains under her eyes, as if she'd been crying. Pain? Sadness? Joy?

Probably all of the above.

One of her arms was outstretched, her hand resting inside a nearby bassinet. Rowan crept into the room, clutching a stuffed polar bear wearing a Santa hat. He'd gotten it at the gift shop downstairs. Hasty gift shop gifts were not the way he wanted to start Uncling, but desperate times called for desperate measures and all that.

He leaned over the bassinet to set the bear inside and his breath caught.

The baby was lying quietly, awake, and staring right at him.

He was pink and round with a fuzz of dark hair that seemed to start at just above his eyebrows and march back under his little knitted cap. His dark eyes shone in the dim light of the hallway. He'd snaked one tiny hand out of his blanket and was pushing his fist against his mouth.

A blue note card affixed to the bassinet next to the baby's head read: Connor Rowan Runyon.

Connor *Rowan*.

Rowan's chest warmed and tears filled his eyes. He already loved this little boy more than he realized was possible. He wanted everything for him. All the happiness in the world. Born on Christmas Eve—that had to mean something, right?

He reached down and brushed the back of the baby's fist with one finger and then curled the finger into the fist itself. Connor had a strong grip. Rowan loved the way the baby's squeeze felt. Trust and need and greeting and acceptance all balled into one reflexive gesture.

A tear plopped onto the baby's blanket, and another on Megan's wrist. She stirred and then woke, peering into the bassinet and then blinking at Rowan.

"You're here," she whispered.

"What, like there was ever a question? My sister had a baby. Where else would I be?" Rowan wiped away a tear, but it was hopeless at this point. He let another tear run down his cheek and soak into the baby's blanket. "Not even a blizzard could keep me away. Merry Christmas, sis."

"Merry Christmas. What do you think?" She winced as she adjusted herself to sit higher so she could reach over the side of the bassinet better. She gently rubbed the baby's belly. The baby grunted and wiggled at her touch.

"I think you did something amazing."

"You can hold him."

Rowan took a step back. "Oh. No. I shouldn't."

"Why not? Of course you should. He has your name, after all."

"He's so little," Rowan said. But he reached into the bassinet and pulled the baby out anyway. He was tiny but solid, heftier than Rowan expected. *Those eyes*, he thought. *If this kid ever cries in front of me, he'll get whatever he wants. Times a hundred.* "Hey, buddy," he whispered. "You sure do know how to make an entrance. Timing, bro, it's everything. Good job." He fist-bumped his nephew's tiny fist. "I'm Rowan, I'll be your uncle. Nope—your funcle. Can you say Funcle?"

"You're already unbearable." Megan chuckled, wiped her cheeks. "I still haven't heard from Johnny," she said. "Have you heard anything?"

He shook his head. He'd tried calling Johnny several times an hour during the last part of his drive, and every time it went to voicemail. It was as if his brother-in-law had simply disappeared off the face of the earth. "Try not to let your imagination take over. We will hear from him."

"I'm scared, Rowan. What if something awful has happened?"

"You can't think that way. I'm sure everything is fine and there's a reasonable explanation for why he hasn't reached out."

"Like he accidentally stowed his cell phone in a checked bag that's headed to who even knows where right now, and by the time he figured it out he was driving a rental car into the worst snowstorm he's ever seen, and so he spent the last, I don't know, hundred hours, wondering why aren't there pay phones anymore?" A shadowy figure spoke from the doorway.

Megan gasped as her husband came toward her. "Johnny! You're here!" The words came out as a half-anguished cry. She held her arms out for him. He fell into them, sinking onto the bed next to her. They held each other for the longest time.

When they finally parted, Megan wiped her eyes again. "How, though? I thought you were stuck."

"It's been a whirlwind. A nightmare, actually, that involves two planes, a rented SUV, and a whole lot of very intense driving. Also, I broke my glasses and stepped in something very concerning in a restroom in Indiana and probably have to burn these shoes now. But none of that matters. I'm so sorry I missed it. Are you okay?"

She buried her face into his chest. "I'm fine. Everyone's fine. We're all here."

"Speaking of everyone," Johnny said, standing and coming toward Rowan. "Who's this little party crasher?"

"What do you mean? You've known me for years," Rowan joked, but even as he said it, he held the baby toward Johnny. "Congratulations, Dad."

Johnny took the baby and cradled him in his arms, cooing. "Hey there, little guy. Sorry I'm late. I promise I'll be early to everything else in your life to make up for it. In fact, I'm gonna leave in about half an hour to get a good seat at your first Little League game." He glanced back at Megan. "He has your eyes. Lucky guy."

"He has your chin," she said. "And your mom's nose."

"And my name," Rowan said. "That's the most important part."

The baby's grunts had turned into fussing as he brought his fist to his mouth with more vigor, pressing it against his lips over and over again.

"I know what that means," Johnny said, bringing the baby to Megan's bed, where he sat next to her again. "I think someone's hungry."

"That makes two of us. And I think I need to

give you all space to get to know each other." Rowan kissed Megan on the top of the head and edged for the door. "It's late."

"You're staying at the house, right?" Megan asked. "You have a key. There's food. Lots of it. And the sheets are clean on the guest bed. And, um, fresh towels are in the hallway closet."

"Stop worrying about that kind of stuff. I'm resourceful. I'm fine. I'll see you in the morning."

The house looked like someone had abandoned it quickly. Lights were on in the kitchen and pantry. The TV was still running. An opened, half-empty box of cookies was resting on the coffee table, next to a box of Christmas decorations.

The top third of the Christmas tree, above Megan's reach, was bare. Rowan laughed to himself. Only his sister.

That's not true. Ellory would also do that, he thought. *She'd rather have a half-bare tree than no tree at all.*

It had been a while since he was last at Megan's house, but he was pretty sure he still knew his way around. He found the guest bedroom—the one their mother stayed in when she bothered to blow through town—and rid himself of his duffel bag and shoes.

When she bothered to blow through town.

Megan could probably say the same for him, couldn't she? And he couldn't really argue it.

He marched back into the living room and peered into the box of Christmas ornaments. Until he'd helped Ellory with the little trees, he hadn't decorated a Christmas tree in years. He supposed a part of him—maybe the biggest part of him—thought he would never decorate one again. But he hadn't hated it. And he wanted Connor to come home to a first Christmas that was...celebratory.

He wanted to break the cycle.

He wound lights and garland around the top of the tree and hung ornaments and placed the star atop the highest branch. He then dug through the box and found other decorations that seemed like maybe they were just meant for a space that was out of his sister's reach and hung those, too. A couple of wreaths. A few caroling dolls placed on a high windowsill, looking down over the tree.

Finished, he found a carton of eggnog and made himself a peanut butter and jelly sandwich. It was late. He was bone tired. He ate his sandwich standing at the kitchen sink, washed and dried the plate and cup, and went back to his room.

He flopped back on his bed and reflected.

He had been resistant to coming here, and why? Because the past haunted him? The past wasn't even a real thing. It was gone. As soon as the second hand marched into the next minute, the next hour, the old time was gone. Already, Connor had time under his belt. Already, he wasn't brand-new. He'd already felt the pang of hunger. He'd felt fear. Maybe even sorrow.

Why do we hang on to the past so hard when we don't have to? he wondered. *Why have I clung to it?*

Suddenly, he felt terrible for leaving Megan behind in his quest to leave the past behind. She was real. She was present. She was always there for him.

She'd named her baby after him.

He'd spent so much time over the past three days thinking about joy and love and the past and the future. It seemed everywhere he turned, someone was there to offer a lesson.

Megan, his past, reminding him of why he'd closed off his heart in the first place. Showing him that it was possible to live with an open heart, even if opening it meant opening yourself to pain, because without potential for pain, there is no potential for the richest stuff of life. Love, happiness, joy.

Ellory, his present, worming her way inside of him, challenging his thoughts and beliefs. Bringing him fun and connection and a warmth that he hadn't known was still ignitable inside of him. *This is temporary*, he'd said. But the present always is. That second hand marches and marches.

That was why you had to continue to choose the present, over and over again. It was no accident that *present* also meant *gift*, was it?

And Mr. Crowley, and that table. How had there been a Rowan miniature on there before he'd ever arrived in Haw Springs? Was it pure coincidence? Was it just a generic figure and he had seen himself in it because it was what he wanted to see? Or was it...Rowan's future?

He checked his phone. Ellory hadn't returned his text. He supposed she was outside caroling her little heart out right now and just hadn't seen it. Or maybe she'd taken him at his word about the temporary nature of whatever was going on between them. Maybe she just wasn't interested.

No. You felt it. You know she felt it, too. And if you wondered, then her reaction when you said the dumbest words of your life—*this is temporary*—let you know exactly how she felt.

His thumb hovered over his keyboard to text again. But instead of texting Ellory, he went to his contacts and pressed a very different button. The phone rang four times. He was just about to give up when a familiar voice answered.

"Hello?"

"Hi, Mom."

"Rowan? I can barely hear you. I'm at a waterfall right now. I gotta tell ya, this place is absolutely gorgeous. Most beautiful place I've ever been. Although I think I wrenched my knee during the hike. I'll probably have to ice it when I get back to the ship. Maybe even see the medic. Of course. Just my luck. I swear if I didn't have bad luck, I'd have no luck at all."

He closed his eyes, tried to muster his patience, waited for her to take a breath so he could squeeze in a word or two.

"Glad you're having fun. Or…at least, I think you're having fun. Medic visit aside. I just thought you'd like to know that Megan is doing fine. So is the baby. I'm here. Johnny is here."

"Huh? Oh. Okay. Very good."

"When will you be coming home? I'm sure you're dying to see them."

"Oh, I'm not scheduled to be home for a few weeks yet."

"Weeks?" This was the mother Rowan knew. He supposed he had been going on the assumption that it was different for Megan. He'd thought they maybe had a closer relationship. He'd probably, he realized, feeling ashamed, used that erroneous thought as an excuse. He didn't need to be more present as long as Megan had their mom.

But she didn't.

Nobody did.

"Yeah, weeks. I don't see any reason to come home early. They'll still be there. Travel is very expensive, and I'm past the time where I can get refunds. Listen, kiddo, I've gotta go. I've gotta be back on the ship in two hours."

"Sure, Mom." He hesitated. "Merry Christmas, by the way."

"Yep, talk to you later."

And that was that. A stark reminder to Rowan that even if he were to change, not everyone would change with him.

Time marched on.

And if he wasn't careful, and he just kept marching with it, he'd end up going in circles.

December 25

OVERNIGHT, THE SNOW STOPPED. The animals could tell that this time it was for good. They raised their heads and sniffed the air. They inventoried the young ones with their noses.

Some of them got up and tiptoed out of their dens, beginning the long, possibly futile search for food. Others, totally relaxed for the first time since the storm began, snuggled in tighter, readjusted.

They stared out at the brightest star in the sky, blinking in the darkness of their dens. They knew that the sun was coming, bright and bold tomorrow.

It was Christmas Day.

CHAPTER FIFTEEN

ELLORY AWOKE THE next morning with all the wide-eyed excitement she'd always worn on Christmas morning.

It took only moments for her to realize that she was alone. There would be no gathering, no parties, no gift exchange. Even Mr. Crowley was planning to spend the day with neighbors. It would be just Latte and her.

She found herself surprisingly unbothered by it.

She got up, took a shower, brushed her teeth, just like it was any other morning.

Sure, it was going to be different. But when it came down to it, the choice she'd made that had landed her here was the same choice she would make again and again. She chose herself. Her dreams. Her future.

She'd been so overwhelmed with joy and love and spirit the night before, how could she have possibly even considered anything different? She was happy right where she was, even if it meant a quiet Christmas Day. She'd been given all the gifts she could possibly have wanted the night before.

Well, maybe except for one thing.

"Yes," she said to her reflection, foggy from shower steam. "Sure. Okay. Yeah. It would have been nice to celebrate with him here. But what we had was temporary." She put toothpaste on her toothbrush and wet it, then pointed it at her reflection, flicking water droplets onto the mirror. "In case I didn't know it, he made sure to point it out. Temporary. There will be no Christmas Days for us and that's okay. A week ago, a month ago, a year ago, I didn't even know he existed. I wasn't planning on spending Christmas Day with him and I was totally happy." She brushed, maybe a little too hard, and spat into the sink, then went back to the mirror, as if it had been arguing with her all along. "What's the big deal about him, anyway? There are a million Rowans in the sea." She put her toothbrush away and ran a comb through her hair, smoothing down all the little frizzies, then picked up the cat. "Right, Latte? We can find another Rowan anytime we want."

Her phone rang.

"Good mooorning," Marlee sang before Ellory could even say hello. "I wish you a Merry Christmas, I wish you a Merry Christmas!" She giggled. "I can't stop singing. Last night got me in the mood."

"Aw," Ellory sank back into bed and scooted under the covers. Outside was brilliant white as the sun shone down on the accumulated snow. The world was lit up as if it was glowing. Ellory loved being inside the glow—the nucleus of joy. "Me, too. Thank you again for, well…everything. And thank Ben, too. That was a long day for him, and I can't tell him how much I appreciated it."

"He loved it. He can't stop talking about it. I think his girlfriend, Annie, might die of jealousy. He promised to take her out in the sleigh today. Between you and me, I think he's got something up his sleeve. He's been very secretive this morning. But first, I've asked him to take me out in it this morning."

"Oh, that's fun! Where will you go?"

"That's why I called. I was thinking we would come get you."

"Oh, thanks, but I'm okay," Ellory said. "I was kind of looking forward to hanging here with Latte today. I'm pretty tired from last night. Besides, I don't want to crash your family Christmas."

"Posh," Marlee said. "You are family. Morgan and Annie are pulling out all the stops on dinner. We need help eating it all. Bring Latte with you, if you want."

"I don't know. I don't have gifts for anyone."

"No gifts. We don't exchange. We think of dinner together as our gift to each other. Nobody's going to surprise you with a gift and make you feel bad."

"Well, if there aren't any gifts for me, why would I show up?" Ellory teased. Then, when Marlee made protesting noises, "Okay, okay. I've been looking for a good reason to try out Latte's new snow jacket anyway. What time?"

"How about we'll come get you around noon?"

"What can I bring? I haven't cooked anything today. I was going to surf for leftovers."

"Just bring yourself, friend."

Ellory jumped out of bed and raced directly to her closet. What would she even choose? She hadn't expected to go anywhere today; otherwise, she would have had her outfit already selected. She flipped through a decade of carefully curated Christmas outfits and finally landed on a soft, emerald-green sweater dress with her favorite white sweater tights and a pair of red bejeweled boots. She topped it with a red bejeweled beret, which she bobby pinned to her hair. She could practically hear her mother's disgust all the way from New Hampshire, but she didn't care. She'd spent her whole life trying to be what other people wanted her to be, and she was done with it.

She twirled in front of the mirror, then decided to send Marlee a photo.

It was then that she finally saw the message from the night before.

Her heart fluttered and she found herself sucking in a quick breath and holding it there. Rowan had texted.

Merry Christmas! It's a boy!

Relief flooded her, and she realized only then that she had been worrying about him, wondering if he'd made it and purposely avoiding her phone, lest she find the urge to check in on him irresistible.

She stared at the words on the screen until she could have sworn they started moving, taunting her. Did this mean *he* found the urge to reach out to *her* irresistible? The very idea made her heart pound harder.

No. He was just keeping her in the loop. Being kind.

But he'd also wished her a Merry Christmas and that had to count for something, right?

Either way, she had to reach back.

Her palms were sweaty as she mulled over what to say, as if it weren't painfully obvious.

"Just say what anyone else would say. Right, Latte? Latte? Ugh. Pretty cowardly of you to hide out at a time like this, I'm just saying." She was stalling, and she knew it. If this was Marlee or literally any other person in her life—save for maybe Danny Wittfeld—she wouldn't think twice about how to respond. "You're making your own life more difficult, Ellory Elizabeth DeCloud. Just answer the text."

Merry Christmas! Congratulations, Uncle Rowan! What's his name? How does it feel to be an uncle? I'm so glad you're safe! I've been worrying about you.

She hit Send before she could overthink it, and immediately began writhing around in her blankets, regretting every single word. She'd said exactly all the things she hadn't wanted to say, expressed worry that she hadn't wanted to express, and—worst of all!—asked him questions.

Now, either he would be compelled to answer and she would feel like she forced him into it, or he wouldn't answer at all, and she would spend days filling in those blanks.

Fortunately, he put her out of her misery right away, with a photo of a beautiful little baby, and the words Connor Rowan, the greatest nephew who ever lived. And a second text right after: Unless and until he gets a baby brother.

"Awww." She touched the photo with her finger, as if she could feel the baby's soft skin through the screen. "He's so cute." Latte popped out from under the bed and began twining his way through her arms, begging for attention. "Oh, so now you come out, when you think I've found something cuter than you, huh?" She idly scratched Latte's ears, contemplating the fact that, while Rowan had responded right away, he'd actually done so in the worst possible way.

He'd left the conversation nowhere to go.

She dropped her phone onto the bed beside her and sighed. "Merry Christmas, Ellory. You made a fool of yourself with your dreams once again."

NOBODY GOT SHUSHED faster than a Santa Claus *ho-ho-ho*-ing as he walked through the doors of a newborn's room. Rowan figured that out very quickly.

"Shhh! We just got him to sleep," Megan said. "What are you doing, anyway?"

Rowan pulled the pillow he'd swiped from an empty hospital room next door out from under his shirt with one hand and the Santa hat he'd found at the bottom of the Christmas decoration bin last night off of his head with the other.

"People complain when you don't celebrate, and then they complain when you do," he mumbled. "Never mind. How's little Rowan?"

"His name is Connor," Megan said.

Rowan pointed at the card on the basinet. "I'm

not the greatest speller in the world, but I do believe I know what *R-O-W-A-N* spells."

"Already I have regret," Megan said. "And he's great. He makes the sweetest little noises. All these grunts and groans, like a little old man. And his cry is just so sweet. He didn't sleep at all, but he's so cute, it was fun being up with him. Like we were having a little Christmas Eve slumber party."

Rowan chuckled as he peered down into the bassinet. "Okay, I'll remind you that you said that in about three weeks, when you're having your twentieth slumber party with Mr. Cute Grunts here." He pointed at his brother-in-law, who was sacked out on a cot next to the window. "Looks like he didn't make it through the slumber party."

"He was so tired," Megan said. "He tried so hard to stay awake. I finally told him to let go, and he was out in about thirty seconds. He had been up for hours and hours. Stress-driving is the worst."

"You don't say," Rowan said. "I also slept like a…well, given the report you gave Connor, like a baby doesn't seem quite right. But you know what I mean. Can I get you anything? Are you hungry? Thirsty? Can I get you a coffee? Water? Christmas ham?"

She shook her head. "They came in earlier with a tray. Stale hospital cinnamon roll and watered down coffee. Not exactly my idea of a traditional Christmas morning breakfast."

"Well," Rowan said, easing down into a chair next to the bed. "We're not exactly a traditional family, so that kind of works out."

She tilted her head and looked at him through squinted eyes. "On that subject," she said. "What's with all this holiday cheer?"

"What? I can't be cheery?"

"On Christmas Day? No. And I know you talked to Mom last night, which should have only made it worse."

Rowan nodded. He stretched out, his shoes, which had tracked in snow, had left a dirty little puddle, and now they squeaked over the wet tile. He and Megan both winced and glanced at the baby and at Johnny. "It did. But, I don't know. Your house was all decorated. You gave the world this glorious little gift. I spent the past couple of days in what seemed like an idyllic snow globe. And it just... I don't know, it feels right, I guess."

"Cheer feels right?"

"Christmas cheer does. On Christmas. Yeah."

She pointed a finger at him. "Don't act like my skepticism is unreasonable. It was only two days ago that you were talking about it being a pointless, commercialized holiday that forced people to be together even if they didn't want to. Ouch, by the way."

"I didn't mean you."

"You kind of meant me."

"Okay, fine. I kind of meant you, but not because it's you. Because it's Christmas, and there's so much expectation to it."

The baby fussed and Megan reached over to shake the bassinet to calm him back to sleep. She did it like she was a pro who'd just birthed her tenth kid instead of her first. Rowan watched in amazement.

"What does that even mean, expectation? I didn't have any expectations of you."

"Sure you did. It just comes with the territory. Instead of Merry Christmas, maybe we should greet each other with, Hey, it's Christmas, hope you make it through! Granted, that's a little clunky for a card, but I'm still refining it. Maybe just, Get Through Christmas! Same number of syllables without the unreasonable demand of also being merry." He pointed at her. "That is cheer, sis, and you can't tell me that it isn't."

"Super heartwarming," she said. "But, see, I know that's what you actually think, so what gives with all the cheer and the fake belly and the hat and ho-ho-ho? That is not the Row-Row-Row I know-know-know." She poked his shoulder.

He swatted away her finger. "It's what I used to actually think. Now I have a new perspective, that's all."

"And does that perspective have anything to do with someone you might have met in Haw Springs?"

He crossed his arms. "Definitely not. I mean, she was nice and all, and definitely into Christmas. But, no. Nothing."

"Rowan?" Megan gave him the you're-not-pulling-one-over-on-me look she'd perfected when they were young.

"What? No. She cooked great meals and she helped me out and gave me a place to stay but that's it. I had to endure her."

"Okay, now you're laying it on thick. Endure her? Like she was a crisis?"

Rowan gave an exaggerated shrug. "Wellll..."

Megan swatted his shoulder this time. "Rowan!"

"Shhh! You're gonna wake the baby! And Connor, too."

"I heard that," Johnny said, eyes still closed.

"Way to go, you woke the baby," Megan said.

In that moment, Rowan was glad he had come. It felt like old times between the two of them. Laughing and teasing. A reminder that sometimes memories treated you poorly. The good ones liked to hide away and leave the bad ones out front, as if they were the only ones to be had.

"Listen, it's no big deal. She gave me a place to stay and some meals. She was really kind to me. End of story. It's not like I fell in love with her or anything."

Now Johnny did open his eyes. He craned his neck to make eye contact with Megan, grinning as if he were a cat with a canary.

"What?" Rowan asked. "Why are you looking at each other like—you can't be serious. You're going to psychoanalyze me, now?"

"He said *love*," Megan said.

"He actually said *fell in love*," Johnny said.

"I said I *didn't* fall in love with her," Rowan said. "Because I didn't. Go back to sleep."

"Neither did we," Johnny said, swiveling so that he was sitting on the cot now, facing them. He rubbed his face dramatically, waking up.

"Gosh, how we both insisted that we didn't," Megan said.

"What? That's not true. You literally introduced him to me as the love of your life."

"That was after we gave up." Johnny stood, paced to the bassinet, started to reach inside to touch the baby, but thought better of it and snatched his hand back.

"Yeah, I knew it was hopeless to fight it. I loved this goofball, and I couldn't hide it anymore," Megan said.

"That's all well and good for you two," Rowan said. "But that's your story. Not mine."

Megan tipped her eyes up to Johnny. He nodded, as if to answer a question that she never asked. "I'm going to run home and take a shower." He stepped into his shoes and stumbled, nearly tumbling head over heels over the cot.

"You should take a nap, too," Megan said. "We're fine here."

"You know what?" he said, putting on his coat. "That might not be a bad idea. I'll come back with a proper Christmas dinner for you, my love." He kissed Megan on the temple.

"Burgers and fries?" she asked, her eyes going wide.

"Burgers and fries. Just like they had at the first Christmas," he said. "I'll even buy you a shake."

"You spoil me."

"Drive safe," Rowan said. "There's still lots of snow on the ground."

Johnny stopped at the door. "I kind of never want to drive again. Especially in the snow. But burgers and fries await." He patted the doorframe twice and was gone.

A nurse came in with a tray of Christmas cookies. "Would you like one?" she whispered. Megan nodded and took two. Rowan passed.

Megan took a large bite out of her cookie and closed her eyes with pleasure. "So good. Much better than that cardboard cinnamon roll. I'm starving. Giving birth takes a lot out of you."

She chewed for a moment, then opened her eyes and took another bite. "Okay, brother. Spill."

He knew better than to try to get one over on Megan. She had always been able to read him like a book. "There's nothing to spill, really. We met, we spent a couple of days together." He took a deep breath and let it out in a gust. "I liked her. And then I left. The end."

"Why?"

"Why what?"

"Why does it have to be the end?"

It was so painfully obvious to Rowan, he wondered what he was missing. "Because she lives in Haw Springs, Missouri, and I live in Tulsa, Oklahoma."

"So move."

"What?" It came out as a bark. Connor squirmed inside his bassinet. Megan reached over and jiggled it again, soothing him back to sleep. "What?" Rowan repeated as a whisper. "Leave my job, my apartment and just go to Haw Springs?"

"They have fires in Haw Springs. Firefighters are needed everywhere. You'll be fine." She took another bite of her cookie. "Okay, maybe she moves. Have you asked her?"

"Have I asked someone I've known for two days if she'll shut down the business that she put her heart and soul into and move to another state with me? No, Megan, I can't say I've done that."

Megan ate the last of her cookie, sighed, and broke the second cookie in half. She handed half to Rowan. "Look, all I'm saying is this. We're fighters, Rowan. But not in a good way. We fight against happiness. Remember when you called and asked me about joy? I thought maybe you were actively dying, by the way, but that's a conversation for another day. When you called, I made it sound so easy, like I feel joy all the time, no big deal. But the truth is I have to choose it for myself. The way we were raised wasn't joyful. It wasn't filled with love. So we both grew up afraid of those things. So we pushed them away. Only you're still pushing. You're still afraid. And do you remember when you called while I was in labor?"

"How could I forget?"

"I was about to tell you what your strength was." She waited for his attention. "Your ability to be alone. Now ask me what your weakness is." She paused again. "The same thing."

Rowan bristled at this idea. He didn't like to think of himself as afraid of anything. He liked to think of himself as fearless, ready for whatever may come his way. But on the inside, the tiniest part of him knew that Megan was right. He hadn't experienced joy and love because he hadn't allowed himself to. And the very thought of letting those things in made him feel anxious and unmoored.

"Let me guess," Megan said. "You two had a moment together. Something really tender and intimate and great. And you were the first one to break that moment. And then you were the first to point out that it wasn't an actual moment."

He thought about the moonlight sparkling over the snow. The moment of pure beauty in the middle of a blizzard. Of the two of them standing side by side, their hands brushing against each other. Of the deep longing he felt, wanting to pull her to him. To kiss her.

This is what perfection looks like, Ellory had breathed. But he hadn't been looking at the snow; he'd been looking at her. *I agree*, he'd said, taking in the soft upward slope of her nose, the length of her eyelashes, the curve of her lips.

And then he'd literally stepped away from her. Because…

Well. Because he was scared.

So what did he do the next morning? *You know this is temporary, right?*

He let out an anguished groan, the uneaten half cookie still in his hand. "I don't need this in my life," he said.

"It's exactly what you need in your life,"

Megan countered. "And I'm about to give you a Christmas gift. Are you ready for it?"

"Are you about to give me some sort of advice and call it a gift? Because, seriously, you've had weeks to buy something."

She laughed, shook her head. "You are too much. You know that, right?"

He spread his free hand across his chest and gave her an exaggerated innocent, wide-eyed look, as if he couldn't believe she was talking about him.

"Yes, you. And, no, I'm not giving you advice. I'm giving you a command. Get out of here."

"Get out of here," he repeated. "And…?"

"And go back to Haw Springs."

He threw his head back and laughed. "You mean reverse the harrowing drive that I just completed yesterday through all the snow and ice to get here. Leave you on Christmas Day."

"You'll come back. I'm not worried about that. You'll come back after we're all settled and you'll help me take down that Christmas tree. And you'll tell me all about the romantic moment that you cruised back into town and swept the love of your life up into your arms and confessed your love for her."

"You're loopy from all the meds they gave you yesterday."

"They didn't give me any meds. And I'm serious. You can go get her, or you can live the rest of your life wondering. And, who knows, you might come back right when Mom happens to be breezing through town, and you'll get to hear her tell Connor all about her problems."

"Captive audience. Poor guy."

"Exactly." She ate her half of the second cookie in two bites. The baby fussed himself fully awake and Rowan got up to retrieve him. He cuddled the baby in his arms while Megan ate his half of the cookie, too. "What? I told you I'm starving. You snooze, you lose, little brother."

"Can you believe this woman?" Rowan asked Connor, who stared up at him with his little gray eyes. It was hard to believe that he, too, once looked out at the world so innocently. Megan got up to use the bathroom.

Rowan went to the rocking chair and sat with his nephew in his arms, feeling the weight and warmth against his chest. Connor squirmed, his face scrunching up, so Rowan instinctively began rocking and humming to quiet him, at first just notes that sounded good together. But soon those notes turned into a tune. And then a soft song. "Good people all, this Christmas time, consider well and bear in mind…"

He trailed off, recalling that night under the moon, Ellory teaching him this song, as if knowing all of the lyrics to a forgotten Irish Christmas Carol was something that everyone did. As if learning this from her wasn't special in just about every way.

"Oh, buddy, I'm in trouble." Connor, who had begun to drift once again to sleep, startled awake at the sound of his voice and stared up at him but, surprisingly, didn't cry. "I think I went and fell hopelessly in love. How on earth did that happen, and what am I supposed to do about it now?"

"You're supposed to go get her," Megan said, coming out of the bathroom. She held out her arms to take the baby.

"What? Right now?"

She put her hands on her hips. "Can you think of a better time?"

When it came to Ellory DeCloud, probably not. Unless, of course, she didn't feel the same way. "What if she doesn't want it? Then Christmas Day is just about the worst possible time."

"Do you really think it's possible for you to have felt the connection that you're describing without her having felt it, too?"

"Well, she definitely made it sound like she didn't feel it." Of course, in that moment, he'd had a pretty good idea that she was just saving face. She had seemed flustered, very quick to change the subject and move on to the next thing. He hadn't believed it in the least.

Megan gave her hands a soft clap. "Hand me

my baby, Rowan Kelly, and leave my hospital room."

"Ouch. On Christmas Day."

"I say this for your own good—get out."

"But little Rowan."

"Is named Connor and will still be here when you come back. Unless, of course, you're not planning on coming back for the next eighteen years. Then I can't make any promises. But since you're going to come right back after you've settled things with this woman, I'm not too worried about it."

"You're serious."

Megan leaned over and took the baby out of his arms. "I'm serious. Go take care of your business. Come back in a few days. We'll be at home. Johnny and I will need someone to take over while we take naps. There will be so many diapers to change."

"Gosh, you make it sound so fun, how could I resist?"

She gave him a peck on the cheek. "We will ring in the New Year together. How about that?"

"We could do that if I stayed, too."

"Get out."

"Love the way you beat around a bush, sis."

"Leave."

"Okay, okay," Rowan got up and walked toward the door, a mixture of excitement and fear making his legs feel a little weak and his heart feel a little fast. "I'll go."

Rowan wasn't sure what any of this meant, really. He knew that Megan was right, that he would regret it if he didn't do this. But he also knew there were a lot of moving parts. A lot of things to figure out. He slid into his car, his breath pluming out in front of him.

Was he ready to give up his apartment, leave Oklahoma, leave the station? Did they even have a fire station in Haw Springs? If not, what would he do? He couldn't ask Ellory to leave her shop. After all, it was her dream. And it was a beautiful dream. Just as beautiful as she was.

"That's if she wants me, too," Rowan said, plugging the key into the ignition and turning. The car started on the first try. "That's the first unanswered question. But I guess I'm gonna get an answer. Let's go."

CHAPTER SIXTEEN

CHRISTMAS DAY ON Decker McBride's ranch was the kind of experience songs were made of. Perched high up on the hillside, Ellory felt like she could see forever. Yet, at the same time, the ranch felt hidden from the world with all the trees that surrounded it. Cozy and majestic. Ellory almost had the same feeling she did that very first day when she drove into Haw Springs and parked on the side of the road to take it all in. The only difference was that now she had someone she wanted to—and couldn't—share it with.

"After dinner, we'll take the sleigh to a spot where you can see over the whole town," Annie said. "It's Miss Morgan's favorite place in the whole world." Annie had come along with Ben and Marlee in the sleigh and was all smiles the whole way.

"I think she might be addicted to the sleigh," Marlee whispered. "But it is a beautiful spot. You can definitely see Main Street from there."

"We should wait until it gets dark so we can see all the lights," Annie said.

"Too tricky to take the sleigh through the woods, especially at night," Ben said. He ducked his head, as if preparing himself for an argument.

Instead of looking disappointed, Annie beamed with pride. Annie was also on the autism spectrum, and was head over heels in love with Ben. "Ben made the sleigh, so he's very protective of it."

"He's also very protective of you," Marlee said.

"That's true," Annie said. "He is. But he's mostly protective of the sleigh because he spent a lot of hours making it."

They arrived at the house. Ben paused at the end of the driveway to let them out, then continued to the barn to park the sleigh and feed the horses. Ellory followed Morgan, Marlee, and Annie up the driveway toward the house, Annie excitedly leading the way.

Marlee leaned in. "I think Ben has other plans with the sleigh today," she whispered. "He's been messing with it all morning. And he said something about needing to do a bit of work after dinner. Annie didn't catch it, but he's not the greatest liar in the world."

Annie paused at the front porch. "Come on, you two. You're walking so slow!"

Marlee and Ellory giggled and hurried to join her. Inside, the house smelled like buttery turkey and yeasty rolls and cinnamon and pumpkin. Ellory's stomach growled as they followed the scents to the kitchen. She hadn't realized she was so hungry until this very moment.

"You didn't bring your kitty," Morgan said, turning away from the stove to give Ellory a big hug. Morgan was a regular at the Dreamy Bean, and while Ellory wasn't as close to her as she was to Marlee, being next-door neighbors and all, she still adored Morgan and was thrilled that Morgan found her happily ever after with Decker McBride, the strong, silent rancher who was currently mashing a big pot of potatoes as if his life depended on it.

Ellory shook her head. "I thought it might be a lot for him. The cold ride, the new people, the new place. He's very social, but maybe he even has his limits. I'm a little disappointed that I didn't get to try out his new coat, though."

"Archer will be disappointed. But I understand completely."

Archer was Morgan's son, a nonverbal boy with autism. Cute as a button and animal obsessed. "Well, you can bring Archer down to the shop anytime to play with Latte on his home territory," Ellory said. "Open invitation. Here, I brought this." She handed Morgan a foil-wrapped sweet potato pie, still slightly warm from the oven, despite the cold ride in the sleigh.

"You didn't have to do that," Morgan said.

Ellory shrugged. "You didn't have to invite me."

"Nonsense," Morgan said. "You're always invited. You're practically family."

Ellory felt warmed by that statement, more than Morgan would ever know. She sort of needed a family to be part of right now. And she could think of no better family to be part of.

Still, the tiniest part of her ached for Rowan. She wanted to be getting ready to sit at the table next to him, their knees touching under the table, their elbows bumping awkwardly as they passed the gravy. She longed for that closeness, for the radiance of his smile, for his goofy jokes and even his grouchy Christmas scowl. What she wouldn't give to hear him say how dumb a lyric was in a Christmas song right about now.

But mostly she tried to concentrate on how grateful she was as she sat down between Marlee and Archer.

Sometimes, your family shows you who they really are and disappoints you.

Sometimes, you make your own family.

And they're just as good.

No, scratch that. They're even better.

DESPITE THE BRIGHT Christmas Day sun, the roads hadn't melted off much. And in the areas outside of the cities, they'd only been minimally plowed, if at all. Rowan tried to follow the tire tracks of the few brave souls who'd ventured out, suspecting that some of them were his own from the day before, but even still, he kept sliding dangerously near ditches.

It took him hours just to reach Kansas City. He was still three hours, on a good day, away from Haw Springs. And if yesterday was any indication, these would be the trickiest hours of the trip.

Just take it slow, he kept telling himself.

But he didn't want to take it slow. Now that he'd confronted his feelings for Ellory, he wanted to get to her as quickly as possible. He wanted to make up for lost time. As much as he had felt like he'd always known Ellory, in reality there was still so much about her to learn. He wanted to begin right away—the world's most eager student.

He especially wanted to know what it was like to spend Christmas Day with her. He was excited and hopeful in a way that he hadn't been since he was a child.

Take it slow. He crawled past Lee's Summit. *Take it slow*. He inched past Peculiar. *Take it slow*.

But slow got faster with every mile. He became confident. Cocky, even. A near miss in Spearville, and still his foot lay too hard on the gas pedal.

He turned off the highway at Riverside, the town he'd heard so much about. He'd been so singularly focused on getting to Megan and the baby, he didn't even remember driving past it the day before. It, too, was charming and quaint, and the people had begun getting out and about, carrying their bright packages and covered casserole dishes as they carefully stepped through the snow.

Seemed everyone he drove past gave him a jaunty wave. He waved back—*Merry Christmas!*—and was so enjoying himself, he didn't even see the snowbank that had been pushed into the middle of the road by a well-meaning plow.

He drove right over the top of it, high centered, and found himself stuck. Revving, but going nowhere.

"No," he said. "No, no, no! Not this close!"

ELLORY SAT ON the couch, her belly full, her hand curled around a mug filled with hot cider, the scent of apple wafting up into her nose. Her eyes were closed as she listened to the joyful sounds around her. Archer making soft animal noises as he played with his new toys, Morgan and Marlee giggling over a childhood memory as they made plans to get down into the valley to see their parents later that evening, Annie softly humming as she knitted in a nearby rocker, waiting for Ben and Decker to come back inside from feeding the animals and completing Ben's mysterious "work" in the barn.

It was the kind of Christmas afternoon that she most loved. Quiet, warm, introspective. Something that couldn't be replicated, not even in the carefully constructed "joy" of the DeCloud home.

She'd been texting her sister all morning. There had been gifts—many of them—but there was something missing, Daphne had said. If she didn't know better, she would suspect that their parents had regrets about their choice to spend Christmas Day with Danny over their own daughter.

Ellory seriously doubted what her sister was saying—mainly because neither parent had yet to respond to her *Merry Christmas* text that she'd sent each of them hours before. But she appreciated what her sister was trying to do, what she was trying to say—that she regretted their choices on their behalf, even if they didn't. That she knew, or at least hoped, that they would eventually see the error of their ways. And that she missed Ellory on an important day.

Maybe Daphne hadn't turned out to be as much like their mother as Ellory thought.

I love you, little sis, Ellory had texted just before sinking into the couch. I hope you have the best day. And she meant it.

"Hey," Marlee said, plopping next to her. Ellory's eyes flew open as she fought to keep her cider from spilling over. Marlee ignored the near spill and gave Ellory an uneasy smile that was half wince. "So don't be mad at me."

"Why would I be mad at you?" Ellory asked, but then she saw the gift bag that Marlee was clutching. "What is this? You said no gifts."

"I know," Marlee said. "That's why I said don't be mad. I couldn't just not get you a gift. You're my best friend. And you give me so much free coffee. And cookies and cake and brownies. And sweet potato pie. Basically everything delicious in the world."

"Awww, that's so sweet." Ellory leaned over and hugged her friend. "I feel bad that I don't have a gift for you, though."

"Seriously, your friendship is gift enough," Marlee said. "Open it!"

Ellory pulled the tissue paper out of the bag, feeling a mix of guilt and delight. "What is it?" she asked, peering inside the bag. She reached in and pulled out a rolled-up cloth. She held it up and let it unroll.

It was an apron with an illustration of a steaming pie on the front. The steam was a twisty, swirly rainbow that rose into a multicolor cloud that was filled with colorful, cursive words. A coffee bean perched on the edge of the cloud, a knife in one hand and a fork in the other, a napkin tied around its neck.

Ellory gasped. "The Baked Bean! It's perfect!"

She let the apron drop in her lap and hugged Marlee again. "Thank you!"

"You know I've been trying to think of the perfect name for your cafe. That one just popped into my head one night. Like, in the middle of the night. I sat up and practically shouted it, so loud I was afraid that you would hear me all the way down at your apartment. You don't have to go with it, of course. I just wanted you to know that I believe in you and want to support you in any way that I can. In fact..." She pointed at the bag. "There's something else in there."

Ellory reached in and pulled out a large spoon. She held it up questioningly.

Marlee took it from her. "Actually, that's mine. For when you're frustrated and you don't want to talk about it, you can call in reinforcements to help you stir a million bowls of cookie dough. No prying, just baking. I'm there for you."

Ellory hugged Marlee again. "You really are the best friend. Thank you for these things. Truly. And thank you for inviting me over today."

"It wouldn't be Christmas without you."

"Mar! Come here. Mom wants to talk to you about breakfast tomorrow morning. She's wondering if we think we can get somewhere to buy eggs on the way there tonight."

"I have eggs," Ellory said. "My Christmas gift

to you." She and Marlee laughed and hugged again before Marlee popped up from the couch.

"Be right back," she said, as she hustled to the kitchen, where Morgan was pacing with the phone attached to her ear.

Ellory stared at the apron in her lap, turning it so the illustration was flat and smooth against her legs. Everything about it was so perfect. A pie floating on a cloud, a chubby, smiling coffee bean plunging in with a knife and fork. It was so utterly ridiculous, how could she even entertain another idea?

"The Baked Bean," she said aloud, turning the words over on her tongue. "The Baked Bean. Yes. It's perfect."

She traced the rainbow words with her finger. *Rowan would hate this so much he might actually love it*, she thought. *I hope someday he comes back through town so he can see it.*

"You've got to be kidding me!" Rowan said, slamming his car door shut. He slipped in the snow and slid to one knee, which gave him an up close view of the hopelessness of the situation. The car was jammed so tightly in the snowbank, the back tires weren't even touching ground.

Stuck. In Riverside. An hour away from his destination.

"I can't believe this." He ran his hand through

his hair and glanced around, wondering who might have seen it happen.

Were Riverside residents as helpful as Haw Springians? He hoped so.

Although…helping a stranger in need was one thing. Spending hours in the cold snow digging out someone who wasn't paying attention to where he was going on Christmas Day was quite another.

Muttering under his breath, he started to walk away from the car, heading for what looked like the closest open business. Déjà vu, he thought. Only he knew that this time the best he could hope for was someone who could maybe call a tow truck, not an angel on earth who baked and sang and made his heart smile.

Before he could get ten feet, he saw the snowplow that had created the drift in the first place. The driver hopped out of his truck.

"You okay?" the plow driver asked. "I saw you just drive right into it. You didn't see that snow?"

"I was distracted," Rowan said. "I didn't expect there to be any plow drifts yet. The blizzard, Christmas. You know."

"Oh, trust me, I know," the plow driver said. "Everybody and their uncle's been calling me, wondering when I'll be plowing. *Junior, when you gonna plow my street? Junior, when you gonna get back in town? Junior-this, Junior-that.*

I told everyone just hold on, hold on. Wait for the snow to end. And then wait for me to get some of my mee-maw's Christmas morning breakfast casserole. I beat the blizzard to Riverside for a reason." He laughed and bumped Rowan's elbow with his own. "I'm willing to work just as much as the next guy, but there are some things I'm just not willing to miss."

"So you're Junior!" Rowan cried.

Junior gave him a curious look. "You've heard of me?"

"Let's just say your mee-maw's breakfast casserole may have changed my life."

Junior chuckled. "I don't have a clue what you're talking about, but if anyone's breakfast casserole could change a life, it's my mee-maw's. Anyway, I can help you out of this spot, but it's gonna be a bit. I've got people waiting for me at home. Take me about four hours, I'd suspect. It's just one main street, but it's the to and from that'll take time. An hour to get there, a couple hours to plow, an hour to get back."

Rowan froze. "Wait a minute," he said.

"Oh, I know what you're thinking. Your car is kinda hanging out in the middle of the street. But it will be okay here until we get to it. Nobody's driving today, really. Plus it's stuck in a big drift that everyone but you will avoid." He chuckled and elbowed again. "I'm just kidding.

But the only thing is, most everyplace is closed with it being Christmas Day and all. I could take you over to the police station. Carl'd probably let you hang out in the lobby for four hours. Might even make you coffee. Or you can go to my mee-maw's. She's always willing to take in a stranger."

"You're going to Haw Springs," Rowan blurted. He gave an incredulous laugh to the sky. "Of all places, you're going to Haw Springs, aren't you?"

Junior looked taken aback for a beat, then nodded with the whole top half of his body, almost a bow. "I am."

"Can I just ride along with you? I have business I need to take care of in Haw Springs. That's where I was headed."

Junior was still a little leery. "I would reckon there's not a single business open in Haw Springs today."

"That's okay," Rowan said. "It's not business business. I have someone I need to talk to. Desperately."

Junior sized Rowan up for a long moment and then nodded again. "Mister, I don't know how you know all that you do about me and my whereabouts, but there's something about you that tells me you could really use a helping hand. Hop on up into the truck, and I'll get you there."

CHAPTER SEVENTEEN

ELLORY HAD JUST gotten home from Marlee's and was hanging her new apron on a peg on the wall when she heard the jingle bells rattle on the front door of the Dreamy Bean—scratch that, the Baked Bean. Oh, how she loved that name!

She hadn't intended to be open—she still felt sleepy and sluggish from dinner—but she wasn't about to kick anyone out on Christmas Day. Besides, she was still feeling so floaty and full after last night's caroling and her time at Morgan and Decker's that morning, she didn't mind firing up her machines for a Christmas cup for someone. Heck, she may as well even make it on the house!

Instead of hanging up the apron, she wound it around herself and was busy tying it when she popped into the lobby. No better time to try out the new name.

"Welcome to the Baked…" She trailed off and froze in place, barely believing what she was seeing.

Junior Feeny stood just inside the doorway, his

plow puffing exhaust into the cold air outside the window. Standing behind him...

"Rowan," Ellory said. Her hands fell away from the ties she'd been fumbling with, and the apron fell loose at her sides.

"Hey, there, Ellory. Merry Christmas," Junior said.

She pried her eyes away from Rowan. "Merry Christmas, Junior." She shook her head, trying to shake herself out of her daze. "You're plowing."

"Yes, ma'am. Gonna get a few good swipes through Haw Springs so folks can get to their families, then head on back to Riverside. Mee-Maw's breakfast casserole has nothing on her Christmas Day bread pudding, and I intend to be bellied up to the kitchen table when she pulls it hot out of the oven."

"Can't say I blame you. Bread pudding sounds delicious. Do you need something warm to get you through? I can fix you one of my famous hot chocolates that you love so much."

"No, ma'am, you don't have to go through all that trouble. I just had a tagalong here who wants to see you, and I wanted to make sure you know him before I leave you with him."

Ellory felt her entire body flood with warmth. Rowan wasn't standing here on accident. He'd come on purpose. "I do. You are totally safe to leave. Thank you for looking out for me, though."

"Of course." He turned and winked at Rowan. "It's what we do in Haw Springs. I'll be just outside if you need anything."

"Thank you, Junior. Let me know if you change your mind about that hot chocolate."

"Will do." Just as quick as he'd appeared, Junior was gone, the jingle bells on the doorknob chattering behind him. When the noise died down, there was nothing but total silence, Rowan and Ellory frozen in their places, gazing at each other. The sun was beginning to go down, dots of Christmas lights beginning to glow on the houses marching up the hill behind Rowan.

Ellory couldn't wrap words around all the questions that were swarming her head, so all that came out was one single word. "How?"

Rowan pulled the stocking cap off of his head. "It's a long story. Basically I'm going to have to get to Riverside tomorrow to dig my car out of a snowbank."

"Oh, my goodness, are you hurt?"

"No, I'm fine and the car is fine. Just my pride is a little dinged up."

"So you remembered about Junior and found him?"

"Actually..." He paused, scratched his head. "His plow made the drift that I crashed into. So, yes, I found him. Just not in the way that you mean."

Ellory pushed her hand over her mouth and let out a little giggle. "I'm sorry," she said. "It's not funny. It's just…"

"It's a little funny. But also I don't care about the car now that I'm here." His shoulders relaxed and he pointed toward the chairs in the back. "Can I…?"

"Of course. I'm so sorry. Where are my manners? Of course you can come in. Have a seat. What can I get you?"

She forced herself to keep talking as she led the way to the cloud chairs that she now had unintentionally begun to think of as Rowan's chairs. She pulled one out for him. "What were you doing in Riverside? Did you never make it to Iowa? But you sent pictures of the baby. Why did you come back here?"

Rowan didn't sit in the chair. Instead, he reached down and gently grabbed her hand. Ellory abruptly stopped talking, immediately lost in his touch. She realized she didn't care about the logistics, as long as he was here and he was okay.

"I don't want to be temporary," he said.

Ellory's mouth fell open, but no words came out. Of all the things she may have expected him to say, she didn't expect this.

"I don't want to be in Iowa or in Tulsa or in Riverside or anywhere other than where you are."

Ellory shook her head. "I don't understand."

He let go of her hand and sank into the chair, running both of his hands through his hair. "I don't either, honestly. I wasn't expecting this at all. I thought I was happy with my life the way it was. I figured that outright joy belonged to other people. I wasn't raised that way, so I didn't aspire to it. And…and I think that I began to resent it, you know? Joy itself." He gazed at her. "Until I met you. You are joy personified, and when I stepped away from it, I felt it." He clutched his heart.

Ellory lowered herself into the chair across from him. Now that his hand was no longer holding hers, she felt so empty. "Rowan, I can't…"

"At first I thought, well, I just hate Christmas. So much bad stuff in my past was directly tied to the holiday. And I was okay with that. Not everyone has to be filled with holiday spirit. It's not a requirement to be holly jolly, as much as the stores and the TV commercials and the movies make it seem like it is. And it's actually pretty easy to be the one guy who doesn't celebrate. The problem is, it grew. It didn't stay about Christmas. I pushed away any potential happiness. I pushed away any potential joy. And…love. I pushed away love."

"Rowan. Please."

"But then I met you. And it wasn't just that I couldn't push away Christmas with you. I couldn't push away joy. And I couldn't push away love. When I left here, I was all set to never see you again. I had it in my head that you would be out of sight and out of mind and all that. About an hour down the road, I realized I hadn't thought about anything but you."

"I've thought about you, too," Ellory said, somewhat shocked that she had the breath to speak. "But…"

He reached over and held both of her hands in his. "I also realized that I no longer want to push those things away. You are joy, Ellory DeCloud, and everything about you is love and light and wonder. Standing next to you is like standing next to the sun, and touching you is like holding a live wire but at the same time is like getting the warmest hug. I can't explain it. But I think you know what I'm feeling. I think you feel it, too."

He was right, of course. She absolutely felt those things, too, but realized she was feeling them with a painful lump in her throat. Tears welled in her eyes. She pulled her hands out of his, and stood, turned away so he wouldn't see her cry.

"Rowan. I'm sorry. I can't."

ROWAN FELT GUTTED. He wouldn't have been surprised to look down and see his heart weakly fluttering on the floor at his feet. His stomach dropped. He'd been so certain that what he felt, she felt. He'd never even considered that she would reject him.

"What?" It was the only word that would form. "What?"

She turned to face him. Tears streaked down her cheeks. She shook her head. "I'm sorry. I have dreams to fulfill. I couldn't abandon them for Danny or for my family. And I can't abandon them for you, either."

He went to her. "What kind of dreams? The shop?"

She nodded. "The shop. And this town. I can't give up on them. I can't just leave. Even for love."

Relief flooded him. He wanted to throw his head back and laugh, or scream in triumph. Instead, he threw his arms up. "You don't have to! I'm not asking you to."

"I don't?"

He held her arms and bent to look directly into her eyes. "No. I believe in your dreams, Ellory. I would never try to take those from you. I believe in you. You are Ellory of the Clouds. Anyone who would take you out of those clouds is a fool. And, worse, unkind. I don't care about Tulsa. There's a fire station in Haw Springs, right? Riverside? Oak Hollow? I'll do something else if I have to. I'll sell vacations or deliver groceries or...or make coffee. I don't care. The point is, none of that matters as long as I have you."

He slid his hands down her arms, leaving a trail of goose bumps behind them. He wound his fingers through hers. She curled hers around his, not wanting to ever let go. He took a step closer and pressed his forehead against hers.

"You are the dream I can't abandon, Ellory DeCloud."

"Oh, Rowan," she whispered, shivering, but not from cold. "I don't want to be temporary, either. I never did."

Without another word, he wrapped an arm around her waist and pulled her to him. With his other hand, he traced her cheek, her lips, her neck, all while keeping his forehead against hers. Ellory closed her eyes and leaned into him, let herself be wrapped up.

This is how it feels, she thought. *This is what acceptance feels like. This is happily ever after.* "I love you," she whispered, not just to Rowan, but to the entire, all-encompassing sense of finally having realized her dream. Her full dream.

"I love you, too," Rowan whispered.

Suddenly, the Christmas music she had playing overhead swelled, and he grabbed one hand and twirled her out to arm's distance, then pulled her back in, holding her tighter around the waist than he had before. Her skirt swirled around her calves, and she smiled warmly as they danced to "The Christmas Waltz."

They didn't need to speak.

And when the song was over, and he lowered her in a dip, she let out a delighted laugh that brought a smile to his face. He pulled her up and into him.

"Merry Christmas, Ellory of the Clouds," he whispered.

"Merry Christmas," she whispered.

THE SUN MADE its final descent behind the farm at the top of the hill, and the Christmas star sparkled and shone with all its might in the night sky. The houses all around Haw Springs captured that sparkle and reflected it back in twinkling and blinking reds and greens and blues and whites. Inside those homes were all manner of turkeys and pies and special recipes handed down for generations.

And if the wind died down and someone listened hard enough, they could hear the hum of laughter and conversation and the ripping of wrapping paper and delighted squeals and togetherness.

They would hear Mr. Crowley tell a story about coming home from the war and proposing to his beautiful Roberta. They would hear Mrs. Crowley, miles away on the other side of town, tell the same story. They would hear Marlee West and Morgan McBride walk into their parents' home, and the jubilant chatter of their parents as they hugged their daughters and pumped Decker's hand and wrapped Archer into their arms and swept them all into the living room, where gifts awaited.

They would hear Ben hooking two horses up to the sleigh he'd built, readying them for a ride that he planned just for Annie, a box-shaped lump in his front pocket.

And they would hear the grind of a snowplow coming to a halt down on Main Street.

Junior Feeny finished his last swipe of snow and turned off his plow. He was warm and cozy in the cab of his truck, but he'd worked up a thirst for some of that hot chocolate Ellory had offered to whip up.

He got out of his truck and stood in the silence of Christmas night, peering up the hillside. Haw Springs sure was beautiful this time of year.

Shoot, he thought. *Haw Springs is beautiful every time of year.*

He made his way up the sidewalk, which hadn't been shoveled, but had been trampled by many snow boots the night before. Part of him was disappointed to have missed the Carol Crawl. He was nobody's singer, but on Carol Crawl night, that didn't matter. Everyone released their voices into the air on that night, and nobody judged. He liked it.

He found his way to the coffee shop, but when he got in front of the window, he stopped.

Inside, Ellory DeCloud was dancing with the stranger he'd brought into town. There sure was a story there that he didn't know. A history, even.

He watched as they twirled and laughed and gazed into each other's eyes. He watched as the stranger dipped Ellory and then straightened and pulled her to him.

Aw, heck, Junior thought. *The hot chocolate can wait.* He turned and walked back to his truck just as the stranger cupped Ellory's cheek and leaned in for a kiss.

364 Days Later...

THE ANIMALS POKED their heads out of their dens, sniffing at the sky.

There was weather coming.

But it wasn't big weather.

It wasn't the kind of weather that would trap the humans in their own dens and nests, cowering against the driving wind and the pelting snow and little bits of ice that hurt their human skin and made them shiver and emit their breathy, surprised human noises.

The animals would still retreat into their dens and nests, though, grateful for their reserves of fat and food and fur. They would curl around their partners and their young, snooze into a comfortable warmth, and hope that they wouldn't have to wait too long for the weather to pass and their life to continue the way it always did.

They would dream of the arrival of the spring, filled with sunshine and warmth and plenty.

And when that time came, they would venture out of their dens for good.

And there would be celebration.

CHAPTER EIGHTEEN

MARLEE STOMPED HER BOOTS, knocking snow off onto the mat of the Baked Bean. "Someone want to grab these poinsettias so I can uncover my head, like pronto?" she called. "My hair is wilting with every second."

Rowan's brother-in-law, Johnny, appeared from the back of the Bean, where he was busy rearranging furniture. "More?" he asked incredulously, taking the plants from Marlee. He spun, as if to figure out where he could possibly squeeze yet another poinsettia. "Every surface is already covered with them."

Marlee gingerly pulled her hood back, then began working on the buttons of her coat. She smiled broadly. "Gorgeous, isn't it?"

Annie clomped down the stairs in her Mary Janes, a matching pair of which awaited Marlee upstairs. Annie also wore the same white sweater tights that Marlee wore inside her boots, and the red dress that Marlee would be changing into right away, now that all the poinsettias had been delivered.

"Oh, good! You're finally here," Annie said.

"Why? Is something wrong?"

"Yes! You're the maid of honor and you're not even dressed yet," Annie said, helping relieve Marlee of her coat and hanging it on the hook by the door.

"I was delivering the flowers. It was a lot of flowers. Just ask Johnny," Marlee said defensively. "Besides, my hair and makeup are done, and I have my tights on. All that's left is the dress. I'm sorry if I'm holding things up," She called up the stairs, abandoning her boots by the door and bustling up the stairs in her stocking feet. "I'm coming now!"

"You're fine." Morgan appeared at the top of the stairs. "Annie is being a worrywart. Now that she's got her own wedding to plan, she's insufferable." She gave an exaggerated eye roll, then smiled and side-hugged Annie.

Annie's face flushed red. "I'm sorry I'm making you suffer, Marlee" she mumbled.

"Oh, no!" Morgan said, hugging her friend even tighter. "That's not what I meant by insufferable. I was just joking anyway. Let me see your ring again."

They'd all seen it a thousand times over the past year. Ben had surprised her by gussying up the sleigh on Christmas Day with twinkle lights and had taken her for a ride to a campfire around which he'd positioned comfy cushions, thick blankets, and a picnic. He'd gotten Annie settled—*holding my hand like I was a princess!*—and had proceeded to get down on one knee. Ever since, Annie had happily and excitedly shown her ring to anyone who asked, and even people who didn't, splaying her fingers wide and proclaiming, "He started saving up for it on the day we met!"

"I don't want to overshadow the bride on her special day," Annie whispered. "That's a thing. I'll show it to you tomorrow, though."

"Okay, deal." Morgan gave her one more quick hug. "Let's finish getting ready."

Annie checked her watch and jumped, visibly concerned. "We've only got two hours until the Annual Haw Springs Main Street Christmas Carol Crawl," she said. "We have a lot to accomplish." With Ellory otherwise occupied, Annie had taken over as the committee chair.

"No need to worry," Marlee said, "The maid of honor is here."

"And we're all here to help you make sure the crawl is perfect," Morgan said. She pushed open the bedroom door.

Inside Ellory's bedroom, Ellory sat at her vanity, in what literally appeared to be a cloud. She was paused, leaning forward, toward the mirror, a tube of lipstick in her hand. She sat back and smiled when her three friends came in. "You guys," she said. "I'm so nervous. My hands are shaking so much, I'm afraid to even try."

"Why are you nervous?" Morgan asked. "You're about to marry the man of your dreams."

"She's probably nervous because her maid of honor was running late," Annie said. "But it's okay, because Morgan and I were here to help you get into your dress, so now you're ready, except for your lipstick. You're probably nervous that it's going to get all over your teeth, though."

Ellory's eyes grew wide. "I wasn't worried about that until just now. Maybe I shouldn't wear it. At all." She began to replace the cap. "We don't have to match. I mean, that's not a rule. I'm not even sure if it's a thing."

"It's a thing," Annie stage-whispered.

"Here, I've got it," Marlee said, taking the lipstick from her friend. She held it up against her maid of honor gown, which was hanging on the doorframe nearby. "It's a perfect match. Just like you and Rowan. I think that's a sign that nothing can go wrong today. Do this." Marlee parted her own lips, and then, when Ellory did the same, began painting the bright red lipstick on her bottom and top lips. "Now do this." She pressed her lips together, and Ellory followed suit. "Perfect. You're stunning. Let's go get you married."

The girls all got into their floor-length, red dresses, pinned their white, faux fur stoles over their shoulders, adorned themselves with pearls, and stood behind their bride, all gazing into the vanity mirror.

"It's time," Annie whispered. "Are you ready?"

Ellory grinned and nodded. Not so much as a speck of red lipstick was on her teeth. "I'm so ready."

TRUTH BE TOLD, despite her nerves, Ellory felt stunning. Her wedding gown was big and billowy, covered with layers upon layers of tulle that made her feel like she was floating rather than walking. Beneath the gown, she wore white tights and silver, glittery Mary Janes that matched her bridesmaids' black ones. Her hair was braided and upswept and pinned in place by a single piece of holly. Her makeup was minimal except for the dramatic red lipstick.

Her shoulder ached from all the stirring, stirring, stirring. Only this year it had been cake batter rather than Christmas cookies, and Marlee, who had been with her for every single layer that went into and came out of the oven, admitted that she, too, had a sore shoulder.

The result of their hard work, though, was

breathtaking, if Ellory didn't mind saying so herself. The new lunch counter downstairs had been transformed into a winter scene, courtesy of Mr. Crowley, who transported his entire town to the Baked Bean for the occasion. In the center of the scene was not one, not two, but five towering wedding cakes, enough to feed Carol Crawlers who might wander into the busiest café any small town had ever seen for a Christmas Eve snack.

Perched atop the center cake were not a bride and groom, but a moon just like the one they'd fallen in love under just a year before. Miniature Ellory and Rowan stood on the next tier down, holding hands, her head leaning on his shoulder. When Ellory looked at it, she could practically hear "The Wexford Carol" floating on the air.

Annie went downstairs first, to scout out the readiness of Rowan and company. The sun had fallen below the horizon. Lights blinked all up and down Main Street. Christmas Eve quiet fell over the town under the light snow that had been falling all day. Hardly a blizzard. Just enough to be perfect.

Annie popped back into the bedroom, breathless, looking worried. "They're ready. But, um, somebody's here."

"Who?" Ellory asked, but before Annie could respond, the bedroom door cracked open and a familiar face peered in. Ellory pressed her hand to her stomach and gasped. "Daphne?"

Her sister opened the door and crept inside.

"You didn't really think I'd miss it, did you?" she asked.

Ellory let out a cry and went to her little sister, arms outstretched. Daphne let herself be enveloped by the cloud that was Ellory, and the two cried and hugged for what seemed like forever. Ellory wasn't even aware that Marlee had quietly ushered Annie and Morgan out of the room to wait at the top of the stairs.

"I can't believe you're here," Ellory said when she finally let go of her sister. She reached over and wiped a red lipstick smear, and then a tear that could have belonged to either one of them, from Daphne's cheek. "Are you...?"

Daphne nodded sadly. "Alone? Yeah. I tried to get them to come, but you know how they are about their Christmas traditions."

Ellory's heart released the tiniest little pang. For the most part, she'd given up on her family for exactly this reason. But Rowan's mother had shown up for the wedding and had even managed to gut out a begrudging congratulatory embrace, so Ellory had hoped that maybe something extraordinary could have happened with her family, as well.

"Well," she said, so happy to hold Daphne's

hands in her own that her chest literally ached. "You're here, and that's all that matters. But if I'd known you would come, I would have made you my maid of honor."

"No, I think you've got exactly the right person in that position," Daphne said. "I wasn't even sure I was coming until yesterday. I had to work up the courage to break it to Mother and Daddy. But I decided that I might have some dreams of my own one day, and who would I be to try to follow them if I never supported you in yours?" A tear slipped down one cheek and she wiped it away. "I'm so proud of you, Ellory. You're so strong and you believe in yourself so much. And look what you've pulled off! This place is amazing! And now you're marrying the love of your life…" She shook her head. "You're my hero."

Ellory let out a choked sob. Maybe someday she would hear these words from her parents, too, but even if she never did, she knew she would be okay. Daphne was right—she was strong and she believed in herself.

And she was about to have Rowan at her side every step of the way for the rest of her life.

There would be no stopping her now.

Daphne leaned over to the nightstand and plucked a few tissues out of the box. She dabbed at Ellory's face with one and then at her own with another. She stood and held out her hands to pull her sister to standing.

"It's time for your happily ever after."

THE BACK AREA of the Baked Bean had been transformed. The chairs and tables were all moved to allow for a center aisle. The rainbows and clouds were replaced with tasteful wedding decor that softly glinted in the candlelight of what seemed to Rowan to be at least a million candles, the overhead lights turned off.

On one side of the aisle, his mom bounced Connor on her knee as he softly burbled and drooled down the front of his adorable little suit. Megan sat with her, every so often fussing over the baby, feeding him one Cheerios morsel at a time, but mostly just taking advantage of the break.

Rowan and his sister had spent hours over the past year, discussing and digesting their mother's reappearance in their lives, and had finally come to an agreement of wary appreciation and willful ignorance. It seemed the safest route.

Also on that side of the aisle sat Ben and the two McBride brothers, along with Lindsay, the car genius who'd gotten him on the road in the middle of a blizzard, and Junior, the big hearted man who'd brought him back to Haw Springs.

On the other side of the aisle sat Daphne, who

looked like a red-haired, uptight version of Ellory. Daphne wore her pedigree on her sleeve but looked slightly embarrassed by it. Rowan was fully aware of the complicated but thriving relationship his bride had with her sister, and he knew that Ellory must be beside herself with joy that Daphne had appeared. For this reason, he welcomed his sister-in-law-to-be.

Beside Daphne was a space for Mr. Crowley, right next to Mrs. Crowley and Ellory's friend Tena from the memory care center. Mrs. Crowley looked attentive and quietly serene. It had been a rough year for the Crowleys, and Rowan was overjoyed that Mrs. Crowley was having a good enough day to make it to their wedding. After all, Ellory was the daughter they never had.

Rowan took his place next to the pastor. Soon, standing next to Rowan would be Frankie—his brother from the Tulsa firehouse—and Salvatore, his brother, captain, and only other firefighter in the nearby Oak Hollow firehouse. His best man, of course, was his brother-in-law, Johnny, who had pledged to text Rowan and his sister every single day for the rest of their lives and had never yet missed a day, even though he never had anything to say.

The first carolers had just begun to walk Main Street when music crackled overhead and Annie appeared at the end of the aisle, looking awkward and delighted as she held on to the crook of Frankie's arm and slowly moved toward Rowan. After she reached the end of the aisle, Morgan appeared with Salvatore and then Marlee, with Johnny.

The music changed to something a little lighter, and Latte appeared, wearing a tiny tux, with rings attached to a pillow on his back. Rowan squatted and beckoned toward his little four-legged best friend, and Latte trotted toward him. Rowan had chosen Latte's tux himself and believed it made the cat look distinguished.

Marlee deftly removed the ring pillow from Latte's back and held on to it with her flowers. Latte leaped onto his favorite cloud chair—the one he'd awakened Rowan on a year ago—and immediately set to grooming himself. A soft chuckle arose throughout the room and then the pastor raised his hands, the music changed, and there was the soft shuffle of people getting to their feet.

Ellory appeared at the end of the aisle, clutching Mr. Crowley's arm. She looked nervous as she floated toward her groom.

Rowan's breath caught.

His heart pinged around in the confines of his chest, behind the prison bars of his ribs, as if wanting to escape and bounce throughout the room in great, joyful leaps.

He felt dizzy.

His stomach clenched and his knees weakened. He knotted his fingers together to keep his arms from going slack at his sides.

And, without warning, his vision flooded. A lump worked its way up into his throat and through him until it escaped in a breathy cough that might have been a sob on anyone else. He had to force himself to inhale, exhale.

Ellory came to him in waves of beauty. Wide eyes. A scent of flowers. A smile, tentative and self-conscious, but growing wide and comfortable the nearer she approached.

He barely forced out a choked whisper. "You're beautiful."

She opened her mouth to respond, but instead simply cupped his cheek with one hand, the way he loved her to do.

Mr. Crowley kissed Ellory on the cheek and then took his seat. The pastor gestured for everyone to sit.

I love you, Ellory mouthed, and the unsteadiness rocking Rowan intensified and then settled, making him feel calmer, more grounded.

This is it, he thought.

This...is joy.

CHAPTER NINETEEN

JUST AS ELLORY and Rowan were saying *I do*, the carolers had begun to crawl in earnest on Main Street in Haw Springs. It was difficult to see all the way to the back of the Baked Bean from the front window, but everyone knew what was going on and several carolers watched with their faces pressed against the glass as Ellory drifted down the aisle, and continued watching until Ellory and Rowan returned up the aisle, their faces flushed with joy and their hands clutched in matrimony.

They paused only for Rowan to twirl Ellory into his arms and press his lips against hers, lean his forehead against hers and hug her around the waist.

The carolers readied and positioned themselves around the door, fanning out until it seemed like all 653 Haw Springs residents were standing outside the Baked Bean, awaiting the arrival of the newly minted Kelly family and the start of the biggest wedding reception anyone had ever seen.

When the door was finally flung open, Rowan

and Ellory standing in it with their arms up in triumph, the entire town erupted into a great cheer, which erupted into a hearty rendition of "Joy to the World," which some would later suspect might have been heard as far away as Rayville.

Everyone had spent a breakfast or lunch over the past year in the Baked Bean, talking with Ellory about family and friends and love and life and dreams as they drank sweet coffee and velvety tea and ate egg salad sandwiches and buttery croissants and Danish that all but dripped jam with every bite. Everyone knew about her love of the stranger from Tulsa, who made a wrong turn and then got stranded on the side of the road. Everyone followed the wedding plans and speculated about the wedding cake, which she would most certainly share with the entire town.

The carolers encircled the couple as they stepped into the snow, singing and patting their shoulders with well-wishes and offering hugs and smiles and gifts. They streamed into the Baked Bean and came out with plates of the most delicious cake they'd ever eaten, cream and vanilla and cinnamon and almond and butter.

They sang and sang until the children grew tired of sliding on snowbanks and drinking hot cocoa and asked to return to their beds so Santa could come visit them.

They trickled away and closed their shops and

their homes and extinguished their lights until all that was left were Ellory and Rowan, standing under the moon, bulky blankets slung over their shoulders, dreams and happiness in their eyes.

"Did you ever think…?" Ellory asked.

"You know I didn't." Rowan pulled the blanket so they were entirely encompassed by it. "I thought I…I don't know…didn't deserve this? Or maybe just that I wouldn't be one of the lucky ones."

She turned to face him, holding him around the waist and turning her face up to his. "Do you think you're one of the lucky ones now?"

He held the blanket tight around her back, pulling her in so that their hearts beat together. "I know I'm the luckiest one," he said.

Ellory snuggled up against his chest, closing her eyes. "I think I knew," she said. "When you showed up at my coffee shop, I opened the door, against my better judgment. I let you sleep here. And even though I pushed all my furniture up against the bedroom door, I wasn't actually scared of you. Something told me you were someone I could trust. I don't know. It just felt right with you here. Even though you were a total Scrooge."

He leaned back so that she would lift her head. He looked her in the eyes. "You pushed your bedroom furniture against the door?"

"In case you were a murderer," she said, as if this were the most matter-of-fact thing in the world.

"You told me then that you didn't."

"Oh, I definitely did."

Rowan threw his head back and laughed. "Fair enough," he said. "But it was the Scrooge thing that bothered you more than the potential murderer thing."

She shrugged. "I like Christmas."

"You know what?" he said, pulling her against him again and settling his chin atop her head. "I like Christmas, too."

"And I like the moon," she said, wriggling out from under him. "And I like you, Mr. Kelly."

"I like you, too, Mrs. Kelly." He clasped both ends of the blanket in one hand so he could rest his finger under her chin with the other. He pulled it up so her face was upturned to his. "In fact, I love you."

"I love you, too." She gave him a quick kiss, then gasped. "This is our first Christmas as The Kellys."

"Well, in that case, Merry Christmas, Mrs. Kelly."

Ellory smiled, her eyes sparkling in the moonlight. "Merry Christmas, Mr. Kelly."

THERE WAS SNOW on the ground, but it wasn't much.

The animals came out of their dens and nests

and hiding places freely, some of them surprised to even find snow at all.

The moon was bright. Just the kind of moon to highlight prey for any of the hunters among them. But they weren't hunting. They were hunkered in the holes of their dens, the bowls of their nests. They were watching.

There will still be humans out, and that meant waiting out whatever storm, because wet and cold they could handle, but humans were things to be wary of. To watch.

The moonlight slid over the sheen of snow, silvery and liquid and illuminating. It spilled over the humans—just two of them left—who seemed to not even notice the cold as they moved their human mouths and made their human noises.

But as the moon crawled higher and higher into the sky, and as the hunger pangs of the animals grew stronger and stronger, their urge to step out into the darkness more and more palpable, causing them to quiver and shake in their hiding places, the human noises quieted and quieted and quieted.

The animals watched as the two humans wound down, their noises softening, their shivers growing.

They watched as the humans melted together. One kiss, and then the night would be theirs.

* * * * *

Be sure to look for Marlee's story—the next book in Jennifer Brown's Haw Springs series—available soon, wherever Harlequin Heartwarming books are sold!

Get up to 4 Free Books!

We'll send you 2 free books from each series you try PLUS a free Mystery Gift.

FREE Value Over **$25**

Both the **Harlequin® Special Edition** and **Harlequin® Heartwarming**™ series feature compelling novels filled with stories of love and strength where the bonds of friendship, family and community unite.

YES! Please send me 2 FREE novels from the Harlequin Special Edition or Harlequin Heartwarming series and my FREE Gift (gift is worth about $10 retail). After receiving them, if I don't wish to receive any more books, I can return the shipping statement marked "cancel." If I don't cancel, I will receive 6 brand-new Harlequin Special Edition books every month and be billed just $6.39 each in the U.S. or $7.19 each in Canada, or 4 brand-new Harlequin Heartwarming Larger-Print books every month and be billed just $7.19 each in the U.S. or $7.99 each in Canada, a savings of 20% off the cover price. It's quite a bargain! Shipping and handling is just 50¢ per book in the U.S. and $1.25 per book in Canada.* I understand that accepting the 2 free books and gift places me under no obligation to buy anything. I can always return a shipment and cancel at any time by calling the number below. The free books and gift are mine to keep no matter what I decide.

Choose one:
- ☐ **Harlequin Special Edition** (235/335 BPA G36Y)
- ☐ **Harlequin Heartwarming Larger-Print** (161/361 BPA G36Y)
- ☐ **Or Try Both!** (235/335 & 161/361 BPA G36Z)

Name (please print)

Address   Apt. #

City   State/Province   Zip/Postal Code

Email: Please check this box ☐ if you would like to receive newsletters and promotional emails from Harlequin Enterprises ULC and its affiliates. You can unsubscribe anytime.

Mail to the Harlequin Reader Service:
IN U.S.A.: P.O. Box 1341, Buffalo, NY 14240-8531
IN CANADA: P.O. Box 603, Fort Erie, Ontario L2A 5X3

Want to explore our other series or interested in ebooks? Visit www.ReaderService.com or call 1-800-873-8635.

---

*Terms and prices subject to change without notice. Prices do not include sales taxes, which will be charged (if applicable) based on your state or country of residence. Canadian residents will be charged applicable taxes. Offer not valid in Quebec. This offer is limited to one order per household. Books received may not be as shown. Not valid for current subscribers to the Harlequin Special Edition or Harlequin Heartwarming series. All orders subject to approval. Credit or debit balances in a customer's account(s) may be offset by any other outstanding balance owed by or to the customer. Please allow 4 to 6 weeks for delivery. Offer available while quantities last.

Your Privacy—Your information is being collected by Harlequin Enterprises ULC, operating as Harlequin Reader Service. For a complete summary of the information we collect, how we use this information and to whom it is disclosed, please visit our privacy notice located at https://corporate.harlequin.com/privacy-notice. Notice to California Residents – Under California law, you have specific rights to control and access your data. For more information on these rights and how to exercise them, visit https://corporate.harlequin.com/california-privacy. For additional information for residents of other U.S. states that provide their residents with certain rights with respect to personal data, visit https://corporate.harlequin.com/other-state-residents-privacy-rights/.

HSEHW25